I0573137

D.A.D.
THE WORLD'S BIGGEST CON

CLARK VIEHWEG

Black Rose Writing | Texas

©2022 by Clark Viehweg
All rights reserved. No part of this book may be reproduced, stored in a retrieval system or transmitted in any form or by any means without the prior written permission of the publishers, except by a reviewer who may quote brief passages in a review to be printed in a newspaper, magazine or journal.

The author grants the final approval for this literary material.

First printing

This is a work of fiction. Names, characters, businesses, places, events, and incidents are either the products of the author's imagination or used in a fictitious manner. Any resemblance to actual persons, living or dead, or actual events is purely coincidental.

ISBN: 978-1-68513-072-5
PUBLISHED BY BLACK ROSE WRITING
www.blackrosewriting.com

Printed in the United States of America
Suggested Retail Price (SRP) $20.95

D.A.D. is printed in Calluna

*As a planet-friendly publisher, Black Rose Writing does its best to eliminate unnecessary waste to reduce paper usage and energy costs, while never compromising the reading experience. As a result, the final word count vs. page count may not meet common expectations.

For my dad and Kimberly
The ones who matter most

"Governments need to have both shepherds and butchers."
–Voltaire

"If you don't scale the mountain, you can't view the plain."
–Chinese folk wisdom

"The afternoon knows what the morning never suspected."
–Swedish words of wisdom

D.A.D.

CERTAIN FACTS

In the spring of 1979, during President Carter's first year in office, OPEC and other Middle East nations imposed their second oil embargo.

Gasoline prices escalated around the nation, eclipsing $1.00 per gallon for the first time in history.

Accusations of oil company profiteering were commonplace, prompting endless congressional hearings and investigations.

Many public officials declared the gasoline shortage to be the most significant national crisis on record.

Auto clubs in many states hired additional staffers to assist drivers running out of fuel.

Truck drivers staged slow-moving convoys in protest of fuel allocations. Two motorists engaged in a New York gas pump riot got shot while drivers brandished knives, tire irons, jack handles, and baseball bats all around the country.

Federal authorities were concerned that our energy and oil supplies had dwindled to a critically low level and could perpetuate an even worse crisis.

–From many news sources

PROLOGUE

July 1945
A small village in southeastern Idaho

A flash of light followed by a resounding bang interrupted a quiet summer evening. Quiet, if you ignored the local symphony of crickets and frogs taking place under a blue-black dome speckled with uncountable brilliant winking lights. The clean, high mountain desert air provided the perfect setting for a blazing display of the Milky Way's sparkling array of stars. The sudden loud noise interrupted the nighttime chorus, bringing the evening's serenade to an instant halt. A quiet stillness filled the night, lingering in the dark shadows under towering pines.

Although the days are dry and hot, nights in this peaceful section of southeastern Idaho were always pleasant if you could ignore the mosquitoes. The cool, damp nighttime air that promoted these parasites also brought refreshing relief for the valley farmers who had labored all day in the blazing hot sun.

Outlined against the star-filled sky was the ridgeline of a log cabin nestled next to a mixed grove of pine and box elder trees. Looking north, the base of the big dipper hung just above the roofline. A luminous, silky white haze floated up from the cabin's chimney into the cool night air, filling the dipper's cup, a sign that not everyone's work had been finished for the day.

A tight spring on the cabin's screen door produced the shattering bang that disturbed the evening's cacophonous symphony. A young, tow-headed boy could be seen following a curving path through a cedar tree grove in the momentary silence. His golden hair seemed to glow whenever he stepped from the shadows under the trees into the starlight. Being perfectly at ease in the world, he hummed *You Are My Sunshine,* a song learned from his mother, his bare feet gliding silently in the grass, stepping in unconscious rhythm with the beat of croaking frogs as they resumed their nighttime refrain. By inspecting the patches of starlight, you could see the faded patches stitched on the knees of the boy's ragged pants. Another shaft of light cut into the darkness as the boy opened the door of a small shed tucked into a grove of Douglas Fir pine trees, filling the evening air with their clean, crisp scent.

"Supper's ready, Dad," the boy said, almost singing the words.

"Thanks, Son, come over here and look at this," the boy's father said while never looking up from his activity.

The big man stood at a workbench. He had the scarred and callused hands of someone used to heavy manual labor. His big-boned frame was covered in a pair of faded bib overalls over a homemade work shirt sewn from old flour sacks. Knowing that the ladies used their bags to make clothing, the flour companies started making sacks with various colored patterns. Cheery good nature radiated from sparkling blue eyes set above ruddy, high-boned cheeks. Surrounding the man were four walls covered from floor to ceiling with the clutter of unusual objects that can only come from the mind of a genius inventor.

Catching light from the naked bulb dangling on its wires from the ceiling, a pair of metal leg braces seemed to gleam with impudence. A wheel was attached to the bottom of each brace. Attached above each wheel was a metal platform for feet through which straps could be laced to hold a shoe firmly in place. Other straps held ankle and calf muscles against the brace so that when standing, the braces acted as leg extensions with six-inch pneumatic wheels at the bottom of each leg. The thought behind this invention was to allow a person the ability to skate quickly, a precursor of today's rollerblades. A fine idea, except that it didn't work. No one has the balance required to stand on one wheel, let alone speed down the road. In the inventor's mind, this contraption could be a replacement for the automobile or bicycle.

The entire shack was full of similar useless inventions. That not one of them seemed to work or have any practical significance had apparently not been a deterrent to future projects. While the walls held the clutter of failed projects, there had been several successes for which the inventor, not being a businessman, had been unable to receive any compensation.

The project of interest tonight had a very different destiny.

Floating in front of the man, a few inches above the tool-covered workbench, was a shining silver globe about twelve inches in diameter. Dancing light from a dangling bulb reflected from the sphere's smooth surface sent shimmering rings around the room. As he spoke, the man reached out with both hands, pulling the bright ball out of the air, and turning, held it out to the boy.

"What do you think of this, aye?" he asked with a broad grin and sparkling eyes.

The boy's eyes grew large with excitement, twinkling like the stars outside. He reached out to take the ball as the man removed his hands, but the ball just hung in the air, suspended between father and son, surrounded by an aura of glimmering light as though it were a magical lantern.

"What is it, Dad?" he asked in awe. "Can I play with it?" he asked with a voice full of wonder, like that of someone observing an incredibly mysterious event.

A big grin spread across the face of both as they stared at the gleaming sphere hanging in space. A building silence grew heavy as the night creatures, seeming to know that something momentous was happening, stopped their chorus. The air and very space within the small shed seemed to hum and pulsate with unseen energy while reflected light danced and flickered on the grinning faces of father and son.

The father finally spoke, breaking the magical spell.

"No, Son, not just yet. Here, let's put it in this box and I'll explain what's happening."

As he spoke, the man reached under his workbench, retrieving a square heavy cardboard box just slightly larger than the silver ball. He had the boy grip the box and then, grasping the ball with both hands, forced it into the box and closed the lid before pushing the box down on the floor.

"There, it will stay put now," he said. "Besides, the gyros are about all wound down."

Gasping slightly from the exertion, he looked his son in the eyes, and with seriousness, the boy seldom witnessed the father explained.

"Son, what you've just seen is our new anti-gravity machine. It's not a toy for you to play with, but it will be yours. One day, when you're much older, we'll use this machine to provide power and transportation for the entire world. You'll build machines to provide electric energy and large enough so people can be inside and travel without gasoline. It won't cost them any money to go wherever they want. You will even build gigantic machines that can carry thousands of people, whole cities."

The boy, impressed by his father's serious countenance, had a look of worship on his face as he asked, "Why can't we build the flying machines now, Dad?"

"We don't have the money, Son. And this is much too important to show anyone else. This is our little secret, just yours and mine. Besides, this just isn't the right time. But the time will come when we can build our flying machine, although by then, it might be just you."

Missing the implied suggestion, the boy continued his questions. "How will we know when it's the right time, Dad?"

The father gave his son one last lingering look.

"You will know, Son, I guarantee, you will know. Now, let's go eat before your momma gets angry with both of us."

The man reached up, twisting a switch on the hanging light, bringing darkness with a quick snap. The little shed seemed to collapse back on itself as the light went out. Just before darkness took over, the boy caught one fleeting glimpse of a square cardboard box resting on the floor under the workbench; the letters <u>rod</u> stenciled on the upper right-hand corner.

As happens in life, a couple of years later, the father died in an accident. The cardboard box lay hidden away, forgotten for several decades.

CHAPTER ONE

Thirty-four years later
July 3rd, 1979, 2:30 p.m.
San Francisco, corner of Lombard & Laguna

In 1979, gas stations occupied every corner of the intersection at Lombard and Laguna. On the third day of July, three of the stations were closed for lack of gasoline. Big hand-scrawled signs propped against sawhorses in each driveway declared, '**OUT OF GAS**!'

The fourth station, Chevron, had three islands with two pumps on each island. Theoretically, six cars could pump gas at the same time. Many drivers wouldn't pump high-octane gasoline, or the gasoline caps were on their vehicle's wrong side, making access impossible or difficult. The number of cars being serviced simultaneously seldom exceeded three or four.

A line of cars stretched from the Chevron station driveway south down Lombard, around the corner onto Gough, and down Gough to Greenwich and around that corner. The day seemed unseasonably warm for San Francisco, adding to the frustration and impatience of drivers waiting in line, many for over three hours, just to purchase their ration of ten gallons. Many of those in line were secretaries or assistants waiting in their boss's cars. These substitutes appeared additionally aggravated because they still had no gasoline for their own vehicles after waiting so many hours in line. Undoubtedly, by the time they got off work and returned, the station would be out of gas. This backup of hot, frustrated, worried and impatient drivers created a recipe for disaster.

Josh Logan sat perspiring in his muggy Mercury Capri, five cars from the island. The Capri's windows were rolled down in an irrational expectation of some minimal air circulation. Running the air conditioning would require gasoline, therefore not a consideration.

Listening to the radio, Josh wiped the sweat from his forehead with the back of his hand while trying to stay alert for any movement in the line. A news announcer discussed the growing gasoline shortage and the devastation this was causing truckers, traveling sales personnel, and others who made their livelihood traveling the roads of America. This shortage hit the golden state hard, where oil derricks and refineries had always meant cheap gasoline and many cars.

Something in the news caught Josh's attention, causing him to sit up. The announcer quoted Speaker of the House, Tip O'Neal, who claimed that the big oil companies, the "Seven Sisters" he called them, had "***manufactured the entire shortage.***" According to the radio announcer, Speaker O'Neal claimed that the third world (OPEC) countries allegedly responsible for the shortage were in fact "***responding to demands for higher payments***" from the "Sisters." Supposedly, the oil companies who had invested billions in drilling for oil and building the refining infrastructure in OPEC countries had a growing impatience for recovering their investments. This led to the big oil companies' embargo being orchestrated, resulting in an unprecedented rise in oil prices.

The announcer continued, "In the local news, long gas lines and motorist frustrations are the top stories."

At least that part of the news Josh had no problem verifying.

Glancing into the gas station ahead, he watched the movement of cars as one driver drove away with his ten-gallon allotment, while the next car in line moved forward. Barely conscious after the long hot wait, Josh nearly missed the small hand-written sign tacked onto a sawhorse.

The misspelled sign scrawled on the side of a scroungy oil-stained piece of cardboard read "ODD LISENSE PLATES ONLY."

Only cars whose license plate numbers end in an odd number would receive the allotted ten gallons of gasoline.

Moving up with the four cars in front of his Capri, Josh noticed an argument developing between the driver of a beat-up VW van that had just pulled next to the pump and the attendant. The dented green van sporting hand-painted flowers and peace slogans made the occurring argument between the driver and station attendant look incongruous.

With his window down, Josh could hear the van's long-haired driver yelling and gathered that the VW's license plate ended in an even number. The pump attendant, in his official Chevron white and red striped shirt, repeatedly pointed at the van's license plate, shaking his head "no." Despite the shabbily dressed driver's protest that he needed gasoline for his overdue pregnant wife, the station attendant held fast, shaking his head no and blocking the driver's access to the pump.

A commotion in the rear caused Josh to glance in the mirror, nearly missing what happened next. The sudden movement and a fearful shout of "no" jerked his vision back to the station just as the hippie drew a tire iron from the van's open door and struck the station attendant on the head. Dropping his tire iron, the driver reached for the pump nozzle even before the attendant in his blood-spattered Chevron shirt hit the ground. Looking back in the mirror, Josh witnessed the scene behind.

As he and the drivers in front had moved ahead, a silver and black Chevy pickup that had been behind Josh's Capri remained stationary. Its driver, an older man, lulled by the heat and lengthy wait, had not been alert. Parked with his engine off, saving gasoline and probably napping, several seconds elapsed before he realized the opening ahead, leaving a gap between his pickup and Josh's Capri.

A young businessman heading down Lombard in a shiny new BMW spotted the opening and darted into the gap. A rugged, tough-looking redhead, two cars behind the BMW, got out of his black Mustang convertible. Shouting obscenities, he advanced towards the BMW. Still screaming, he opened the driver's door and started throwing punches at the driver. Watching in his rearview mirror, Josh didn't have the best angle for observing the details of this ugly scene; however, subsequent events spoke volumes.

A loud, shattering explosion echoed up and down Lombard. The brawny redhead stumbled backward, clutching at his chest, a shocked expression fixed on his ridged features. Time seemed to move in slow, jerky steps as though caught in the freeze-frame action of a movie camera.

The redhead began sinking slowly onto the pavement with blood seeping through fingers clutching at his chest. Pulling his eyes back to the station, more blood caught Josh's attention. A large pool of bright red blood reflecting the glaring sun formed around the gas station attendant's head. Everyone at the pumps concentrated on getting their gasoline, ignoring the chaos and violence.

Josh pounded both fists against the steering wheel while shaking his head in agony.

"Oh, God! Oh, God! No!"

It seemed to Josh as though the entire world stood still. Then suddenly, he felt at peace. A strange calmness spread through his body. He seemed to hear his father speaking in his head. When he finally spoke, it felt like he was reciting a prayer with the greatest reverence.

"Okay, Dad, I guess the time has come," he whispered in the empty car. "You were right. I do know it. The time has come."

An hour later, he appeared in the attic of a beautifully restored Victorian near the top of Nob Hill. Kneeling on the bare floor, he dragged a square cardboard box out of an old green Army trunk. The heavily soiled and battered cardboard looked ancient. Faded dark from age, even darker patches from various stains made random Rorschach patterns on the sides and top. The box looked squished in spots, producing wrinkles and dents, but if one looked carefully, one could barely make out the small faint letters "*rod*" in one corner near the top.

CHAPTER TWO

Late July, 2000
Burbank, California

In the early fall night, a slight chill barely registered on the tall man in a gray and green tweed suit walking down Constitution Avenue looking for street signs. With a dark soft felt trilby hat tilted slightly sideways over silver hair, he carried a very unusual cane featuring a shining silver ball at the top. The ball, nearly three inches in diameter, about the size of a softball, appeared unusually large for a cane. The man turned the corner at Howard Street and, spotting his objective, moved slowly towards the rear of a dilapidated wooden warehouse that had once been an orange sorting shed. The faded old-style lettered words "*CALIFORNIA ORANGES*" could still be seen if the sun was just right on the old warped weathered gray board siding. The man stood hesitating briefly just outside of this weathered ramshackle building before stepping quietly through the doorway.

Inside, angry voices were heard coming from the other side of a stubbed-out wall. The room lived in darkness except for two lights. A ceiling spot shining down behind the short wall gave the room an eerie, otherworld quality. The man in tweed did not go towards the sound and light but stayed in the shadows by the outside wall. Slowly moving away from the door, he moved down the wall before turning towards the room's center.

Towards the light, he could see a table lamp resting on an overturned wooden crate, adding its dim glow to the spotlight. Ten men and women in street clothes held scattered positions in a semicircle on a raised platform. Sitting on folding chairs facing the makeshift stage, another group dressed similarly eagerly watched the events on stage. Everyone in the trade would recognize this as a tryout reading for a new play.

The people standing reading lines for a new Pasadena Playhouse production were taking their turn trying to impress the director. Included among those sitting by the director and a few assistants were several strangers off to the side. These observers wore the anxious expression of actors still waiting for a chance to read. Scattered throughout the audience, a few Hollywood agents, producers, and directors who often used the Pasadena Playhouse as both hunting and training grounds for new talent sat silently observing the action.

Many years ago, a generous patron had purchased the warehouse for the playhouse when developers started chopping down orange orchards for housing tracts and strip malls. While the troupe performed in a small theater in downtown Pasadena, they did most of their rehearsals and tryouts in the old packing shed. This arrangement allowed the theater to continue with performances while new productions were being prepared. While functional and cost-effective, the site produced many jokes, primarily by those envious of the playhouse's reputation. Recognizing that the experience far transcended the ribbing, most actors spending time with the group didn't mind being called *"orange packers."*

The man in shadows stood unobserved, watching and listening as various men and women took turns shouting lines concerning an epidemic about to strike Los Angeles. He couldn't help but smile as he listened to different actors shout their lines concerning the plague. In his mind, Los Angeles had been struck by several plagues over the years. First came too many immigrants, later the oil industry followed shortly by Hollywood and finally the smog. For his money, a little plague-type crisis thinning out the population might be a blessing, not a curse.

Sensing that the readings were about over for the evening, the quiet man retraced his steps, stopping just outside the door. A faint light from the street made his highly polished shoes look like miniature sidewalk moons in the otherwise dim alley. Soon, men and women started leaving, many talking excitedly about their chances for a role in the upcoming play. Others hung their heads and marched stoically into the evening; whether in despair or fatigue, it was hard to tell. As one particular young man left the building, the tall, quiet man moved forward.

"Mr. Langham, Joseph! May I have a word with you?"

Joseph stopped and looked at the man before replying, "Who are you? How do you know my name?" he asked, curious and slightly uneasy.

"Oh, sorry if I startled you," the man said quickly. "My name's Abraham Weinberg, but my friends all call me Abe. I'd like you to call me Abe as well." Knowing the magic words that command attention everywhere in tinsel town, he hastily continued, "I'm an agent. Here's my card." He said this with a winning smile as he handed over a plain white business card.

Joseph had visited several agents in the past six months, trying to find one interested in helping advance his career, with no takers. Yet, here was an agent searching for him? This just didn't happen. On the other hand, what actor doesn't have an ego, secretly believing themselves a star just waiting to be discovered?

"Yeah, so how can I help you?" he asked, hurrying to catch up with Abraham, who had turned and started walking. Although Abe looked old, he moved at a brisk pace, tapping the silver-headed cane on the sidewalk, causing Joseph to hurry to keep from falling behind.

"I'd like to buy you some dinner and perhaps offer an acting job," Weinberg responded without missing a step.

There is absolutely nothing in the world that will get a starving actor's attention faster than the words, "let me buy you dinner," unless it's the words, "acting job." Including both in the same sentence has the effect of making a struggling actor trying to break into the business momentarily insane. Either phrase is guaranteed to command instant and complete attention. Including both statements in the same sentence is not only incomprehensible, but it's also close to irresponsible. Already weak from hunger and suffering weeks of rejection, many actors in Joseph's situation would faint hearing Abe's pronouncement. After a few moments of stunned silence, Joe began regaining his composure. Stammering and out of breath, he croaked, "Wha..., wh..., when and where?"

With a broad smile, Abe said, "My car's right over there," pointing to a Silver Shadow Rolls Royce. "Jump in, and we'll go over to Marne's for a bite to eat," he said, referring to a local hangout where *wannabes* hung out, hoping to get discovered. "I'll tell you about the job over dinner."

An average person would have heard alarms going off at this point. An agent shows up out of nowhere, offering dinner and a job. Although well dressed, the man somehow came across as seedy by Hollywood standards, even if he appeared to be driving a Rolls. These should have all been definite warning indicators.

However, aspiring actors aren't typical, and insanity isn't out of the question when you add the hunger factor. While the average person might question the wisdom of getting into a Rolls Royce with an absolute stranger in the middle of a dark night, Joseph never even hesitated.

Seated in a corner booth at Marne's, Joe got his first good look at the man offering him food and a job. Abraham Weinberg appeared to be in his early sixties with curly white hair framing a square, well-tanned face. His chiseled face featured the bluest eyes Langham had ever seen. They reminded him of some robin eggs he had once seen as a child in a display at the Oakland zoo. While his wrinkles and gray hair indicated a man in his sixties, Abe seemed younger. As an actor in training, Joseph studied people he met, observing their actions and mannerisms. Something about his host didn't seem quite right, but then the man was buying dinner and wanted to talk to him about an acting job. The ornately decorated cane with the large silver ball on top stood leaning against Abe's seat.

For his part, Abe openly studied the young man seated across the table. Joe kept dumping extra sugar and cream in his coffee, as though coffee might be the only food on the table he could have. Ordering coffee and then loading it with spoonsful of sugar and cream was an old starving actor's trick dating back into antiquity. As Abe watched the comely young man with blond hair doctor up his drink, he considered the possibility that actors as far back as Shakespeare probably did the same thing; spiking tea with honey and lots of cream. Being absorbed in his own doctoring and evaluations, Joseph didn't notice how closely the older man watched his every move and expression.

"Yes," Abe thought, this young man with his clean, good looks and honest face in the right suit with a power tie would make a great company president.

With his mind made up, Abe pulled a bulging white business envelope out of the inner breast pocket of his suit coat and laid it on the table in front of his companion. Joe glanced at the package curiously, wondering what mysteries the envelope might contain but unsure of what to do.

"Pick it up and look at it, Joe. It won't bite," Abe said with a chuckle as the young man reached hesitantly for the envelope. "Let me tell you about the job."

A thick bundle of hundred-dollar bills neatly stacked inside the envelope next to a folded sheet of stationery caused Joe's heart to stop beating momentarily. He felt paralyzed and short of breath for the second time that evening. "*This guy is gonna kill me if I'm not careful,*" he thought. It would be several weeks before Joseph realized the accuracy of his unspoken prediction.

CHAPTER THREE

A slender figure dressed in black kneeled shivering next to a large green garbage container behind The Capitol Avenue Plaza Shops, CAPS to San Jose residents. He wished for the warmth of his car instead of the chilly morning air. His watch read 2:30 a.m. He kept thinking August shouldn't be this cold.

He looked one more time up and down the alley to make sure there was no one around to witness his actions. Satisfied he was alone, the dark figure raced to a power pole near the mall's rear corner.

CAPS had eight stores occupying nearly 400 feet of prime Capital Avenue real estate. Over the years, so many businesses had occupied the mall requiring new services that the power and telephone company who shared a utility pole left the climbing pegs permanently installed. The power pole had been conveniently placed next to the rear corner of CAPS. As the man hurried up the pole, he thanked the stupid phone people for making his job so easy. The exertion and adrenalin rapidly warmed his body so that when he reached the louvered ball vent on the rooftop, he felt sweat running down his forehead.

He quickly loosened the holding screws and lifted the louvered ball from its vertical mount with practiced knowing. He placed the vent quietly on the flat roof. He unclipped a rope dangling from his waist and hooked it over the vent mount. The rope had large knots at three feet intervals. Crawling into the opening, he grabbed the rope and lowered himself to the false ceiling eight feet below. Fifty seconds after climbing the utility pole, he disappeared out of sight.

Half-inch plywood, two feet wide, located directly below the vent, ran down the entire length of the mall, providing a walkway for service personnel. The man crept silently along the board, counting the two by six rafters. After reaching thirty-six, he dropped to his knees and crawled along the ceiling supports before lifting some insulation. After putting it to one side, he slipped a knife under one corner of a two-foot square ceiling panel, prying it up high enough for him to peek into the room below. Satisfied this was the correct shop, he lifted the panel quietly out of its bracket with both hands, setting it aside. With another knotted rope pulled from his belt, he quickly clamped one end to a ceiling brace, throwing the rest through the empty square. Straddling the hole with the rope in both hands, he climbed down the knots into the room below.

He stood behind a jewelry counter with the front door and glass display windows fifteen feet away. Ducking behind the counter, out of view from anyone who might pass by on the street, he pulled a soft black sack from under his belt. All the easy items like cheap watches and earrings on the countertop got scraped into the bag. Once that was done, he tried opening the doors to the expensive merchandise below. These doors were locked as he had guessed, and out came his handy knife with a six-inch blade. The locks proved to be better than expected and didn't give as easy as he had hoped. After much jabbing and prying, the first lock finally gave way with a loud crack.

Not to worry. Who could hear? The sound couldn't have been heard outside or even next door.

The burglar began grabbing diamonds and wedding sets, stuffing them into his rapidly filling sack.

He planned to start on the next cabinet door when something made him turn around. There, right behind him, stood David Chen, the shop owner, rubbing his eyes, still trying to come awake.

"Hey, what are you doing?" Chen yelled, flapping his hands still half in a dream.

The old man started reaching towards a drawer in the counter where he had a gun. Still groggy, he didn't realize what his actions signaled until it was too late.

The burglar, thinking the old man had a hidden gun, turned and used the knife he had been working with on the locks, shoved upwards, straight into David Chen's heart.

The shop owner slumped to the floor, spurting blood, dying on the way down.

The panicked burglar fled back the way he had come, leaving everything behind.

CHAPTER FOUR

A few nights earlier, Lisa Ogden relaxed at her favorite table in La Gaston's courtyard, a Greenwich Village espresso house. She had just spent a trying day making the rounds of casting agents and production companies looking for another acting job. She sat under a Beringer Winery umbrella with Mousy on her lap, the proprietor's Siamese cat. Lisa was sipping a glass of champagne with her aching feet propped up on another chair when a distinguished older man in a tweed suit and felt hat tilted rakishly to one side approached the table carrying a hand-carved cane topped with a sizeable gleaming silver ball.

"Good evening, young lady," he said with a smile and courtly bow, doffing his hat. "May I sit and join you for a few minutes?" His smile and mermerizing blue eyes swayed her towards saying okay. Even though they were in New York, where you didn't even look at strangers, much less talk to them, Lisa felt at home here in familiar territory. The people at the surrounding tables were primarily regulars, people she was comfortable to be with. And while most customers seemed withdrawn and reserved, she relaxed, knowing someone would come to her aid if necessary.

"Certainly," she said, "but I have to warn you that my boyfriend is very jealous, and he's due here any moment." Nothing in her pretty but tired Oklahoma farm girl's face with peaches and cream complexion suggested a lie.

The man's smile broadened, deepening the crevasses in his cheeks and around his eyes while revealing even white teeth.

"Come now, Miss Ogden," he said while slipping into a vacant chair opposite hers, "if we're going to be friends, let's not start out by telling fibs." Relaxing into the seat, he rested the beautiful cane with a gleaming silver ball for a head against the table.

A slightly worried frown creased Lisa's smooth forehead, and a shadow passed through her sparkling eyes as she replied, "Who said we're going to be friends? And how do you know my name?"

Although surprised and curious how the stranger understood her non-existent boyfriend wasn't coming, Lisa experienced more surprise that she didn't experience any real fear, just some sort of small apprehension, the sensation you get while waiting to read for a new part in a play. The man seemed too nicely dressed and acted much too easygoing to be much of a threat, and besides, this was her turf and the place was very public. Nothing about the situation made her anxious; still somewhere in her consciousness registered the thought this man seemed unusual, and she felt wary.

"Well, I said friends, but actually, friends may not be the correct term. Associates may be more accurate, and even that is incorrect. You see, I represent someone. Here's my card," he said, handing her a plain white business card bearing only the words ABRAHAM WEINBERG - AGENT.

"I've been looking for you, well, someone like you, for several days. My ah..., employer needs a talented young woman to play a certain role. The role may entail a slight danger, but he is willing to pay generously." He emphasized the words pay and generously.

"How dangerous and how generous are we talking?" She responded quickly while laughing at what she assumed had to be some kind of ridiculous proposal. Someone was playing a joke on her. Perhaps one of her audition friends. However, she straightened up, putting her feet down, causing Mousy to leap off her lap, seeking quieter quarters.

"And you didn't answer me. How do you know my name?" The strange man and suggested part seemed unusual, and she had to admit, made her more than a little curious.

The man hesitated for a moment before leaning across the table, looking into her greenish-blue eyes while noticing the little flip at the end of her otherwise long, straight blond hair. This brought him the closest he had been to her, and then relaxing back in the chair, he took a second to study her in more detail. "*Nice symmetrical features, honest face with down-home farm girl looks still keeping that country girl innocence and dimples, for God's sake, not to mention a good figure. She'll be perfect,*" his final assessment.

"I've been following you around," he finally answered, "asking questions, listening to your tryouts. As for the danger part, it's real. Potentially very dangerous. You could get killed."

He delivered the lines atonic, with nothing showing on his face.

Lisa's eyes glittered with excitement when death got mentioned; her fatigue forgotten, she seemed suddenly more alert as the agent continued. "That possibility, although real, is very remote and highly dependent on your acting skills. As for how generous, how does one million dollars sound, plus of course, expenses?"

Lisa gasped as though choking on air. She couldn't believe she heard correctly. To a little country girl from the dirt-poor farming town of Oakdale in the middle of Oklahoma, a million dollars sounded like a fortune. Hell, a million dollars would sound like a fortune to most people. As for the danger, what actor wouldn't be intrigued, and possibly challenged, by a role where death could be the penalty for a poor performance.

"When do I start?" she asked after only the briefest hesitation.

With a knowing chuckle, the man reached inside his jacket pocket, extracting a thick white business envelope. As he handed the envelope over to the girl, he replied, "Here are fifty thousand dollars, a list of items you will need to purchase, and a plane ticket. I have taken the liberty of making an appointment for you with Alexis Makin at Neiman Marcus. She will assist you in selecting the necessary wardrobe. Details are inside of the envelope."

The girl's immediate acceptance came as no surprise. She had been followed and studied for many days, her every move carefully observed. Abe had suspected that the thought of danger would be precisely the bait he needed to seduce her into accepting the role. He experienced a bit of shame for using the girl's weakness, so he hastened to add, "I did tell you that this job was not without the possibility of danger, that you could get killed."

Lisa still had a dazed look in her eyes as she moved forward in her chair, visibly sparkling with vitality, her fatigue now forgotten. She nodded affirmatively, sweeping hair back from her face with the left hand, the right hand firmly gripping a thick white envelope.

Abe continued, "However, every precaution has been taken to minimize the risk." As though putting a salve on his conscience, he added, "Once you learn the complete details in California, you will be given a chance to back out if you think it's too dangerous. I believe you will find the job most exciting."

He waited for a response and seeing Lisa still appeared too stunned for speech, he continued, "We won't be seeing each other again, so I can only wish you the best of luck."

With that, the man grabbed his cane, stoop up quickly, and left before Lisa could even say thank you, goodbye, or go-to-hell. She sat, sitting stunned and speechless, looking into an envelope stuffed full of hundred-dollar bills.

CHAPTER FIVE

Soft rhythmic chimes from the telephone gently eased King from a deep slumber into a state of semi-consciousness. Jangling bells and harsh buzzers were banished from his life. As a boy on the farm in Wyoming, his father always woke him for the four a.m. chores by coming into his basement bedroom, moving around quietly, picking up books or pictures, then settling them back in place, making only gentle, rustling sounds. This quiet process never failed to bring King out of even the deepest sleep, usually fully alert and ready to begin the day. On those rare occasions when his father was away, his mother would stand at the head of the basement stairs and yell harshly, "**Carl, time to get up and do chores.**" He swore that when he had his own place one day, every damn alarm would be soft, gentle, and pleasing.

Fumbling with the bedside telephone while still half asleep, he heard himself mumble, "Yeah?"

A cheerful baritone voice greeted him with an insincere, "Good morning," then added insult by saying, "oh, did I wake you up"?

"You know damn well you woke me up, Larry," King barked, now fully awake. "I, like most sane people, enjoy sleeping at four-thirty in the morning. I'm not on the farm anymore. What's so important it couldn't wait for a decent hour?"

Given the time of day and his rude awakening, this constituted a mild retort for the King.

"Thought you might like to know another one of your strips got hit last night," the voice answered. There was no longer any humor in Detective McCutchen's voice. Larry's position as a senior detective in the San Jose Police Homicide Department meant he rarely made calls announcing robberies. This incident made the fourth King strip mall hit in the last twenty-seven days, about once a week. The detective continued, "They hit CAPS," he pronounced with the same serious tone.

"So? Why is a homicide detective calling me about another robbery, even if it is number four?" King, now fully awake and getting concerned by the tone in his friend's voice, slid out from under the covers of his custom-made bed.

"It wasn't just a robbery this time, King," he answered. "They hit Chen's Jewelry. The owner, David Chen, appeared to have been sleeping in the shop. Apparently, Chen's presence surprised the burglar who killed him. A knife right in the heart, very messy."

King had known Larry McCutchen before there was a King and before Larry had joined the San Jose P.D., and long before he became a homicide detective. Back then, King went by his given name, Carl Tanner. He worked as an aerospace engineer at Lockheed Marietta in Sunnyvale, California. Larry moonlighted as a bouncer at Spence's, a local titty bar, while studying law at Santa Clara University. Carl had gone to Spence's on a Wednesday night with a group of engineers to watch amateur night, a weekly feature in which female patrons were encouraged to expose their breasts while gyrating to some taped rock-and-roll. The winner, chosen by receiving the loudest audience applause, received $50.00. A full-breasted Lockheed secretary had entered and naturally, all the Lockheed nerds, Carl included, went in to gawk. Feeling self-conscious and uncomfortable, Carl sat by the door in case he wanted to make a quick exit.

He started talking with Larry, whose job required his presence at the door, and before the night ended, a friendship of sorts, began. Larry soon quit both the law and Spence's for a job with the San Jose Police Department, and Carl started to acquire strip malls. These actions occurred during the late 60s real estate slump, which is when Carl began looking for failing malls.

King took over the mortgage, cleaned up the garbage, resurfaced the parking lot, and gave the buildings a jazzy paint job, a new name, and a bright, catchy sign while never spending over five thousand dollars out of pocket. Before long, he owned ten malls, and people started calling him the mall king. Later it just became King. He quit engineering to become a full-time landlord and developer. His friendship with Larry never really got beyond the occasional cocktail together, but somehow, they kept bumping into each other on either a professional or personal basis. The early morning call today appeared to be a little of each.

"What in the hell was David doing in the shop?" King asked as much to himself as to the detective.

"That's another reason I'm calling you at this ungodly hour. The wife doesn't know yet. I'm assuming he's still married. Knowing that he became one of your first tenants and a longtime acquaintance, I hoped you might volunteer to go see her. Find out what made him be there at that time of night. He may have just been worried about his jewelry, but I doubt it."

"God, Larry, you got a lot of nerve getting me out of bed for this kind of lousy job. But okay, yeah, I'll do it."

Already sitting up and throwing back the covers, he quickly left his inviting bed.

"I don't want some ham-handed police dork rousting her out of bed at four-thirty talking about somebody knifing her husband," King muttered into the phone. "You still at the mall?"

"Yeah, we're bagging and tagging. The thief left the goods. He must have been spooked, but other than that, it appeared to be just like the others. It has to be the same guy. It's a real shame that Chen had to get caught up in the middle of a robbery spree, but that's life. You going to meet me here?"

"Yeah, and please don't let the news have it until after six. I don't want Mrs. Chen to hear it on KGO until after my visit, and I don't want to wake her until at least six. It may be the last decent sleep she'll have for a while," King said.

"You're still the bleeding heart King. You need to spend a few weeks down here with me in homicide and get a few calluses on your emotions. But I agree. No need to hurry the bad news. It will not get any worse by waiting for an extra hour. How long before you get here?"

"I'll be there in thirty-five. Just keep the news quiet. See ya," he said with a sigh, while dropping the phone back in its cradle.

CHAPTER SIX

Two days earlier in San Francisco, Howard Trent missed his first mid-week rehearsal for *Phantom of the Opera* in two years. An understudy for one of the lead roles, Howard earned just a little less than two thousand dollars a month. This included the bonus he got for regularly working matinee performances twice a month. Two thousand dollars doesn't go very far in San Francisco, and with the show about to close, the options amounted to either find another job or move with the show for a few weeks run in Honolulu. Howard had already made his choice. While Honolulu and the warm ocean sounded great, the cost of living over there wasn't any better and living in crowded quarters sharing everything but a toothbrush had gotten old. This was often the only way struggling actors could live and many couldn't, or wouldn't, tolerate the required sacrifices year after year after year with no guarantee of a bright tomorrow anytime in the future, even for the love of their chosen profession.

So, when an old washed-up agent with a plain white business card stumbled into him on the street one afternoon and started blathering about a million dollars for doing a little acting job, Howard said, you've found your man. That the job posed a little danger only added to the mystery. After all, there aren't any guarantees in life. What's a slight danger here and there? The old man said if he possessed decent acting skills, the threat would be minimal, and he damn well knew he was good. He should have been playing the Phantom lead years ago instead of that asshole Wally Pierpont. All the people he called friends told him he looked better than Wally, had more acting skills and had a better voice. At six-one, he had the perfect height although a bit slim, and his dark, brooding eyes and long blond hair made him everybody's favorite, but Wally's father had sunk a bunch of dough in the original Broadway production, and he couldn't be replaced as long as the show continued to sell.

Oh well, that's show biz and the end of the run, at least for now. That crazy old Weinberg with a carved cane featuring a grossly oversized silver ball for a head had given him nearly fifty thousand dollars to get clothes and a car plus rent a large furnished house in San Jose. Everything had to be set up under new names with papers supplied by Weinberg. What the hell, he could play Billy Westlake, computer genius, as well as or better than any other actor he could name. So, he had to develop a new look that none of his associates would recognize as him—no big deal. Hell, makeup and costumes were his forte.

He couldn't help but wonder about the other two people who would live in the other bedrooms. The old man had told him everything would be explained shortly. What was a little danger, anyway?

He still had to call *The Phantom's* director, Jacob Steinman, and tell him he wouldn't be coming back. Although the man would be pissed, Howard couldn't just walk away and not say anything. You never know when you might want another job with the director, and quitting without notice was bad enough. Walking away saying nothing would be fatal. Picking up the small pathetic bag of belongings he had collected over the years from the room he shared with six other cast members, Howard left searching for a public phone and the beginning of a new role. He couldn't help thinking speculatively about his new partners.

CHAPTER SEVEN

Ten oil ministers, each in their own bulletproof Mercedes sedan provided by the Venezuelan government, arrived for the quarterly OPEC meeting in the Canaima National Park. The entire park had been closed for several days, giving all OPEC member nation's security forces time to secure the area. Mr. Jose Barrera had explicitly chosen the park as it featured Salto Angel, the highest waterfall in the world. It seemed only fitting to Barrera that Venezuela, one of the founding members of OPEC, and home of the world's sweetest oil, should display its magnificence. The world's highest waterfall was symbolic of the heights to which Barrera considered his ascendency in world politics.

The sedans being used to transport OPEC's visiting dignitaries were paid for by Barrera using funds he had siphoned from Venezuelan oil revenues. Barrera, the Venezuelan oil minister, and President-Elect was an ambitious man. Gaining the Presidency made only one small step in his overall plan of world domination. His next goal was to govern OPEC. He believed that control of OPEC, which provides over forty percent of the world's oil, would give him an international platform for gaining superpower status. The world as a whole needs oil, and he who controls the oil controls the world.

To control OPEC, he would first have to deal with Mohammad bin Salman, the current president from the United Arab Emirates. As an original member of OPEC, Venezuela had more claims to leadership than many of the newer members, including the Emirates. All the oil companies in the Emirates didn't produce as much oil as any one of the four companies comprising the former Venezuelan Petroleum Corporation. A fact the portly Barrera found particularly annoying since he had served as the President of VPC before being nationalized in 1977 and divided into four different companies. That the world's oil production leadership should be in the hands of this newcomer Salman was more than the fat, newly elected South American leader could tolerate. He had accordingly used all of his powers as an oil minister to arrange for the safe housing and transportation for his fellow OPEC oil ministers.

Carlos, the name under which he began his career in manipulation, extortion, and bribery, started working in the oil business as a geologist for Exxon. As Exxon and British Petroleum oil interests in Venezuela grew, they helped form a private company called Venezuelan Petroleum Corporation with the support of Hugo Andres Velasquez, the country's corrupt dictator. The Barrera family interests coincided with those of Velasquez, and after discovering that President Velasquez had two illegitimate children with a well-known prostitute, Carlos found himself installed as president of VPC with the blessings of both the government and the oil companies. Several leadership changes later, when democracy was given a chance, VPC became nationalized and broken apart. Carlos, who always had a keen eye and ear for the political winds of his country, began using the name Jose Barrera and got himself appointed as the country's oil minister with Petroleos de Venezuela S.A. (PDVSA), the oil industry company. When OPEC began in 1982, Jose Barrera announced himself one of the first ministers to speak out in favor of oil quotas, limiting oil production to drive up prices. It appeared unclear just how much influence his old comrades in Exxon had in this position. What is clear is that oil companies in every country benefited. Some have even suggested that OPEC was the brainchild of Colonel Otto Conrad, the president of Texaco.

Barrera stood in the shade of the park's grand lodge portico to welcome his ten guests. He breathed slowly and deeply to remain calm and prevent sweat from staining his new white Armani cotton suit. He wore a smile plastered on his bloated face, a difficult feat given his vast jowls. A thin dark mustache with curled ends broke up his otherwise bland features. An aide stood by his side to remind him of the exact pronunciation of the difficult Arabic and Muslim names. Winning current favor with other oil ministers was his primary aim. Making Venezuelan Tia Juana Light crude oil the world's primary choice his second.

CHAPTER EIGHT

The outside of King's home in the southwest corner of San Jose, known as Almaden Valley, would win no Better Homes and Gardens awards. The basic look of a rustic Montana sheepherder cabin deliberately made the entrance appear squalid and uninviting. Located on ten acres of scrub rangeland nestled against the coastal foothills, an old-weathered railroad caboose covered with faded Union Pacific yellow paint served as the entrance to a ten thousand square foot mansion invisible from the road. A gravel drive circled a few scattered cactus plants in front of the old railroad car, which with clever landscaping, hid the main house. Creosote railroad ties lined a walkway from the road and served as terraced steps leading to a small aggregate concrete porch. A large front door tiled with apple crate boards still bearing their faded lettering had been cut into the side of the railroad car, completing the picture of desperation. It didn't have the appearance of wealth and indeed not the home of a king. One small step inside the ugly board front door took away the breath from the few visitors ever invited inside.

The entire caboose served as a foyer with sand-colored marble flooring sprinkled with potted palms. Directly ahead were two turquoise marble steps leading down to the lazy room decorated with soft leather tan couches facing a two-sided river-rock floor-to-ceiling fireplace surrounded by stacks of multi-colored throw pillows. The house branched off on both sides of the fireplace with 18 rooms covering ten thousand square feet. This did not include the indoor swimming pool. No expense had been spared decorating each room with a different theme.

There was a Japanese room, the mountain room complete with babbling brook and pine trees, a Hawaiian beach, and an indoor swimming pool complete with pounding surf and the white room used for meditation. The King bored quickly and wanted a space to complement each mood. Whenever he found himself in a particular frame of mind for an extended period, he just called Ester, the decorator, and had a room redecorated to match the feeling. Whatever the current mix of themes, they always seemed to flow seamlessly into each other without creating a choppy mixed-up confusing effect. King remained a bachelor who pampered his every whim. Fortunately, most of his unusual delights showed excellent taste.

After cradling the phone, King hustled out of his round king-size bed into a serpentine shower. At 58, he groaned a little as the aches and pains that came with growing older pulled on his body. Standing six feet tall, he kept his weight at one-eighty by working out twice a week and jogging three miles every other day. Although streaked with silver along the sides, his hair, still dark and curly, hung down over his forehead. The ladies considered him ruggedly good-looking, but his wealth formed a barrier keeping him single. While lathering up with coconut oil soap in the shower, the murder of Dave Chen kept preying on his mind. It seemed like his strip malls were the only ones being targeted, and that bothered him. With a waiting list for vacancies, his occupancy rate almost always hovered around 100 percent, but news like this could empty buildings fast.

The early morning sky had grown into a silver-gray mirror when King pulled out of his garage and headed uptown. Leaving home, he took Cherry Ave north through patches of madrone in the foothills towards Almaden Expressway. Following the road up and down the gentle hills, he let his mind wander, looking for answers.

Why just his malls? Was there any other common thread? Each entry had been different, but in each case, only one store had been hit. What did that mean?

Thinking about it, King began wondering about the builder. It seemed like the Cabrini's had built each mall where a robbery had occurred. Brothers Dario and George Cabrini were the developers, sons of one of the city's oldest families. They still owned hundreds of acres, although they had made their fortune as developers, not farmers.

King would have to check to be sure, but it seemed like they had built every mall that had been targeted. If so, what did that prove? The Cabrini's surely weren't hitting their own malls. They were probably one of the wealthiest families in the area; besides, they had built over fifty percent of the valley's strip malls. Still, it was something to think about.

His mind kept rambling on his drive to meet Larry at CAPS. Maybe he should ask Ann to go with him to visit Chen's wife. Ann Chou was practically the only woman in his life. Her shops, ***OUTRAGEOUS STYLES,*** were the preferred hair styling shops for the moneyed. At the tender age of 22, she kicked her abusive Chinese husband out the door and went to beauty school so she would not have to depend on a man ever again. After graduation, she found space in a strip mall that had just been redecorated and charged reasonable rates. Hanging up her sign, she started out being true to the name by charging outrageous prices. Believing that if you pay more, it must be better, the upper-class clientele started coming, and before long, she had three shops serving the valley's elite and prosperous matrons.

King was the landlord for all three of her shops. They began dating shortly after she rented her second shop and had toyed with the idea of marriage for over twenty years. Both had loved and lost during their first marriage. They each loved their privacy, so they did the mating dance, although neither one took it seriously.

Ann was Chinese, a stunning beauty with a soft heart, and a genuinely lovely person. She would be a big help in consoling Mrs. Chen. King punched a button on the steering wheel while giving her name to his hands-free built-in telephone system. King worried that this early, she would be furious, but what the hell. Duty calls.

CHAPTER NINE

After Weinberg left, Lisa found herself trembling with an envelope full of money clutched in her hands. It had happened so suddenly. One moment her life was sailing along, taking voice lessons, waiting tables, attending tryouts; then- Bam! Out of nowhere, a man came along with a life-changing proposition and stuffed an envelope full of money in her hands.

Did taking on this new role make her stupid? Just how dangerous could it be? *I mean, what do you have to do to earn one million dollars?* These thoughts and fears kept running through her mind when she finally loosened her grip on the envelope and peeked inside. Along with the stack of bills, several other items had been included, along with a folded piece of regular office stationery. It had her name right across the top, clearly addressed to her.

FOR: Lisa Ogden
THIS IS YOUR ROLE:

CHARACTER: Janet Hills
OCCUPATION: Executive secretary
EMPLOYER: TRANSTECHNOLOGIES INTERNATIONAL LTD. (Transtec)
PRESIDENT: Mr. Theodore Blankenship

BACKGROUND: Janet Hills is twenty-eight years old with three years of experience as an executive secretary. Before that, she worked as a file clerk, office manager, and girl Friday. She graduated from Billings Business School in Atlanta, where Miss Hills was born and educated. She speaks with a slight southern accent. She has a father and mother, both alive and a sister that models in Paris. She has been in her present position at Transtec for three months.

IMPORTANT NOTE

Consider this as just another role, with the following exceptions:

1. Do not discuss this job or your new name with any of your current friends or family. This precaution is necessary for their safety and your own for reasons that will soon become clear. You were told that this role had potential danger. You will have one last chance to back out in San Jose. This assignment should last only two weeks, but could last a month. Tell everyone who may need to know that you won a free cruise and will contact them when you return.

2. Apply your Stanislavski studies to this role and develop a thorough background for Janet, including your parent's names, the name of your sister and friends, the schools you attended, etc. As a method actor, you will need to understand the role of the executive secretary thoroughly. Learn all you can about this position, the argot (if you don't know this word, look it up), duties, responsibilities, and behavior patterns. You will be given the appropriate lines when this becomes necessary, but you must be capable of delivering a believable performance.

3. Begin rehearsing this new role immediately, however, not in the presence of your current associates. Come to think of yourself as Janet Hills.

4. Leave all your present identification in New York, taking only those items included in this envelope pertaining to your new identity, (drivers license, credit cards, and social security card). The credit cards all have the minimum limit being provided primarily for identification. Use cash whenever possible. Receipts will not be required.

5. Upon reaching California, stay in character **at all times**. Your associates will also be role-playing, and it is most imperative that you all use and maintain your assigned identities. Failure to do so will unnecessarily risk the lives of yourself and everybody you know. You must use your assumed background whenever talking about the past. DO NOT FORGET. Once you leave New York, **NO ONE** is to know your real name, *especially* the other characters in this drama.

Be at 458 Dilbert Avenue in San Jose, California at exactly 1:00 p.m. on Wednesday, August 11th. The enclosed, one-way airline ticket is valid anytime; however, you must make your own reservation. You may leave for California at the time of your choosing as long as you make the Dilbert Avenue appointment. Your appointment with Neiman Marcus here in New York is for tomorrow at 11:00 a.m. Please ask for Miss Ainscroft on the third floor. Housing in California is arranged and will be explained along with the project's details at your Dilbert meeting. Use some enclosed money to lease a vehicle in California under your new name. You must pay cash, so choose wisely. Miss Ainscroft will see to your beauty appointment for hair colorization and styling. As an actor used to stage makeup and costumes, you must develop a new look for your role as Janet Hills. When you get to California, you will understand the reasons behind this necessity. When in costume and full makeup, *it is imperative* that no one in your present life would recognize you on the street.

Memorize this letter, then burn it. VERY IMPORTANT!!!!

Good Luck, Abe

Lisa read the letter several times, and each time had more questions than the time before. Just what had she gotten herself into? The envelope contained a new California driver's license with her picture and the name Janet Hills. Now that was interesting. The picture barely resembled her. She appeared much older; her face seemed more significant, with pronounced eyebrows half-hidden by designer eyeglasses. There were several other differences, including her hair color. She could barely recognize herself and wondered if anyone she knew would recognize this as her picture.

Then, the envelope contained fifty thousand dollars plus several credit cards, although the note made it pretty clear that the cash should be spent on new clothes.

What if she just took the money and ran? She could cash in the ticket and buy a new one for the Caribbean or someplace. But then what? What about the million dollars? How much danger could there be?

Despite her questions and second-guessing, in her heart, she already lived in California. It all boiled down to curiosity, an actor's occupational hazard. She had always been that way. Her mother's voice echoed in her mind, telling her about curiosity and the dead cat. But hell, life was to be lived, wasn't it? Still, those three little sentences were hanging around in the back of her mind. Just thinking about it resulted in a bit of fear, causing a slight twinge in the back of her neck.

Receipts will not be required. It could be very dangerous. You might get killed.

Okay, time to get moving. She had a lot of things to do in the next couple of weeks and a plane to catch.

CHAPTER TEN

Shit!

Shit! Shit! Shit!

Shit, hell damn.

Why'd that old fucker have to be there? Goddamn!

Why'd I leave the shit there, anyway? Should-a kept the crap. They ever catch me, I'm gonna get it anyhow. Now, what am I gonna do for money? Got that key coming. If I don't get the grease before tomorrow, I've got more than cops to worry about. Shit, hell damn.

Think!

Did I leave anything there?

Ropes!

They don't matter. Just Orchard Supply junk.

The sack!

Oh, God! Nah, never mind, just an old pillowcase. Don't mean nothen.

You sure?

Yeah. It ain't nothen. Just an old pillowcase. They can't trace it to anybody.

Still...,

Yeah, shit.

I'm more worried about some cash. Need some serious shit before tomorrow night.

Might as well hit the next one now; no sense saving it.

We're not ready.

Course we are. Seen the plans. Know their schedule.

What about supplies?

Don't need no fucking tools. This one's easy. Go right in the back door. Jimmy the lock with my knife. Oh shit, I got to get another knife, but the place is ready; I got it scoped.

Okay. Let's do it. Better hurry. It's starting to get light.

Shit!

CHAPTER ELEVEN

A dark, square wooden table with twenty-five foot sides dominated the large second-floor room of the Canaima National Park's main lodge. Originally a space for dancing and parties, Barrera had it redecorated to serve as a war room. Large maps covered the walls between windows below which desks sat with computer monitors where Barrera's aides could study news reports from around the world. Oversized soft cushioned leather-covered chairs were along each side of the enormous conference table. Several hard-wooden chairs for the minister's aides sat behind each member's cushioned seat. Many of the aides chose to stand and observe the news monitors rather than sit in uncomfortable chairs. Sitting or standing, they were alert for any signal from their leader should their attention be required or some task needed to be performed.

Mohammad bin Salman was a small, thin man with a cruel face. A knife fight in his late teens had left a large white scar extending from his left eye to the corner of his thin-lipped mouth. A peaked nose separating dark hawk-like eyes gave him the look of a perpetually hungry predator. Salman knew his looks were intimidating and used this to help maintain control over others. He not only looked mean; he had proven repeatedly that opposition to him in any form could spell disaster. Many former enemies had simply disappeared. No one asked where they had gone. One man not intimidated was Carlos Jose Barrera. He also knew how to make adversaries disappear.

As the meeting progressed, it became clear that Salman was campaigning for another oil embargo. He wanted to further slowdown the world's economy by reducing the oil supply. Many OPEC members had significant cash reserves, and a crippled world economy would make it easier to buy into other industries and reduce the price of real estate. While

Carlos respected this position and even agreed with it in principle, he could not let Mohammad win this battle. He believed the time had come for him to claim OPEC leadership, which meant he had to oppose the proposed embargo. Fortunately for Carlos, Indonesia, Qatar, and the United Arab Emirates needed increased production to cover short-term debts. These countries had some allies among the other Muslim members, so Salman had difficulty selling his position. Those who needed money were more passionate than those sitting on fortunes, simply looking for a bargain. The battle raged around the table, with minister after minister shouting to be heard.

Carlos, happy with the way things seemed to be progressing, kept his smile hidden while he plotted his next moves. He had already decided that it would be better to wait until tomorrow before revealing his strategy. Give the hungry OPEC members a few more hours to work on their brothers with more financial reserves. The girls and forbidden alcohol had been waiting for the meeting to adjourn. Carlos wanted to suggest adjourning the meeting. Let that idiot Salman make one more outrageous demand. Their host would suggest they postpone the discussions for now and enjoy a rewarding interlude with beautiful young girls and refreshments.

CHAPTER TWELVE

The early morning sky above the eastern San Jose foothills was streaked with hints of red and purple when King arrived at the CAPS. A lingering chill in the air caused him to shiver when he got out of the Mercedes. *I should have grabbed a sweater,* he thought. It didn't matter that he had lived here for over thirty years; he always forgot to bring a sweater for the cool mornings during the summer.

Detective McCutchen stood leaning against an unmarked car, writing in a notebook when King arrived.

"Morning, detective," King said, faking a sour look.

"Good morning, King; what took you so long?" This jab by McCutchen seemed to be his standard way of greeting whenever the two met and was one of the reasons they weren't better friends.

Ignoring the long-standing jibe, King asked, "What do we know?"

"Looks like one guy. He climbed the utility pole at the back. Took off the heat vent and dropped to the ceiling on a rope. It looks like he went directly to the jewelry shop. Like the other robberies, he hit only the one shop." Larry folded up his notebook and put it away.

Still shivering trying to get warm, King asked, "How much did he get? I assume we're talking about a guy. Any idea?"

"Nothing," Larry said, frowning in disappointment. "It looks like Chen surprised him, and he just left everything. The thief probably surprised Chen too. The thief stabbed him in the heart." King nodded in understanding, not feeling the need to comment, so the detective continued.

"It looks like the thief was kneeling behind the cases, jimmying a cabinet door with his knife when Chen walked in, probably rubbing the sleep out of his eyes. Our perp hears something, whips around, sees Chen, and panics. He already has the knife in his hand, so he just shoves it up, right into Chen's heart."

He paused to see King's reaction. "Then the thief panics and splits, leaving a pillowcase half full of jewelry." The detective paused again while watching King's response to the news.

"Anything that will help us find this asshole?" King asked.

"Nothing beneficial; he wore gloves. He left some rope and that old pillowcase I mentioned. The rope looks like a standard Orchard Supply product, impossible to trace. We might get lucky with the pillowcase but don't hold your breath. In any case, it will take some time."

"Hey Larry," King said. "I got to wondering on the way over; it seems like Cabrini built these malls that are being hit. Does that help us in any way?"

McCutchen rubbed his chin in thought. "I didn't realize that, but I don't see how that solves anything. They built practically every damn thing in the valley."

"I know it seems that way," King said, "but lots of other developers built stuff. It just seems like at least one strip built by somebody else would have been hit."

Detective McCutchen again scratched his chin in thought. It reminded King of Mr. Magoo, the nearly blind character in those old cartoons. "You might have something," he said. "Although every mall that's been hit has been one of yours, maybe they just don't like you." He added with that infuriating cop grin that implies they know more than they're telling. McCutchen thought the look would piss King off, which was one more reason they could never be closer friends. "Let's go look at the scene," he said, "and then you can go talk to the widow."

CHAPTER THIRTEEN

Joe decided to drive up Highway 101 to San Jose instead of taking Interstate 5. It would take a little longer, but he had all day and most of tomorrow before his meeting at Dilbert Avenue. Going north out of Los Angeles, Highway 101 was infinitely more interesting than I-5, and besides, driving his new Ford Explorer made the whole adventure a trip all by itself. It was not actually new, but the 1996 white V8 SUV looked and smelled fresh. Fully loaded with every option available, including a moon roof and CD changer that held six disks, it had to be the perfect executive vehicle in the driver's mind. Cruising along 101 north of Santa Barbara, Joe had no trouble pretending to be Theodore Blankenship, president of Transtecnologies International Ltd. Even if he got picked up for speeding, the ticket would go on the Theodore Blankenship driver's license stored in his new executive wallet. This thought made Joe smile, but every time he started getting comfortable or feeling smug, he kept thinking disturbing thoughts like *receipts will not be required,* or *you were told that this role had potential danger. You might get killed.*

What in the hell did old man Weinberg get him into? And how had that old man created his driver's license? According to old Abe's instructions, he had made himself up to mirror the looks depicted on the license and was comfortable playing any part in a drama. Still, he wondered about the requirement that no one he presently knew could recognize him in his new role.

He had taken 101 to view the sights and enjoy the trip but instead found himself only semiconscious, driving more on autopilot than with intent. The warnings in Abraham Weinberg's letter kept recycling through his brain; *Danger! Do not tell anybody! Be sure and stay in character!* Not that he felt necessarily afraid or anything. He thought of himself as no more or less a coward than anybody else; that he didn't know the danger's source caused his angst. What is it about this role that could be so dangerous? The unknown is frightening just because it is unknown. Fretting about it wasn't helping. But it seemed impossible to keep any other thought in mind for more than a few seconds before coming back to the same questions. Questions without answers kept pounding at his brain. In many ways, the trip to San Jose was one of the longest in Joe's short life, but in another way, by spending the entire trip inside his skull, the trip ended before he realized it. Using the internet while practicing his new role of Theodore, Joe had previously located a Red Lion Hotel conveniently downtown just off 101 and close to Dilbert Avenue, his ultimate destination. His research had confirmed the presence of a nearby bar where he could get comfortably smashed while rehearsing his new role as company president.

He slept late the following day, and there were still several hours of anxious, pre-curtain jitters ahead of his one o'clock meeting. The hours seemed endless. He drove the Explorer aimlessly around city streets, getting familiar with his new home. On the road, close to the hotel, he came across a very modern glass and steel sculptured high-rise. A large grassy area dotted with Japanese maples, blue spruce, and old redwood trees surrounded the building. Out front, an elegant six-foot sign made of aggregate concrete announced the building. Imbedded in cement, large brass letters reflecting the sunshine glittered like golden neon lights:

TRANSTECNOLOGIES INTERNATIONAL LTD.

Joe's heart started racing when he spotted the sign. He immediately pulled over to the curb and jumped out for a better view. Glancing around the grounds he didn't see anyone except for an old gray-haired man sitting on a bench about two-hundred feet away down a sidewalk that curved in and around raised flower beds full of multi-colored pansies, yellow mums and bright red gardenias. Curious, he walked up to the building and tried the big glass doors to find them locked. His mouth seemed extra dry, swallowing became difficult, and he noticed his hands were shaking.

"My God, could this be his company? Surely there wasn't more than one TRANSTECNOLOGIES INTERNATIONAL LTD. in San Jose. Was he safe being here? Was he being watched? Confused, excited, and still frightened, Joe returned to the Explorer and left with even more questions.

He didn't notice the smiling face of the old man on the bench holding a silver ball-tipped cane as he drove away.

When it became time to locate Dilbert Avenue and meet his supporting cast, opening night jitters set in, making him a shaking wreck. The time had come for opening night; he was about to enter stage left, and he had never felt less like a company president in his life. The unassuming ranch-style tract home at 458 Dilbert Avenue did little to settle his jangled nerves. He flipped down the visor to check his makeup and hair one final time before opening the car door to begin a million-dollar performance.

CHAPTER FOURTEEN

San Jose had been chosen as the meeting place for several reasons. One, it sat in the heart of Silicon Valley, the high-tech capital of the world. And two, it just happened that a new modern office high-rise right next to the San Jose airport was vacant while waiting for the city's final occupancy approval. That King owned the building resulted in several conveniences, not the least being that it was available for other, less approved uses until the city granted the building an occupancy permit. That King had one real friend from his past meant another even greater convenience. Allowing this friend the undocumented use of his new office complex for a few weeks while the city, as usual, kept dragging its feet before granting the basically proforma occupancy permit, proved a convenient way for King to stick it to the city.

A furnished house on Dilbert Avenue leased to William Westlake had been chosen for the three actors' initial meeting. After getting the lease and settling in, Billy would have been amazed to learn that his house had been visited by several other individuals unknown to him and totally unauthorized by the lessee.

On the drive towards the meeting, Howard kept thinking about the past two weeks in his role as Billy Westlake. Finding a vacant three-bedroom, three-bath house near the Cox Industrial Park in downtown San Jose had taken more time than he had expected. The dot-com revolution created a severe housing shortage, jacking up prices faster than a Japanese bidding war for a rare Van Gogh at Sotheby's in New York. The rate he was going through money caused a bit of unease. Although it wasn't his, being a poorly paid actor didn't lend itself to feelings of affluence. While enjoyable in one sense, spending thousands of somebody else's money still brought twinges of unease. Getting the house furnished while completing other assigned tasks had pushed him to the limit. With growing anxiety over completing all the chores assigned by Weinberg, he hadn't had the time to worry about his new role or the upcoming meeting with his other cast members.

At a stoplight, he took a final quick glance at the folders on the seat. One last chance to make sure he had checked off all the chores on his folder. A half-smile wrinkled the corner of his eyes as he caught the outside label.

William Westlake (Pre-op Instructions)

In capital letters, just below the name, you could read the warning, **"USE THIS NAME EXCLUSIVELY."** This folder contained his preparation instructions. The material in his pre-op package had been highlighted in many places for obvious reasons. The first, to ensure his personal safety; the second to protect the integrity of the project. His associates' names were included in the list, the same ones he was heading to meet. The final warning stipulated that *any* failure to use his assigned name would mean immediate dismissal and the forfeiture of the million-dollar bonus for participating in the project.

Also, inside had been complete documentation for his new name, including credit cards and a California driver's license featuring a holographic photograph appropriately doctored to match his new look. Now how in the hell did that happen? Looking at himself in the rearview mirror, he didn't think that anyone in his present life would recognize him on the street.

The last item contained a reminder to destroy the folder and all instructions once the chores had been completed. Three other folders containing additional role instructions also sat on the seat. These folders had just magically appeared at their rented house the previous evening.

Being familiar with the area after having leased and furnished the house on Dilbert, Billy discovered a Chevron station two blocks away. He used the restroom to tear up the folder and its contents to be destroyed, then flushed the pieces down the toilet. After checking his makeup and costume one final time, a lazy, devil-may-care smile crept into the corner of his eyes; he became, officially, William Westlake.

Driving down 10th street towards Dilbert, he began having severe misgivings for the first time, wondering if he had made a mistake by agreeing to play the creative inventor genius. A million dollars was a lot of money, but you only have one life. Before his thoughts became fixations, he reached Dilbert Avenue, a broad palm-lined avenue in the heart of old San Jose, the garden city. This area had once been the most significant truck garden soil on planet earth. The rich soil producing some of the world's greatest harvests had been covered with asphalt, cement, and extensive business complexes producing the world's most desired electronics. Turning towards the railroad tracks, he dodged potholes in the neglected street before turning into a wide circular driveway fronting a stately old plantation-style house. Ordinarily, the house would rent for at least three thousand dollars a month; however, a developer had purchased the property intending to put in condominiums. While waiting for the city's final building permit, the developer made it available for rent on a month-to-month basis at a significantly reduced price.

Howard picked up the three folders from the car's front seat before getting out and locking the door. As he strolled up the walk to their temporary home, he began putting on his stage face. The front door glass reflected a cocky grin below wide-set dark-brown eyes framed by long streaked blond hair in a ponytail. He was wearing Michael Jordan sneakers without socks, faded jeans, a sloppy sweatshirt complete with ragged holes, Silicon Valley's image of an eccentric genius. William Westlake, wild Bill to his friends; a genius, he knows computers, he will compute. Unlocking the front door, he left it open, waiting for the other two cast members to join him on center stage.

CHAPTER FIFTEEN

In his Mercedes 450SL with the top down, King was halfway between the murder scene at CAPS and Ann's house in the East Hills when his cell rang. It was McCutchen, letting him know that another strip mall had just been hit. Apparently, the thief who had left Chen's shop empty-handed stopped on the way home to hit another one of King's malls. This time, a computer shop in the Mediterranean Village got hit. No telling yet how much cash was stolen. Still, several computers were missing, along with many memory chips, modem cards, and other miscellaneous items quickly convertible into cash if you weren't concerned with getting top dollar. Larry had received the information over his police radio and called King just as a favor. With a homicide mixed in with the robberies, burglary and homicide would work together to solve this current rash of break-ins. Another Cabrini built mall. King decided this needed investigation, whether his friend Detective McCutchen agreed that this was a relevant factor or not.

Ann appeared dressed in a stylish beige pantsuit with a warm woolen wrap and headscarf. She thought King would drive his Mercedes with the top down. This seemed always to be the case unless it was raining. She stood waiting by the front door when King drove into her driveway and was standing by the car door by the time the car stopped moving. Sliding into the passenger's seat, she leaned over and brushed a kiss on King's cheek while exchanging greetings. Although the occasion was grim, the smile on King's face and the twinkle in Ann's eyes made it apparent that they were happy to see each other.

The meeting with Mrs. Chen had been depressing, and King felt the need to get involved somehow. Ann had done most of the talking, taking the widow in her arms and offering condolences along with a warm hug.

King mostly just watched, nodding at appropriate times, looking sorrowful and feeling helpless. After their visit, he and Ann had eaten a late breakfast, during which neither one ate nor said much. Talking seemed out of place and irreverent while events of the day had killed their appetites. During one of these silent moments, King remembered telling McCutchen how strange all the malls being robbed had been built by the Cabrini's. After taking Ann back to her home in the foothills, King decided to visit the developers.

Dario and George Cabrini were the grandsons of Marcelo Cabrini. Through hard work and clever management, this Italian immigrant ended up owning over a thousand acres of orange and prune orchards. For nearly a hundred years, the Cabrini's were one of the area's largest farmers producing fruit that graced tables worldwide. Dario and George inherited the family business when old Marcelo died in 1958 at the age of ninety-eight.

Silicon Valley remained a dream in Hewlett and Packard's eyes at that time, although their company was rapidly expanding and attracting other businesses to the region. Sensing change and tired of being farmers, the two brothers started selling prime parcels of land for commercial development. Someone suggested that they could put up their own buildings on the property and make even more money. Not only that, but banks were willing to finance the buildings and assume the entire risk. They became small commercial developers and with success larger and larger until, by 1980, they were one of the two most prominent developers in northern California. Much of the old land and orchards had been sold during their ascendancy, although they still owned over two hundred acres of prime Silicon Valley real estate. Their twenty-acre compound of elaborately fenced orange trees spoke volumes about their wealth.

Cabrini's offices and construction yard occupied only a tiny part of their large prime real estate parcel in the heart of Willow Glen, one of San Jose's oldest and most prestigious districts. Tall old palm trees reaching over sixty feet high lined a wide paved boulevard leading from their arched adobe gateway on Meridian Boulevard to their two-story Spanish-style headquarters. A six-foot high adobe fence enclosed the entire estate, which still included hundreds of orange trees planted by the first Cabrini's over a hundred years earlier. The adobe fence and gate were painted a blinding white, making the estate stand out distinctly from the million-dollar houses lavishly spaced on the surrounding streets.

As King drove around the fifteen-foot fountain in the masterfully landscaped courtyard, he passed Dario's son Marco just pulling out in his shiny red Ferrari. The two men waved at each other in recognition. Parking his Mercedes under a couple of massive old-growth palm trees, King followed a red sandstone walkway to an inner courtyard where he paused a moment in front of the eight-foot high dark wooden doors before passing through into a spacious, fabulous foyer with another bubbling fountain surrounded by lush plants in ornate terra cotta pots. Graceful classical statues and a soaring roof created a feeling of wealth and power. Indirect lighting from overhead windows and skylights created a bright, welcoming atmosphere. Going around the fountain to the reception desk on the opposite side, he stepped up to an old Spanish desk that looked big enough to serve as a carrier launch pad.

"Hi Arlene, is Dario or George around?" he asked, faking a smile.

"Hello King, long time no see," she said, fluffing her hair back with both hands. Pulling both hands and arms back simultaneously stretched the tight pink sweater across her large breasts in what she hoped was a sexy, provocative, and suggestive move. Although married, it had long been her fantasy that the single King would be smitten by her big boobs and whisk her away to a secret island where they could live forever in sexual bliss.

"I don't think George is busy right now; let me check," she purred.

Punching a button on the sleek, sculptured white intercom box, she spoke into the machine, "Mr. Cabrini, the King is here to see you, okay if I send him in?"

She looked up with a sly, conspiratorial smile as though she had just done him a favor and expected something sweet in return.

"Yeah, send him in," a deep baritone voice came from speakers hidden somewhere overhead. His voice sounded normal and nearby, as though the man was present in the room. Obviously, the Cabrini's were not stinting on their communications budget.

Dario rose from behind a big gleaming solid teak desk with an outstretched hand as King entered the large, designer-decorated corner suite. Floor-to-ceiling windows formed two walls, revealing a private inner courtyard where palm trees and colorful flowing hibiscus plants lined a small river-rock brook complete with ferns and green moss. Crossing an acre of deep rust-colored carpet, King shook hands with one of the Valley's most influential builders, a man of real strength, physical and otherwise.

A flowered Hanalei shirt retailing for four-hundred dollars didn't hide the muscles bulging in his arms and upper body. Loading crates full of oranges as a youth in the orchards had filled out a large frame with hard muscles that Dario kept up with frequent workouts both at home and in a gym behind his office. His bald bullet head with piercing blue eyes made for a formidable look that he used at city hall and with county commissioners to get projects approved rapidly.

"Hey King, what brings you to my humble palace," Dario asked with a grin. He and King had been working friends for years. While they didn't run in the same social circle, they had a deep respect for each other's brains, stamina, and business sense. Sitting in one of the soft, high-backed red leather side chairs without being asked, King replied.

"I've been trying to figure out why it's only my stores that are being robbed. We had two more hits this morning. You guys built every strip mall that has been hit recently. Is that a coincidence, or what? I can't figure out why only malls built by the Cabrinis seem to be targeted."

"You don't think we're robbing your stores, do you?" Dario asked, sitting back in his rolling desk chair with a grin on his face that suggested no one could take that proposition seriously.

"Of course not, Dario; hell no," King quickly replied. "I know you're not knocking off my stores. But something weird is going on." King leaned forward in the leather chair, looking earnestly in his friend's eyes. "How come they're just robbing the malls that you've built?"

"My God, King," Dario said, surprised, "you sure?"

"Yeah, I'm sure. I even talked it over with McCutchen. He's going to be looking into it as well."

"I don't have any frigging idea," Dario said. "Why just our buildings?" he mused, then stood up, flexing his arms in a movement that strained the buttons running down the front of his colorful Hawaiian shirt, then stretched sideways both left and right with his arms reaching overhead before sitting back down. "That helps clear the mind," he said with a wry smile.

"Anything that helps," King responded. "I like to breathe myself," he added with his own tight smile in a mocking gesture.

Dario caught the tease but, realizing the seriousness of the situation, went back to business.

"How can we help King? What do you want us to do? What *can* we do?"

"Well," King began cautiously, realizing that he was about to start something that could alter their friendly relationship. "I just wondered if maybe I could look at the blueprints of the old malls you built twenty and thirty years ago. Several of my malls were built years before I bought them. I have prints for the ones we've built the last fifteen years, but it's the old ones I'd like to look at. They are the ones being robbed."

He looked in Dario's eyes as he asked for the favor to see how his friend took the request. Would the developer be offended, as though somehow King was blaming him for the robberies? King was relieved to see nothing but interest and concern in the big man's eyes.

"Hell yes, let's look at them together," he boomed. "I'll have Arlene fetch em right now." Punching a button hidden somewhere on his side of the desk, Dario spoke into the room as though his receptionist was standing right by his side.

"Hey babe, get us the prints for S- M-0-1, S-M-0-2, and S-M-0-3. Pronto. Mucho, quicko."

With a big grin displaying a mouthful of brilliant white teeth Hollywood actors paid thousands of dollars to duplicate, he stood up and waved to an old antique drafting table standing in a dark corner across the carpeted room. Dario merely spoke some command, and the corner instantly blossomed into light, revealing the highly polished brass swivel and turn screws on the old table. Its surface had been refinished with a hard-thin white plastic coating. They had barely reached the table when

Arlene sashayed into the room, swiveling her hips carrying three large rolls of old vellum drawings.

Thanking her, Dario took the rolls and laid two rolls down on the floor, removed the protective sleeves from the other, and then began unrolling it out on his restored drafting table.

"Well, come on, King, don't just stand there," he grunted. "Let's get to work."

King moved over and helped hold the curled drawings flat so that they could be studied. If only he could figure out what in the hell he was looking for.

CHAPTER SIXTEEN

After spending nearly ten minutes dodging potholes while looking for house numbers on Dilbert Avenue's sad excuse for a street, Lisa finally found the numbers 458 in faded black paint, nearly obscured by overgrown juniper bushes. She had yet to discover that the entire neighborhood was soon to be demolished and replaced by townhouses or condominiums. Wearing designer clothes from Neiman Marcus, giving her that groomed executive look, Lisa settled into the role of Janet Hills as she approached the ridiculously shabby front door of the old mansion. She was still adapting to the black wig, which seemed to add years to her appearance besides making her sweat. Fortunately, she had given herself plenty of time to find the address. A quick glance at her new Citizens Charmer wrist watch showed the time to be 12:59. One minute to the main entrance. Lisa Olsen was about to disappear for a while. That sudden thought gave her the chills, making the skin on her head feel tight, and goosebumps suddenly appear on her arms. She hoped Lisa's disappearance would not be permanent.

Receipts will not be required; you were told this role had potential danger.

Using an old acting technique to steady the nerves, she deliberately thought of an antidote to fear, in this case a one-million dollar acting fee, as he took the three steps onto the front porch and the wide-open door.

Billy Westlake paced the sitting room inside, anxiously awaiting his co-stars. He expected a tall man in his late twenties who looked like an all-American college boy turned businessman and a beautiful young woman with long, black, straight hair. She posed as an office manager with brains to match her good looks. The man he expected to see should appear as an ex-football jock turned Silicon Valley executive. Their first names were

Janet and Ted. While not being told for sure, Bill assumed his associates were also actors and Ted and Janet were assigned names. They should arrive separately but within moments of each other.

Looking through the open door, Janet saw a large foyer that branched right into a comfortably arranged sitting room and left into the dining area. A beautiful parquet floor extended throughout all three rooms. Billy had hired a low-priced decorator to help furnish the rooms with furniture that, although used, looked like good quality and seemed to go well with the old house. Abe Weinberg had suggested the big-screen television in a note left in his mailbox. Bill was not aware of the other hardware that had also been added. Besides the television, the note included sealed instructions to be opened only when Billy met his other two partners at one o'clock. In the corner of the room, Billy was hidden from the front door when a banging suddenly jerked him from his anxious wandering by someone banging on the door knocker. Putting on a practiced stage face, he walked across the room to the open front door and the beginning of scene one.

Janet saw a lanky young man with dark, brooding eyes crossing the room. Looking at his shabby clothes, she felt terribly overdressed, and a twinge of stage fright tightened her stomach. There is always that little familiar flutter, followed by a dry throat and slight tremors in her legs, precisely the same as the first stage entrance on opening night. The man's casual attire was topped by sun-bleached blond hair pulled back in a ponytail, setting off classic Nordic features, high cheekbones, and clear blue eyes. *"My God,"* she thought, *"surely this isn't the local dress code?"*

"Hi, are you Janet Hills by chance?" he asked.

At least his voice had excellent timber, full and resonant.

For a second, she stood, feeling confused. This wasn't a theater stage. It was a personal residence in downtown San Jose. Hearing her stage name from strange lips in this unorthodox setting took her by surprise.

"Oh, ah, yes. And you are...?"

".... William Westlake, but just call me Bill, Wild Bill," he said with a grin, ending her misery. "Come on in. You're the first to arrive, but Theodore should be along momentarily."

He understood why she had hesitated. He had been having the same problem using a new name in public. It is different running around town using a strange name, not at all like being on stage. Having another name on stage in a theater behind the proscenium arch is one thing, but remaining in character while doing real-world activities is a different matter. Getting used to this kind of acting could take a little time. He was suddenly struck with the thought that there would not be any rehearsals. It never occurred to him that certain operators in the criminal population had been assuming false identities on the run for centuries.

"Well, I'm delighted to get here finally," she said, trying to regain her composure. "And how is it you know my name and this Theodore guy?"

"Oh, that's easy. I was given your names to put on the lease. I've got a whole packet here for you as soon as Ted arrives. Speaking of which, I think his car just pulled in behind your Mercury."

They both watched as a handsome man with dark hair and the sculptured features of a Greek statue got out of a Ford Explorer and stood in the driveway, drinking in the scene. Oozing charisma by the bucket, he appeared perfectly at ease in the body of an athlete, moving with the grace of a ballet dancer. Wearing a thousand-dollar cream-colored Harvey sharkskin suit over an open neck brown silk Italian shirt and a pair of five-hundred dollar black loafers, he looked every inch the successful Silicon Valley executive.

Ted had been exposed to plenty of beautiful women in the theater, but there was always something artificial about their appearance. Even offstage, the theater women seemed contrived as though they were still acting. Standing in the driveway surveying the house and open door, he could see Janet standing in the doorway, and she appeared in a whole different realm. Wearing very little observable makeup and dressed for the business world, she seemed so secure, so official somehow. Here in real life, without all the glitter, glare, lights and props of the theater, she appeared so wholesome, a real natural beauty. Not realizing how badly he misjudged her composure, a tribute no doubt to her acting skills, he thought it would be tough playing up to her standard. Stunned by Janet's appearance, he almost failed to see the lean, ponytailed man standing behind her in the doorway. He knew they were watching him as he approached the sidewalk, walking towards the front steps.

"Are you Theodore Blankenship?" Billy asked as Ted made it halfway up the sidewalk.

"Yes," he answered without hesitation, along with an award-winning smile. "Call me Ted, and you are....?"

"I am William Westlake, and this is Janet Hills," he responded with a devastating smile of his own while indicating Janet, who was still standing on the porch, "My friends call me Bill or Billy or wild Bill."

"Let's all go inside where we can get to know each other, and I can give you each a package containing your new lives," Billy said while he and Ted shook hands. He turned and led the way inside, shutting the door once they were all in the foyer.

Taking stock of the sitting room and sparse furnishings, Ted asked, "God, who chose this place?"

Billy took his time answering while indicating places to sit as he studied his new partner. Ted had the look of someone born into money and title, yet something in the depth of his eyes suggested he was not just another empty suit. It would be a mistake to underestimate him. Old Abe had done well, choosing Mr. Blankenship to run their corporation. Ted had the casual look of a successful Valley executive and he wore it well. He simply oozed charm and success.

Bill was slightly envious, but then he didn't get to choose his role.

"You can blame this meeting place on our illustrious leader," he replied, finally answering Ted. "This is our temporary home, and I can show you and Janet your rooms after we've finished with this meeting. We each have our own bedroom with a private bath."

"You mean Abraham Weinberg chose this?" Janet asked.

"Yeah, he's the guy I spoke to," Ted said.

"No," Bill responded. "I said our leader. He gave me instructions for the kind of place to look for, and this is what I found with the help of a realtor."

"Then who are we working for?" Janet said impatiently.

"Ah, the fun begins," Bill responded with a wicked grin. "I don't really know."

His companions both looked stunned and somewhat uncertain about what was happening. How could they not know who they were working for? Who was going to give them one million dollars?

"I have some folders here for you," he said. "They will explain a lot about who you are and what you will be expected to do. You'll get them as soon as you agree to continue with the project. I'm instructed to tell you all I know, which is practically zilch. My orders are to turn on the television, and supposedly all will be explained."

A playwright never wrote a better opening scene and lines. Bill had the total and complete attention of both parties in his audience. Walking across the room, he pushed a button turning on the television. Within seconds a man's image appeared, and he said with a broad grin, "Good afternoon Janet, Ted, and Billy. Have a seat there on the couch so I can see you all at the same time, and we'll get acquainted."

All three people were stunned, speechless. None of them expected to be greeted remotely by someone through a television set. Obviously, the man on the television screen could see them just as they could see him. Unsettled and unsure, they each took a seat on the couch with Janet sitting between the two men.

"Ah, you make a handsome threesome," the man joked. "You may refer to me as Gene, although we will not be meeting in person. We will communicate electronically when necessary. Are you comfortable? Want a drink or something before we begin?"

The three actors looked at each other, and although they all had dry mouths, none of them wanted to delay the proceedings for the time it would take to get a drink.

"No," they said in unison. "Let's just get started," Ted suggested, speaking for all three. He couldn't help staring at the man in the picture. He seemed like an older Victor Mature, but somehow familiar.

"Okay then, let me tell you what you have been chosen to do," the man began. "In just a few minutes, you will each be given your last chance to quit this scene and return to your former lives. If you stay, the next few days will be the most interesting, exciting, and dangerous time of your lives."

Three confused and insecure actors sitting on the couch all had the same thoughts running through their minds; *receipts will not be required-you were told it could be very dangerous, you might be killed.*

CHAPTER SEVENTEEN

After putting in a long day, homicide detective Larry McCutchen was heading home when, on an impulse, he decided to stop by the Cabrini brother's offices and ask a few questions. Marco's bright red Ferrari sat parked in the shade of an old cypress tree, and the young man himself could be seen lounging on one of the visitor's couches in the foyer. Although they had never formally met, Marco recognized the detective from his irregular appearances on the news. Of course, McCutchen knew a lot about young Cabrini and his exploits with the Ferrari. While traffic was not his interest or passion, police officers talk among themselves, and Larry had heard a great deal about Cabrini's efforts to keep Marco out of jail for his misuse of the public roads.

As the detective entered the building, Marco had a sudden chill run down his spine, reminding him of a spooky expression he had heard on television about somebody walking on your grave. Trying to shrug it off, he bounded to his feet while putting on a smile, much like donning a hat before going outside.

"Hi, detective, what brings one of San Jose's coolest cops to our humble home?" he chirped, extending his hand.

"Hi Marco," he responded, letting the youth know that recognition was a two-way street as they shook hands. "Is your father or uncle around?"

"Dad's here. I had hoped for a chance to have a little father and son chat, but since you're here, I think I'll try to catch him later. See ya around," he threw over his shoulder as she slumped out of the building.

Larry wearily strolled over to Arlene's desk, who watched him approach. "Is there any chance I can have a few minutes with Dario?" He asked, smiling at the comely and very sexy young lady.

"I already buzzed him about your visit. He said to send you right on in. Just go straight ahead through those big double doors."

Tired from his long day, the detective reluctantly tore his eyes away from the voluptuous vision sitting at the desk and trudged ahead as directed.

"Hi, Larry, it's been a long time stranger," Dario boomed out in his normally effusive loud manner, coming around an acre of desk and shaking the detective's hand. "I haven't seen you in years. Ever since that night at the Greek's place, what is it, Zorras, no Zorba's; yeah, that's it, Zorba's. We got drunk together on Ouzo; ain't touched the stuff since," he said, grimacing at the memory.

"Lord, that seems like a long time ago, Dario," McCutchen said. "Since then, you've gotten rich and fat, or should I say richer and fatter?"

"And look at you, Lars," Dario retorted, returning to his desk, "still mean and hungry? What brings a homicide detective to my humble digs? It can't be pleasure, and I haven't killed anybody, so it must be some kind of business."

"You been paying any attention to the news?" Larry asked. "Heard about all those shopping mall robberies? One of the robberies turned into a murder last night. As it turns out, I think every mall that has been robbed is a mall that you built. That's the first thing I want to check."

"They're all my malls. The King made it by here earlier with the same question, but hell man, we built half the damn malls in the valley."

"Yeah, I know, still with five malls hit in as many weeks, the laws of average say at least two or three should have been malls built by somebody else. Why do you think they're just hitting your malls?"

"Damned if I know; we pulled all the plans when the King was here earlier trying to figure it out. Couldn't find a thing."

Larry looked around the large spacious office, trying to imagine being rich enough to afford an office like this. Larger than the average home's living room, the office was surrounded by glass on two sides, with one whole wall opening into an enclosed courtyard with a fountain and lush plants obviously well tended. Seated behind a teakwood desk about the size of the bathroom in Larry's house, Dario looked very much at home in his custom-made Cabrera chair.

"King," Larry snorted. "I should have known he'd have been around. Mind if I look at those plans of yours? Maybe something will occur to me that you guys didn't think about."

"Fat chance," Cabrini smirked. "Hey gorgeous," he barked into the room, holding down the intercom button, "bring back those drawings I had you file a little while ago. The ones you got for me to look at with the King."

It wasn't long before Arlene entered, carrying several rolls of vellum drawings. "These drawings are surely getting a workout lately," she said. "Everybody wants to see them."

Larry and Dario looked at each other as suddenly a light came on in both brains. "Who's everybody?" Dario barked.

"Why, a few months ago, Marco started looking at these old drawings. It seemed like every week, he could be found poring over them. I thought it was some kind of project for you. Then this morning, you and King, and now you and Detective McCutchen."

When Arlene finished, Dario's face had turned dark with anger. Hastily excusing herself, she deposited the vellum rolls on the old drafting table, then wheeled around and left the room. She saw that look on her boss's face and was glad that his wrath wasn't directed in her direction. Still, if you stand around and watch a tornado, there's a chance you can either get hit by flying debris or sucked into the vortex. She chose to get out of Dodge before bullets started flying.

"Goddamn," Dario exploded after Arlene had left. "It can't be Marco. Hell, that kid has got all the money he needs and then some. There must be some other explanation."

Even though he wanted to believe his own words, Dario knew in his heart that somehow Marco was involved. He didn't know why, he didn't know how, but he damned well was determined to find the answers.

CHAPTER EIGHTEEN

As the meeting dwindled down with the two sides locked in a battle over whether to impose another embargo, Barrera interrupted to suggest that they table the discussion for the day and retire for a few drinks and enjoy their surprise guests. He led the way out of the conference room to an elaborate bar under massive wooden beams surrounded by tables loaded with appetizers. Playing the ever-gracious host, Barrera had provided everyone's favorite liquor or wine and food. Although most ministers were publicly Muslim, in private or surrounded by their peers alcohol was more than welcome.

The lounge opened onto a large deck featuring a spectacular view of Salto Angel Falls which sparkled in the afternoon sun, with water falling several hundred feet into a radiant pool. The falls truly made an incredible sight captivating everyone fortunate to have the experience. Fueled by a few drinks and the pleasant aroma of hand-rolled Cuban cigars while enjoying the fantastic environment, the oil ministers were ripe for an encore, and Barrera did not disappoint. Wanting the guests to be forever in his debt, he had arranged for twenty of the most beautiful courtesans in the world to be in attendance. As the oil ministers mingled in the lounge and out on the open deck, the girls filtered into the room, all dressed in provocative gowns that revealed much while concealing everything. They were there clearly to amuse and entertain the guests, yet they played coy while flirting outrageously at the same time. The men were captivated and could not wait to take advantage of their host's generosity, but first, dinner. Each minister had to choose one of these gorgeous creatures for their dinner date. The fun was in deciding which girl to choose. Every nationality and every race were represented. There were blonds, brunettes, redheads; Asian, European, Nordic, African, and middle eastern. Each man wanted them all, yet they could only choose one.

This dinner partner selection process played a part in Barrera's strategy. Making the ministers choose yet providing them with a delicious choice was preparing them for tomorrow when he would provide them with another delicious option. Hopefully, they would prefer him to succeed that asshole from Egypt.

Tomorrow was going to be an exciting day. Nobody would guess precisely how interesting it would become, including, and especially, Barrera.

CHAPTER NINETEEN

The marquee sign read Valley Electronics, which is where they had been doing business selling high-end computer peripherals for five years. Their business had outgrown their 3000 square-foot facility, and the other fronts were occupied, leaving no room in the East Hills strip mall to expand. King had provided the owners 5000 square feet in a newly built mall only two miles away at the same price for one year, plus he paid their moving expenses to keep them as a tenant. The move was almost complete with a few boxes of inventory still located at the East Hills mall, plus the display windows that continued to feature the company's high-priced products with a discrete sign in the window directing customers to their new location. For anyone passing by on the street, the business still appeared to be operating at this location.

Marco still needed another ten thousand dollars to pay for the kilo of Peruvian flake he had been fronted earlier. Dealers in the illicit drug business rarely fronted their distributers or sub-dealers. This business is cash upfront, and if you don't have the money, you don't get the product, period. This one time, Marco's dealer let him take a whole uncut kilo of pure Peruvian white without upfront cash, simply because Marco would always make good; otherwise, there were consequences which Marco could not tolerate, such as having his Ferrari appropriated and held hostage. Even worse, the dealer could go to Dario and demand that the father make good on his son's drug debt.

Unfortunately, Marco had thrown a big weekend bash and gone through the entire kilo instead of selling off half or three quarters, his usual method for covering an expensive drug habit. Having already gone through the monthly allowance provided by papa, he had counted heavily on the jewelry heist to pay off the ten thousand owed his dealer. Getting panicked and leaving the jewelry behind hurt badly, and his next hurried robbery had netted almost nothing. High-end electronics were always a hot ticket, easily fenced. Marco had avoided the East Hills mall because they provided no easy access to the roof, and its location was highly exposed. Running out of time to pay back his dealer, Marco decided to hit Valley Electronics. It might take two or more trips inside to haul away enough to cover his debt, but he couldn't see any alternative. Equipment being fenced didn't bring in the top dollar, especially hot equipment and a desperate seller. The jewelry store could not be hit again, and every other option proved just as risky.

He drove by the mall several times, building up his courage while checking out the neighborhood and storefronts. At three a.m., everything seemed quiet. There were no pedestrians around, nobody out for a late-night walk, and no homeless dudes sleeping in the doorways. There didn't appear to be any security cars driving around and no cops. Marco debated whether to park close to the rear of the mall so he would not have to carry a heavy bag of electronics a long distance or hide his rather noticeable car in the shadows under the trees near the wall at the back of the property. He decided that hiding the car made the most sense. There was always the possibility of a cop or security car driving by, and a car parked by the mall was an invitation to investigate the circumstances, especially as there had been a rash of mall robberies in recent weeks.

Marco came prepared with a grappling hook attached to a rope with his trademark knots every three feet. A sling over his back carried the tools needed to remove the air vent and enter the shops below, plus some heavy bags for carrying the electronics. Although the parking lot was well lit, Marco wasted no time getting inside the roof and finally through the ceiling of Valley Electronics.

Surprise.

The store was practically bare, just a few boxes of extra components, plus the display. Marco knew he could not go near the front windows; the risk of being spotted was just too significant. The boxes of modems and routers would not bring enough money to make it worth his while, but two boxes held iphones and accessories, which would almost make him well. A locked office seemed strange, so Marco forced the lock to gain entry. The only thing in the office appeared to be a square cardboard box holding a glistening round metal ball. He did not know what he had found, but since it had been stored in a locked room, Marco decided to take the ball on a whim. It might be worth a lot since they kept it in a locked room.

Happy with his evening's work, Marco made his way back to his car undetected and drove away, trying to decide the best way to fence the stolen phones. He needed to make a quick sale, but it couldn't be too cheap. He needed ten grand. And what about that silver ball? Maybe it would bring a high price if he could only figure out what it did?

CHAPTER TWENTY

The man on the television who called himself Gene smiled before beginning. Dressed in gray slacks with a cardigan sweater over a plain white shirt, his benign expression enhanced by silver hair and faded eyebrows gave the impression that he was somebody's favorite old uncle. Still, something about him seemed to stir memories of someone else.

"You three are here at my invitation and expense," he began. "I have been working on an extraordinary project for more years than you have been alive. That project is now ready for its next step, which begins with an essential demonstration. The project's further development requires considerable funding. I intend with your help to steal this money from OPEC, the large oil corporations, and a few other huge corporations. The theft is more on the order of a big con, a sort of scam, some would call it a big hustle, but it is still stealing. If we get caught, the results will be devastating, a catastrophic event. Any one or all of you could lose your lives. After we succeed in obtaining the money from these people, they will spare no expense or effort to find and punish those responsible."

The three people sat on the couch, speechless. Each person's eyes were dilated with the adrenaline coursing through their veins, while dazed looks covered each face.

"Good, I see that I have your attention," the television man said with another whimsical smile.

"Now you might understand why I stressed secrecy and why none of you know each other's real name. This is why you are all in costume and why you all traveled here under your stage names. Hopefully, you all followed my instructions and told none of your old friends or family your stage name or where you were headed. If any of you have violated this rule, speak up now. Your future safety and the lives of your fellow actors next to you on that couch depend upon your truthfulness. You can leave now, keeping whatever money you have not spent with no fear of an adverse consequence, even if you slipped up and told someone. You will simply be replaced. By not knowing who the other players are in this drama, you cannot cause any of us damage." He had a somber look on his face.

"Did any one of you tell anybody about your new stage name or where you planned on being for the next few weeks?"

Billy, who had spent more time working on various projects for the leader, spoke first.

"No. I didn't tell anybody. My last job was ending anyway and leaving the group I lived with is just a natural progression in our lives. Nobody keeps in touch. We're all too busy trying to hustle a new job."

Janet spoke up next in a somewhat shaky voice. "No one knows the name of Janet Hills except for these two guys and you. Everyone back home thinks I won a cruise."

"Yeah, I'm clean," Theodore said, speaking up last. "The folks back in Pasadena probably don't even realize that I'm gone. There are so many actors pounding the pavement they never really pay any attention to who's there and who isn't."

In a commanding voice, looking very stern, Gene asked, "Does anybody want to leave at this time?"

Nobody spoke, but the three actors on the couch looked at each other, then all shook their heads in a negative motion.

"Okay, that's great, then we can proceed," said the television man.

It was kind of hard to figure out his age. He appeared to be middle-aged at one moment, and seconds later, you would swear he appeared as an older man. A minute later, he looked like a young man in his mid-twenties. Seated in a big padded brown leather chair with indirect lighting and many shadows, it was difficult to determine his height or weight, as there didn't appear to be anything in the picture that provided a reference. Only his upper chest and head were visible, and to a trained actor, he was obviously wearing a disguise. He took this security thing seriously, and this emphasis was not lost on the three actors studying the screen. They could assume as well that Gene was not his real name.

"I am going to review each of your roles, so there are no misunderstandings, okay?"

The three spellbound actors all nodded again, bobbing their heads up and down.

"Speak up. I don't want you just to nod your head. I want to hear each of your voices."

All three actors immediately spoke up, affirming that they understood his request.

"Okay then. Billy is the President and principal owner of TRANSTECNOLOGIES INTERNATIONAL, LTD. This is a real company, properly and legally organized. Billy, Wild Bill, invented and developed the anti-gravity machine, which will be used to con ten billion dollars out of OPEC and the large oil corporations of the world. Yes, I said ten billion dollars. To make this con work, we need a corporation front which explains Transtec. Billy hired Ted as the CEO and frontman for the corporation for which he received some founder's stock. This will show up in subsequent investigations by anyone interested, and there will be a lot of interest." He paused to make sure they were all paying attention.

"Ted has the business and leadership acumen to organize and run a major Silicon Valley research and development corporation. His background resume of experience will satisfy a very in-depth investigation and analysis by anyone snooping into his history. Actually, the same thing can also be said for Billy and Janet. The media and our government, not to mention those who are about to be scammed, will be very interested in who they are dealing with. Hopefully, this will explain a little about why you must stay in your roles at all times."

Gene took a drink of some amber-colored fluid before continuing.

"Janet is a real girl Friday. Not only is she the office manager, but she handles personnel and public relations, for which she also received founder's stock. All correspondence goes through Janet. Corporation ownership is hidden and will take considerable time and talent to discover what you have just been told, but this information will be uncovered since everything is legal. Additional digging, which our victims will certainly do in the future, ultimately proves that the corporation, while legal, is a fraud. Before this occurs, you three will have disappeared with your million dollars, using another safe identity."

He had their attention. Visualizing a million dollars in your hand is always an attention grabber.

"In public, Ted will assume the leadership role and act as company spokesman, while Billy will act as his subordinate. Billy's public role is that of an eccentric genius inventor. Only when you three are alone and in a secure location can Billy's true nature as the real boss be exposed. I know this sounds kind of crazy talking about true nature for an acting role, but hopefully, you all get the picture. While you may think of yourselves in a protected environment, and it is safe to let your guard down, in reality, there is no offstage for this production. Every scene is live, no matter where you are. There is no such thing as privacy, given the scam we are perpetuating. Our adversaries will go to any extent possible to probe for even the most intimate details of your lives. Any questions so far?"

"How come I can't be the open leader?" Billy asked.

"Billy, you are a Silicon Valley inventive genius. You have great engineering talent, but business is not your forte. Ted has the bearing, skills, and educational background to run a successful corporation. Supposedly, Transtec has some venture capital behind its development. The development of the prototype you will be demonstrating took a great deal of money, although who provided that funding will remain a mystery. These mysterious venture capitalists insisted that Ted be the CEO. Ted will insinuate as much, if and whenever it becomes necessary."

The three actors fidgeted in their chairs as they assimilated the information and tried visualizing their roles.

"If there are no more questions, we will proceed. Starting this afternoon, Janet will send out a press release to several media outlets that I have identified announcing Transtec's proprietary development and a public demonstration to be held in two days. Special sealed monogrammed invitations to this demonstration will be sent via registered courier to each OPEC member, the giant oil companies, other large corporations, and of course, the media. That means television, newspapers, etc. This information has all been prepared. You guys with me so far?"

They all nodded at first, then remembering the admonishment from their earlier reaction, each was quick to voice an affirmative response.

"Over the next two days, Billy will become familiar with his invention and learn how to operate the controls. The invention is real. You will demonstrate an actual working model based on an invention dating back more than half a century. A live demonstration will take place at Transtec in front of worldwide television viewers and several very interested parties. Since this event will be on television, and various newspapers will print photographs of the demonstration, you now understand why no one in your real life must recognize you in the pictures."

Here Gene paused momentarily while letting the words sink into their thoughts.

"Ted will rehearse the demonstration sequences and learn how to control his audience. Janet will become familiar with the office equipment and how to become an effective event organizer. Tomorrow, you will all have tutors and experienced instructors for your various functions. However, none of these peripheral employees will know anything about your business or what you are doing. They have been hired for their specific expertise in a given area, and once that has been accomplished, they will be on their way. At no time will anyone other than you three individuals be apprised of the true nature of this enterprise. Is that crystal clear?"

They all nodded simultaneously while voicing understanding.

"No!" the television man said. "I want to hear each of you individually say that you get this message."

"The message is crystal clear," Ted said, speaking first. "Only the three of us in this room, plus you, of course, know what this is all about."

"Very good, and you Janet?"

"Oh, I get it in capital letters. No one else is to know about us, period."

"Good answer," the boss said, smiling, "and you, Billy?"

"Hell, I don't even want these two guys knowing that I'm trying to pull a scam," Billy responded. "Yeah, I get it. It's just us three amigos and the boss."

"I have devoted over thirty years planning this adventure. That does not mean that something cannot go wrong. I will be astonished if something does not go wrong. You three were chosen because you are all intelligent and have demonstrated an ability to improvise on your feet. From what I have witnessed, you are all accomplished actors, even if you lack experience. Impromptu scenes may be required. Given our script, the tools we have to work with, and our D.A.D. machine, plus the circumstances in which we are operating, I believe we have an excellent chance of pulling off the greatest con in history."

"If you three play your roles properly, no one will ever know your true identity. None of you have fingerprint records. I checked. You are each acting outside of your comfort roles and normal daily lives. When this is finished, in roughly two weeks, you will each have earned one million dollars and be given a first-class ticket to three different destinations under other names and passports to be provided. Once you have arrived at your final destination, you will destroy all false identification, costumes, wigs, and makeup used to create your character and resume your old life. It would be in your best interest to forego splashing money around."

There was a brief pause while Gene took another sip of the amber-colored liquid, contemplating his following words. Before speaking again, his countenance took on a severe, extremely stern appearance.

"Listen up and pay attention."

His following words, while spoken quietly, boomed like amplified sound waves vibrating every cell in each actor's body.

"After this is over, under no circumstances are to you contact any of your fellow actors in this drama. Do not try to learn where your fellow actors are from, anything about their previous lives, or where they are going. As you intermingle with each other, exchange information about your stage persona as though it was your real background, making that person more real for you and your fellow actors. Remember to **always** stay in character. Always be aware that any slip about your real identity or plans could ultimately be disastrous for you and your acting mates. Any questions?"

Billy squirmed in his seat for a second before asking, "Yeah, if we are going to be scamming ten billion dollars, it doesn't seem fair that we are only going to get one million each."

Gene's face took on a sad look with a whimsical smile.

"Greed is the destroyer of souls, groups, and corporations. You are being offered a handsome wage for roughly one month's work. True, there is some danger, so the wages are priced accordingly. If you do your jobs as required, the risks are minimal. More money will not ease these risks. I have not planned this exercise because I need more personal finance. That I have personally funded each of your presences here today should confirm that fact. The money we will receive will be used on a greater project requiring considerable funding. The ten billion dollars is not an arbitrary amount. If you do not wish to perform in this drama for the proffered wage, please leave now. You may keep whatever monies you have left from your advancement and simply leave. I do not want disgruntled or unhappy cast members. This project requires your full attention and devotion. Unless you are fully committed and content with your role, and the offered rewards, then now is the time to leave."

The three actors sitting on the couch looked at each other, but no one moved. They all wanted to take part; in fact, they were eager to get started.

When no one said anything, and they all remained seated, the boss continued.

"Now is the time you were promised by Abe when you received your original instructions. You know the proposed drama and have some understanding of the risks involved. When OPEC and big oil discover the scam, they will squeal like pigs locked on a nose ring for the first time. It will take two to three days after you have safely left San Jose before they discover that they have been conned."

"You can also bet that our government wants this device, and many other governments worldwide would like to own this technology. Naturally, they will scour the earth looking for you and, of course, me. Over the next few weeks, I will plant several false trails for them to follow. I will disappear along with the money. If you have followed instructions, you too will disappear, and your true identity will never be discovered unless you foolishly reveal your role in this little adventure. Because we are all human, you each must guard your true identity from the others. If someone slips, their life will be forfeit, and you do not want them telling the rest of the world who or where you are. Is there anyone who wants out at this point? From here on, it will be tough for anyone to leave without compromising the overall project. Everything we have accomplished to date will have to be scrapped. Does any one of you wish to go?"

"No, I'm in," Ted said, looking at first Janet and then Billy.

"Me too," Billy chimed in quickly. "I can't wait to get started."

"I'm a player," Janet said. Then, showing the brains behind her beauty, she continued, "You undoubtedly discovered that danger attracted me and knew I could hardly refuse this role. On the other hand, I can think of a lot of useful things that one million dollars will add to my life."

A big smile spread across Gene's face on the television as he concluded the broadcast. "In that case, I suggest you all take a little break and get familiar with your lodgings. You have an appointment at Transtec in about two hours for a meeting with D.A.D. Goodbye for now."

As the television went silent, the three actors sat overwhelmed without speaking for a few moments. Ted recovered first, standing up to finally break the silence. Tracing circles as he paced in front of the couch, he asked, "Did you guys notice the cane sitting beside Gene's chair?"

"No, I missed that," Billy responded. "What of it?"

"It was a fancy wooden cane with a large gleaming silver ball for its head. When he propositioned me in Pasadena, I saw a cane that looked exactly like that in ole Weinberg's hand. I'm betting that Gene and Weinberg are the same people."

While describing what he had just witnessed, Ted became more and more convincing, and by the time he had finished his statement, he no longer had any doubt about the truth of his observation.

"It makes sense," Janet added. "The fewer people involved, the less chance there is of a leak. If this thing is as dangerous as we are being led to believe, Gene, or whoever he is, does not want us to know his real name. In case something bad happens, who could ever locate a non-existent agent. And we already suspect that Gene is a fake name; plus, it's pretty obvious that he wore full makeup for our little presentation."

"Yeah," Billy said, jumping in, "I missed the cane as well, but we are dealing with a pretty smooth operator. What do you suppose the deal is with that cane? That silver ball on the top seems to be too big for an ordinary cane. It appears to be very awkward, yet he always seems to have it by his side."

"He said this caper has been in the works for many years," Ted said. "You can bet that he has tried to cover all the bases."

"Aren't you guys just a little curious about D.A.D.?" Janet asked. "We're going to be meeting him, it, them or whatever in a couple of hours."

Both guys looked at her with the same bemused expression, like, of course we're interested, but we'll know soon enough. It was up to Billy, the creative genius, to give words to the thoughts in everyone's mind.

"I can wait a few more hours before seeing just what it is that is creating the danger we'll all be facing. Remember, receipts will not be required," he concluded, sending chills racing down everybody's spine.

CHAPTER TWENTY-ONE

King drove his 450 into an unpretentious-looking garage entrance behind some trees and shrubbery on the west side of the house. The door and driveway invisible from the street led to an underground garage that looked like a showroom for great classic cars. The first models of Ford's Thunderbird and Mustang were displayed with the 1957 Chevy Bel Air and his favorite, a 1967 red Cadillac Deville convertible. He had just parked the Mercedes and headed for the elevator when his phone rang.

"Yeah, this is King."

"King, Josh here. I just heard that one of the stores in your Mediterranean mall got robbed. Is that true, and which one?"

"Oh, hi, Josh. Yeah, it's true. Someone hit Valley Electronics. It sounds like they stole a bunch of phones and stuff. Why, are you interested?"

"Oh, God! Yes, I had some equipment stored there. Deke was helping me out with a little computer project, and I left one of my prototypes there for him to tweak. Maybe I'm lucky, and the thieves left my project alone. I'd better get on over to his store and check it out."

King stood waiting outside of his elevator to continue talking with Josh as telephone reception in the elevator was weak to non-existent. "I talked with Larry McCutchen earlier, and all he mentioned were some phones and a bunch of missing chips, so maybe your project is just fine. I hope so."

"Me too. Thanks, King. I'd better run and go check it out anyway. Later man," he finished, but before ending the call, King got in a final word.

"Let me know if I can help Josh," King's words slipped through the receiver before Josh killed the call.

King knew why his friend seemed so upset. Josh, a fellow former Lockheed engineer, was the only individual King considered a real friend. They had both left their old aerospace company at about the same time.

Both had been briefly married, but each had lost their brides shortly after marriage. King's wife had been killed in a tragic accident when a drunk driver rammed head-on into her car, and Josh's wife died of leukemia six months later. Josh had invented many useful electronic devices over the past thirty years, making him a very wealthy man while the King had become wealthy through real estate and commercial development. Their mutual backgrounds, shared losses, and wealth brought them together, but their genuine love and respect for each other had only grown over the years. If one of Josh's latest inventions had been stolen from the computer shop, it could mean the loss of perhaps millions, and King felt for his old companion. It might prove very difficult to get the stolen property back.

Josh had also invested heavily in some of King's commercial projects, including the new building near the airport. Josh had exclusive use of King's latest office building for a few weeks in exchange for a solid granite sign and a few inside improvements. Josh's investment in the building had not been disclosed. It was a side agreement between the two friends. The temporary access contract with Transtec was a legal agreement between Transtec's Theodore Blankenship and King. King knew this to be a sham agreement with a non-existent entity, but he trusted Josh to keep him out of trouble with the law. While it is technically illegal to lease the building before receiving an occupancy permit, it is legal to have a contract providing access to decorate and provide interior improvements. Josh had explained there would undoubtedly be a great deal of subsequent interest in the bogus agreement with Transtec. It would, however, be easy to document the improvements made to the building's interior by Transtec and absolutely no way to prove that King had any idea Transtec was just a sham and Theodore Blankenship a fake. While the King suspected that his old friend had some kind of highly illegal and possibly dangerous project, he also thought Josh protected him by intentionally keeping him in the dark as to whatever was really happening. King had his own problems with these robberies, and his friend's recent problem seemed best handled by the police, anyway. He only hoped that his friend's 'project' would be found quickly.

CHAPTER TWENTY-TWO

The clock read shortly after two o'clock in the afternoon when Ted, Billy, and Janet met on the steps of Transtec. Meeting in front of the etched front doors proved nearly too much for Janet. Although she had lived and operated in stylish New York for several months, this modern sculpture serving as a new temporary home brought up the thought that she might be inadequate to play the role she had been chosen to play. It was just too much, too soon. Looking around to see if they were noticed, she wrapped the blue suit coat across her chest as a sudden chill tensed her body. Billy pulled a simple brass key from his pocket and handed it to Janet with a bow, failing to notice her discomfort.

"Your pleasure, madam," he said, grinning.

Trying to keep her trembling hand steady, Janet accepted the key with the same mock solemnity with which it had been offered, giving her own half bow from the waist. As she touched the lock, Ted reached out, putting a hand on her shoulder, keeping her from opening the door.

"Shouldn't we get a picture of this or something?" he said, looking around as though expecting the press to be swarming all over the sidewalk.

"Nah, let's just get this show moving," Billy responded. "We have to call the boss and get a news announcement placed this afternoon. From now on, we are going to be on a real tight schedule. If we are going to play this scene correctly and keep our lives, we'd better follow orders. Besides, who would you show the picture to anyway?"

Janet opened the door without waiting for Ted to respond, and they entered the building. A glowing panel on the wall to the right just inside the etched glass door had many blinking red lights. Bill hurried over and started punching in a code.

"Hey!" Ted said. "How come you know the code so well?"

"It's today's date, Transtec's birthday," he announced. "Gene decided that today would be the company's official first day. I just entered today's date."

Janet and Ted stood mesmerized just inside the front doors. A soaring atrium going up ten stories took their breath away. Large thirty-foot palms softened gleaming glass, marble and stainless steel. A silent laminar-flow black marble fountain fifteen feet in height fed a small stream that wandered in between potted ferns and large elephant ear philodendrons serving as both privacy screens and decoration. Soft leather couches in earth tones separating the plants were located around the lobby under the palms. A large central stairway towards the rear split into two arches curving towards a mezzanine on the third floor.

"Come on," Bill said with the excitement of a new homeowner giving his friends their first tour. "Our main offices and stuff are on the third floor. Just let me lock this door to keep out the riff-raff."

While speaking, he pushed a button electronically locking both doors, then waving an arm forward, started leading his small party upstairs. As they climbed the stairs, Janet asked, "What's this thing about a news announcement?"

"Ah!" he said. "That's one of Ted's masterpieces. It's a monogrammed press release that you put in today's outgoing mail, plus an email that goes to every news agency and publicity firm listed in the telephone directory. Actually, the boss wrote it, but Ted gets the credit. All we have to do is make sure it goes out today and that we're prepared for our big demonstration in two days."

"My God!" Ted said, wincing. "Nothing like an opening night, is there? I don't want to sound picky or anything, but don't you guys kind of at least miss the dress rehearsal?"

Janet grinned. "When Abe talked about this job, he said I would find it most exciting. I'm beginning to see what he was talking about."

A few minutes later, after examining their offices and the large conference room in which they would demonstrate D.A.D., Transtec's CEO Ted Blankenship leaned back in his oversized leather executive swivel chair and grinned at his two associates as they all shared in the company's first pot of homemade coffee.

"I think it's time we gave our fearless leader a call on that telephone of yours, Bill."

"No need," Bill responded. "The one on your desk works just fine. Just hit the start button three times before dialing, and that activates the system. Push the conference button, and we can all take part at the same time."

"Hey, that's pretty slick," Ted mused while searching the pad for the correct keys to punch. With a life and interest centered on the arts, he felt somewhat technologically challenged, but he had always been a quick study and rapidly came up to speed. It only took a few seconds to punch in the correct code and the speed dial number for Gene.

"Good afternoon folks, I wondered when you would check-in," a voice boomed around the room. The sound came from the receiver on the desk but was also piped into speakers around the room so that it seemed to surround the listeners. Although slightly distorted by the empty-barrel sound of speaker-box electronics, plus some additional unidentifiable interference, something sounded hauntingly familiar about the voice filling the office.

"Hello Boss," Billy said into the room, "how did you know we were all on the speaker?"

"Just lucky, I guess. Have you all roamed around a little and checked out your new playpen?" Although the content of his words seemed friendly and well-meaning, Gene's voice sounded severe and cold.

"Yes," they all responded, almost in unison. Then Janet added, "This is really a very impressive setting," completely unaware of the theatrical allusion.

"Well, we are going to be putting on a pretty impressive show in a few days. Speaking of which, it's time to send out our formal announcement. If you open the center drawer of your desk Ted, you will find the formal invitations plus the press release and a list of addressees. There are several copies there, so give each of your partners a copy and let's get down to business."

Ted opened the sliding drawer and retrieved a small stack of papers. Barely glancing at the papers in his hand, he gave Janet and Bill each a copy of the top sheets. As the three Transtec officials read over the press release, you could see the color slowly drain from each face. It was Billy who put words to their feelings.

"Oh my God!"

CHAPTER TWENTY-THREE

Barrera had momentum running his way and sensed that the opportunity to gain control was at hand. Sweat ran down his neck and under the arms, staining his new white linen suit, despite the well air-conditioned room. He worried that this might make him look weak or timid. This fear caused him to hesitate in exploiting the debate to his advantage. While wrestling with these thoughts, one of his aides handed him a news story that had just come over the wire. This was a story released by UPI for worldwide dissemination. Taking some time to grasp the significance of what he had been reading, he stopped for a few moments before realizing that conversation around the table had ceased.

He held in his hand a gift from God. This paper could be far better than his plans for wresting control of OPEC from that Egyptian bastard. He took a moment to plan his next move. Everyone looked at him to see what had captivated his attention. He looked up apologetically, then wiped the sweat from his brow with an already soaked handkerchief. He handed the paper back to his aide, giving him instructions to make copies for the other ministers.

"While we wait for copies to be made, let me just say that we may have another problem to deal with," Carlos said, sounding authoritative and commanding. "I thought about making a proposal to resolve our disputes, but I think we should consider this new event before going on to the next step in our oil production efforts."

"What kind of problem?" Salman demanded, sensing and at the same time hating the shift in momentum. He could already feel his control slipping away and realized that this Venezuelan upstart could take over control of OPEC unless he did something drastic.

"You will all have a copy in a moment," Carlos responded. "We can discuss the implications of this new development as soon as you have all read the news release." Within seconds, his aides began handing copies around the table that were quickly snatched up and hurriedly scanned.

Reading the news release, a heavy frown twisted Salman's cruel face into an angry, menacing vision of hatred. He believed Carlos had a good chance of becoming OPEC's next leader by staging the meeting in Venezuela coupled with this new information.

DATELINE: AUGUST 10th 1998
CITY OF ORIGIN: SAN JOSE, CALIFORNIA
SUBJECT: ANTI-GRAVITY DEMONSTRATION

TRANSTECNOLOGIES INTERNATIONAL LTD. (TRANSTEC), A SAN JOSE CORPORATION SPECIALIZING IN FUTURISTIC MODES OF TRANSPORTATION, ANNOUNCES THE DEMONSTRATION OF ITS NEW ANTI-GRAVITY, FREE ENERGY MACHINE. A DEMONSTRATION AND NEWS CONFERENCE WILL BE HELD AT THE COMPANY HEADQUARTERS.

111 SHORT CREEK DRIVE
SAN JOSE, CALIFORNIA
AUGUST 13TH
TEN A.M. PDT. (10:00 A.M. PACIFIC DAYLIGHT TIME)

COMPANY PRESIDENT, THEODORE BLANKENSHIP, SAYS THAT THEIR ANTI-GRAVITY MACHINE, CALLED THE D.A.D. MACHINE REPRESENTS THE NEXT MODE OF TRANSPORTATION. THE D.A.D. MACHINE, WITHOUT USING FUEL OF ANY KIND, WILL EXHIBIT ITS UNUSUAL FLIGHT CAPABILITIES, INCLUDING THE LIFTING OF OBJECTS. BLANKENSHIP CLAIMS THAT THIS NEW MACHINE CAN ALSO BE DESIGNED TO PROVIDE FREE ENERGY, POTENTIALLY A TREMENDOUS ASSET TO THIRD WORLD ECONOMIES.

THOSE NEWS AGENCIES, GOVERNMENTS, AND CORPORATIONS RECEIVING THIS NOTICE ARE INVITED TO APPLY FOR ADMITTANCE TO THIS SPECIAL EVENT. SPACE IS LIMITED, AND ATTENDANCE WILL BE LIMITED TO THE FIRST TWO

HUNDRED CONFIRMED APPLICATIONS, INCLUDING THOSE GIVEN A SPECIAL INVITATION.

Carlos Jose Barrera looked around the room as his guests read the news release. He couldn't help but smile inwardly, knowing that this event was exactly what he needed to oust Mohammad and gain control of OPEC, and ultimately, the world. OPEC and their allies needed to attend the demonstration, seize the D.A.D. machine and destroy TRANSTECNOLOGIES and all those involved, including this Blankenship. Carlos believed with all his being that he should be the man to lead this activity. Salman looked cruel and had the reputation of being ruthless and had indeed killed his share of adversaries in a long life of cruelty, but Carlos had no peer for sheer brutality. The time had arrived for a ruthless leader to assume control. The wattles under his chin began quivering as the pending excitement started building in his mind. He had a plan. He had the people. Sensing that the ministers had absorbed enough of the news release to appreciate the need for action, Carlos slammed his beefy fist on the table for attention. "Gentlemen, we must act quickly. I know what must be done."

He had their attention.

CHAPTER TWENTY-FOUR

They were eating dinner in Washington D.C. when the UPI news item came over the wire. White house aides eating sandwiches in the Roosevelt Library saw the announcement as it came over the wire and promptly ignored it as being just another west coast, California kook story. Some military aides in the Pentagon took it a little more seriously at first, but after talking about it, they decided just like their White house equivalents, this seemed like merely another stunt. Probably just another ploy by some kooks trying to get their fifteen minutes of fame and glory. The story got filed and forgotten after a few crude jokes about California nuts.

***

Colonel Otto (Outrageous) Conrad, Rageous to his friends and just plain Ray to his wife and close confidants, was getting ready to head for home from his swank corner office when Lilly, his personal and very private assistant, buzzed his "hot" line, the one only used when something scorching hit the news. Ray served as Texaco's CEO, with an office headquartered in a tall office building on the corner of San Jacinto and Rusk in Houston, Texas. Once one of the largest oil companies in the world with operations all over the Middle East including Saudi Arabia and Bahrain; in 1985 it merged into the Chevron Company. Texaco still carries a big stick in the oil business throughout the world. Lilly loved being one who could use the three-letter R-A-Y when addressing her Boss, but both she and he knew that Mrs. Conrad, the wife of 38 years, would have conniptions if she ever heard Lilly use that familiar greeting. To keep peace in the family, Lilly always said Mr. Rageous whenever anyone else was present.

"Ray, I've just put an email on your screen that you should look at before heading home. You may want to consider some action."

Lillian Dempsey, a spinster, like many executive assistants, loved her Boss. There had been a Mr. Dempsey twenty years ago, but unable or unwilling to compete for his wife's affections, he had long since escaped into the willing arms of a local cocktail waitress. Lilly subsequently devoted herself to a life of denial and false hope. Her friends were all sorry for her as they understood she would forever be denied the love she so passionately sought. On the other hand, Ms. Dempsey wielded more power than many of Fortune's Top 500 CEOs. An unlimited expense account, a million-plus annual compensation package, and exercising more power than all but a handful of world figures enabled the lonely assistant to live comfortably without a mister in her life. Beautiful and intelligent, with a lifetime of "street-smarts," she was worth her weight in gold to one of the world's most powerful shadow figures.

"Thank you, dahlin, what's yer take on it?" squawked the speaker mounted in the ceiling overhead.

"It's probably just some of those California west coast nut cases we keep hearing about," Lilly answered, talking to the microphones hidden all over the room, "but it wouldn't hurt to have one of our guys on scene go check it out, you know, just in case there's some kind of fire behind this anti-gravity smoke."

"That's another one of your splendid ideas, and just fer being so danged smart, I'm gonna let you call somebody out there on the coast and set it all up. I've got to get home for Mary Beth's charity auction or get scalded. Give me a buzz if you need any help. Otherwise, I'll see ya tomorrow."

Rageous knew he wouldn't have a call from Lilly, and he was also confident that Texaco would have one of the brightest technical experts on alternative energy available in attendance at the scheduled press conference, even if it meant buying somebody else's press credentials. He had absolute faith in his assistant's capability.

CHAPTER TWENTY-FIVE

Nearly an hour had elapsed since their last talk on the speakerphone with Gene as Ted hit the speed dial button to call their Boss. They still had not seen D.A.D. but had instead been busy studying the schedule of activities for the next two days.

"Oh, and by the way, good job on getting that press release distributed. It's already gone around the globe. Tomorrow is going to be very exciting."

"But Boss, we have nothing to demonstrate," Ted complained.

"Okay, people, remember that you all volunteered for this. Here is where it gets nasty. If anybody has any doubts, right now, this minute is your very last time to duck out and play it safe. In a few more minutes, it really will be too late."

The three actors all looked at each other and could see both the fear and excitement on the opposite faces mirroring their own feelings and thoughts.

"I think we've all signed onto the big show Boss," Wild Bill intoned in his best hippy drawl.

"I still want to hear each one of you say it for yourself. Go ahead, Janet."

"I'm in, Boss. I couldn't quit now, even if I wanted to."

"Count me in, too," Ted echoed a little too loudly. "I think we're ready for Act II, scene one."

"Okay, and welcome aboard. Let me take this opportunity to wish us all success in this venture. Break a leg."

"Hear, hear, I'll drink to that," and "luck" filled the room momentarily, followed by silence.

"This is where it gets dangerous, people. An armored van will pull up out front in about ten minutes, followed by four other vans, all carrying guards. They will unload a small crate from the armored van and collectively enter your building. You are to greet them at the front door and escort them to the demonstration room next to your office. There, they will deposit the crate. Questions so far?"

"Who are these guards, boss?" asked Theodore.

"They were recruited and trained over the past ten months for precisely this task. Their primary function is to protect and control the D.A.D. machine and their secondary tasks are to protect your lives."

"Isn't that extreme?" Janet said, feeling a little insulted that her life was taking a back seat to some stupid machine.

"Not a bit. Starting tonight, possibly, and definitely by tomorrow, there will be several groups trying to either steal or destroy both the machine and your lives. Once the machine is secure, the guards will focus their attention on preserving your lives. Towards this end, they will not leave the building until after this whole affair has concluded. You will find that living quarters have been provided for them next to the demonstration room, along with a secure storage vault for D.A.D. They have already been divided into watch groups to maintain round-the-clock surveillance."

"It sounds like you've covered everything," Billy sputtered, still a little unnerved by the revelations and the rapidity with which events seemed to move. Even 'on stage,' things never moved this fast.

"Oh, by the time this is all over, we'll all discover just how fallible I am. That's one of the reasons you guys were all chosen. You've shown an ability to think on your feet when somebody else forgets their lines. You all must remember to stay in character and react to situations as they develop. The complete dialogue for this little drama has not been written. You will have to do some improvisation as we proceed."

"What do we do after the guards and the machine arrive?" Janet asked.

"Good question. The guards already know the building and will sort themselves out according to tasks. Some will go off duty, some will go on patrol, and others will stay with the crate. You guys will open the crate and learn how to operate the D.A.D. machine. There are written instructions along with the remote control. I want you to practice putting the machine through its paces until you can do it in your sleep. Ted needs to learn his opening speech for the day after tomorrow. Billy needs to bone up on the details of the machine's operation, at least those that we choose to explain, and Janet needs to make sure that everything is in place for the big show. A checklist of tasks is in the center drawer of her desk."

"How many people do you expect to attend this demonstration day after tomorrow, boss?" Ted asked.

"There will be many more that show up than we have invited. The guards have a list of those who may enter. A security gate will be installed tonight, so everybody entering the building will be scanned for weapons. Only those on the list of 200 invited guests and media representatives will be allowed into the demonstration room. However, we can expect that at least a few of them will have bogus credentials. OPEC and the Seven Sisters won't let a chance like this pass without finding a way to crash the party."

"The seven sisters?" Janet said, looking around at her two companions, who were both shaking their heads negatively.

"Once there were seven big oil companies in the world. They were called the seven sisters, although today, only five control sixty percent of the world's oil supply. At any given moment, about twenty-five major oil companies are supplying 95 percent of the oil. They are constantly being bought out by competitors, confiscated by their government, or joined in partnerships. We are going to steal from ten of these companies."

"Do we sleep here at Transtec along with the guards?" This question came from Bill, who seemed confused after spending so much time looking for a house they could rent.

"You can't. There will be too many people watching your every action. You will be driven home each night pretending to be just your average Silicon Valley entrepreneurs. However, once you pull into the garage, I've arranged a little surprise. You won't be staying there, although it will appear to be your residence. Don't worry about that for now. Your safety is my paramount concern, regardless of what you might think after listening to my discourse concerning the guards. I am only referring to the guards who will arrive at Transtec at any moment now. The other guards soon to be in your life are there solely for your safety. More about that later. For now, you need to go down and meet your new comrades."

As the line went dead, they looked out of the windows to see a caravan of black vans slowly arriving on the street at the front entrance. Although unspoken, each wondered just how the boss always seemed to know what was happening.

Ted, Billy, and Janet watched the caravan of three black SUVs stop opposite their front door. Four young men in dark blue uniforms resembling those worn by the San Jose Police Department exited each vehicle. The men all appeared muscular, moving about easily as though they spent a lot of time remaining fit. All were heavily armed, including some kind of semi-automatic rifle. The eight men exiting the lead and rear vehicle each carried rifles, apparently ready for instant use. Their eyes continually scanned the street and sidewalk for any kind of potential threat. Two men in the middle vehicle also carried their rifles, and the other two had rifles slung over their shoulders. All twelve men wore Sam Brown Belts with many devices attached, including pistols, mace, and tazers. Some had billy clubs, others had tear gas, and all had extra sealed compartments around their waists, concealing God only knows what. If the three watchers had any doubt about the seriousness of the situation, the military precision of their movements and professional appearance of their guards dispelled any lingering doubts.

Two men riding in the rear seat of the middle SUV got out and went to the back cargo door, extracting a large metal box with carrying straps on each side. The two men carried the box up the sidewalk towards the front door flanked by the other ten guards, all holding their rifles in the ready position with their eyes continually sweeping the surrounding area. They were met at the front door by Ted and the others, who stood by as the twelve guards entered the building.

One of the rear guards looked the three Transtec people over, settling on Ted as the apparent leader. Gripping the rifle in his left hand, he extended his right hand towards Ted, "Hi, I'm Captain Wilson, and these are my men. We're here to deliver this box to Ted Blankenship. I presume that's you?" he said in a crisp, deliberate voice.

"Yeah, I'm Ted," he responded. "I'm the CEO of Transtec, and these two are William Westlake, although we call him Billy or Bill, and the young lady is Janet Hills, my executive assistant," he said, indicating Billy and Janet with his other hand.

"Okay, Ted," Wilson continued, "Gene Abel showed me around here a few days ago and instructed me to give you this box for the rest of the day. Apparently, you need the contents to prepare some kind of presentation. I am told instructions for you are inside, plus a way to contact Mr. Abel if you need further assistance. We will collect the box this evening when you are finished and keep it under our protective custody until you need it for your demonstration. Is that your understanding as well?"

Ted and the rest were clueless, but Ted recovered quickly. "Yeah, I mean yes. Would you mind putting the box in our conference room upstairs where we are going to hold our demonstration?"

"Sure thing, no problem," Wilson responded. "There will be four of us on guard duty around the clock until after this assignment has been concluded. The other eight will be camped out upstairs when not on duty. None of us will be leaving until after this is over, except that right now, three of my men need to get our vehicles off the street and into the parking lot behind the building. We will lock the doors at night, and there will be four of us on constant patrol. As the situation demands, other guards will be added."

Even though Gene had briefed them, the three actors had just learned his last name and were still basically clueless. Not wanting to appear incompetent, they all improvised as good method actors are taught, pretending that they had known the procedures all along. They followed the box upstairs to the conference room on the second floor while three of Wilson's guards left to move their vehicles. Two men positioned themselves by the front door, and the other two left to ensure that the building was secure. Ted, Janet, and Billy couldn't wait to see what in the hell D.A.D. looked like.

Feeling like children on Christmas morning getting ready to open presents, Ted and Janet watched Billy unwrap the eighteen-inch cube. Under the butcher-wrap paper glistened a handsome, dark wooden box reflecting light from many layers of penetrating varnish. A hinged lid secured by a simple fish hook clasp held the cover closed, which Billy fumbled open in his excitement to see what the box contained. After Billy opened the lid, three Transtec executives saw a white foam lining, like those protecting a new DVD player, concealing whatever lay underneath. Tension continued to grow in the room as the excitement became almost unbearable. Whatever the box contained, it held the reason for all the mystery, all the fake names, and hidden agendas, and all the planning and the danger. White foam insulation covered their future, and Billy seemed awed and almost reluctant to remove the final layer, shielding their eyes from destiny. He struggled to get his fingers between the foam insulation and wooden box sides before finally digging his fingernails into foam, sliding up the top half of the foam covering, revealing the D.A.D. machine.

The three onlookers gasped at the beautiful shiny silver ball nestled in the bottom half of the foam insulation. Light from overhead shimmered and danced around the sphere like something alive. Although stationary, the ball seemed to pulse and breathe. All three onlookers believed the globe to be inanimate, yet it somehow appeared to exist in another dimension, as something with a soul and spirit. It did not seem frightening, yet the three viewers experienced a sense of awe as though what they were seeing held some magical power.

One corner of the foam lining contained a remote control device resembling those used by model airplane enthusiasts. From another corner, Billy removed a rolled-up set of instructions for operating the remote. Billy quickly scanned the document before handing it to Ted.

"Read this and make sure I'm doing this right," he said while picking up the remote studying its controls. After making sure he understood the function of each button, Billy put his index finger on the top green button.

"Okay, guys," he whispered while depressing the button. "Let's see what this little fellow can do."

All three Transtec executives were mesmerized for the next ten minutes as Billy used the controls to fly the sphere up out of the box and around the room. The globe made no sound as it zipped up and down while zooming around the room.

"Careful," Janet said as D.A.D. zoomed around the room. "Don't run it into the wall or anything. I don't think our beloved leader would appreciate a smashed-up machine."

"Yeah," Ted chimed in and, trying to lighten up the room, continued, "he probably doesn't have it insured."

"Don't worry," Billy responded. "I don't think I can crash it if I wanted to. It seems to steer away from any other solid object. It appears whatever makes it resist gravity also repels it from other physical matter."

***

After the guards had secured the D.A.D. machine for the evening and taken it away to a vault somewhere on another floor, Bill and Ted went back into the office to pick up Janet before heading home. They were greeted by four new guards, who informed them that their job was to see them safely home. Two new Ford Explorers waited for them on the street.

Two of the actors sat in the first vehicle with one guard driving and one riding shotgun. The actors sat in the rear seat. Janet and Billy rode in the lead car while Ted, the CEO, rode solo in the second as befitted the boss. The drivers took alternate routes to the house Bill had rented and furnished. They had been expertly trained at detecting surveillance, plus they had their overhead spy camera looking for other air or ground snoops. The vehicles remained in communication with each other, plus a remote communication center controlled the overhead surveillance. Each driver had been instructed to take their passengers home only after making very sure that there was absolutely nobody on their tail. The cars were all scanned for hidden transmitters and would be under constant surveillance until after the actors were safely out of the country. Their house had also been put under twenty-four hour guard by hidden members of the boss's team, although neither the occupants nor the guard drivers knew this other detail.

CHAPTER TWENTY-SIX

It was almost midnight in Washington D.C. when Army Sergeant Luke Waters, the on-duty communications officer for the Pentagon, was startled to discover the Transtec announcement. Waters immediately grasped the potential significance of this information if it should prove to be genuine. With no hesitation, he picked up the telephone and called his commanding officer despite the time. Within forty minutes, a hastily assembled group of angry, embarrassed officials stood gathered in the Situation Room, in the West Wing basement of the White House.

"Why in the hell are we just now finding out about this God-damned wire?" President Carleton's voice, usually soft and measured, sounded angry. This manner of speaking signaled a sure sign that he was immensely pissed and somebody's ass could be on the cutting block.

Admiral Whittaker, current Chairman of the JCS, one of the first informed about the message, was probably the best equipped to answer the President's question and did not hesitate to speak. "Communication clerks in both the White House and Pentagon assumed the information represented a hoax and didn't want to bother anyone with such useless information. I've already taken care of the Pentagon situation. The White House is not our responsibility. Our analysis, while tentative, suggests that the information is genuine. Whether Transtec is what it appears to be, and regardless of the claims being made, we cannot afford to sit back and watch this unfold from a distance."

The President's cabinet and military generals surrounding the conference table all nodded and either grunted or voiced their concurrence.

"What do you propose, Admiral?" the President asked.

"We must have people attending that demonstration to assess the situation. If the Transtec claim is accurate, all equipment, notes, and drawings must be confiscated. All individuals with pertinent information concerning this program must be taken into custody under threat to National Security. I assume we can sort out the legality later and maintain the cover-up as required."

"Do we have the right personnel available to evaluate this technology, and can they be on site for the demonstration?" the President continued asking the questions, but his tone relaxed into the soft, comforting drawl that made him famous.

DOD Secretary Marcus F. Bachelor spoke as though the question had been asked of him directly. "We have several scientists at DARPA," (Defense Advanced Research Projects Agency) "looking at free energy and related subjects. They can be on site in time for the demonstration. I assume Admiral Whittaker can provide the manpower on site to take control of the equipment and people involved."

"Absolutely, Mr. President," Whittaker responded quickly. "We have a SEAL team doing advanced equipment training at the Naval Air Weapons Station in China Lake. They can be at the demonstration in time to take control of the situation as required."

"That's settled then," the President responded. "We cannot afford to have this technology in the hands of civilians or any foreign power if this information is valid. We have spent years lying to the American people about unidentified flying objects and hiding their advanced technology. This upstart Transtec bullshit has got to be quashed. We cannot allow this information to gain traction with the American public. I'll leave it to you to make sure this does not happen."

There could be no mistake in what the President had just said. If anyone should fail in accomplishing the tasks outlined by Admiral Whittaker, their careers and possibly their very lives were forfeit.

CHAPTER TWENTY-SEVEN

After ensuring that his Transtec actors had been safely tucked away for the night, Josh drove over to Valley Electronics to check on his other D.A.D. machine. He needed to have the backup, as the one being used for the demonstrations would be sold. Without the backup model, he would have to spend another year putting together the necessary components to model his future dreams. A year he didn't want to spend. In addition, the spare model could be used in many innovative ways to shorten the development time for full-scale models. The buyers attending the big demonstration day after tomorrow would have no idea that he had a second machine. While it remained mandatory that they never found out about this secret, it was equally vital that this machine be available.

Valley Electronics looked undisturbed as Josh drove up to the front door. The display electronics in the window were all sparkling under discrete spotlights, building up hope for a happy outcome. Using the spare key given to him by the shop owner, Josh entered the store and quickly went to the shop's back to the extra room where he had stored the D.A.D. Before getting halfway to the rear, he could see that the door to his storeroom had been opened and his heart stopped beating. Within seconds, he determined that his reserve ball was missing. Despair filled his soul, sinking him to his knees. Without this backup, his whole plan could quickly fail. And failure could not be an option. Not now. Too late now to back out of the demonstration; besides, he didn't have the resources to start over, even if he could halt the entire proceedings. No, he had to keep on the schedule, but God, what was he going to do?

King had mentioned Larry McCutchen's involvement because of the recent homicide at another King strip mall where an attempted robbery had also taken place. Getting control of his fears and apprehension, Josh gave the investigator a call.

"McCutchen here," the voice sounded stern, although extremely tired.

"Hey Larry, this is Josh Logan. I hope this isn't an inconvenient time to talk with you about some robberies, although I know that isn't your primary interest."

"Nah, it's okay. Just a little tired. Early mornings and late nights make me a little ornery. Talked with King earlier, and he said you might call. What's up?"

"I had some precious personal property stored at Valley Electronics, which has been stolen. Do you have any leads about the thief or thieves?" Josh hated the desperation that leaked out in the tone of his voice.

"I might have some good news and some bad news Josh, but first, why in the hell did you store valuable property in an electronics shop that is moving to another location?"

"Arnold Hicken, the shop owner, is a friend who has been helping me out with some special electronic testing and evaluation. He had a spare room with its locked door, and it seemed pretty safe. I had only planned on using his store for another day or two at the most. Who in the hell robs an almost vacant store?"

"We're not altogether positive, but we might have a suspect. There's an all-points bulletin out for his questioning, but he seems to have disappeared."

Feeling a bit of hope, Josh asked, "Who is it, Larry?"

With a weariness in his voice that could not hide the reluctance in his answer, Larry responded. "Sorry, Josh, but until we're sure about this suspect, I'd rather not give out his name. He's from a very prominent family that would make life very uncomfortable if we started making accusations before having all the facts."

"Dammit, Larry, I'm dying here. I've got to recover my property within the next two days, or I could be in serious trouble."

Josh's desperation came through the telephone. While the detective and his caller were not close friends, Larry knew much about Josh and his various enterprises. His reputation as an inventor and Silicon Valley entrepreneur was legendary. Understanding the frame of mind that produces such a frantic call for help, McCutchen relented just a bit.

"Look, Josh, why don't you come on down to the station and let's see what we can do to help you. I can't promise anything, but at least you will see what we're doing, and if we get lucky, you'll be on hand to recover whatever you're missing."

Although faint, a flicker of hope made its way to Josh's mind. "Okay, thanks, Larry. I'll be at the station in twenty minutes."

CHAPTER TWENTY-EIGHT

Shortly before midnight, the first group of black-clad figures arrived at 111 Short Creek Drive. Lillian Dempsey, Colonel Conrad's lady Friday, had wasted no time in contacting Skipper Walls, a contract troubleshooter often used by Texaco to solve those minor niggling problems best left to someone in the underground. Someone unknown. Unsuspected. But most importantly, someone with no affiliation to Texaco, so the company would get no blowback if anything went wrong. That had never been a problem with Skipper Walls; he always succeeded in handling those nasty minor problems requiring muscle and discretion. There sometimes appeared the unexplained corpse here and there, but mostly the problems just disappeared. Texaco never asked questions. The company wired funds to an off-shore account ostensibly set up to facilitate overseas contracts and purchases. The system had worked well for several years.

Skipper had two men with him for his initial reconnaissance excursion. Skipper stood six-five, had fair skin surrounding a slender, wiry build. Jesus Madero was a short, almost fat, dark-skinned man, who could move like a subtle breeze despite his bulk and awkward body. He had partnered with Skipper on several previous jobs, where the two men had developed a mutual appreciation for each other's skills. The third man on their team was a first-timer. Criss Hanson just turned twenty-nine, but he looked and acted like a seasoned veteran. Two tours in Vietnam had aged him far beyond his standard years.

Criss had been destroying a disputed Texaco oil well when he came up against Skipper and Jesus. The company that hired Criss told him that Texaco had drilled sideways under an oil field that belonged to someone else. When Texaco refused to acknowledge their error, the company hired Criss to solve the problem if it could be called such. It was only by pure luck that Skipper noticed the explosive bundle attached to the oil pumping platform. He and Jesus had just finished disposing of another Texaco problem by burying the miscreant in the oil field. While returning to their car, they passed the oil well wired by Criss.

Criss, fifty yards away, laid flat on the ground behind a pumping station waiting for the explosion when he saw two men stop by the old pump where he had planted his explosives. With no way to stop the explosion, Criss called to the two men to run like hell. No stranger to strange happenings on a mission, Skipper and Jesus didn't hesitate to take off like they had rockets in their back pockets. They were forty yards away when the explosion occurred. Both men were knocked down and rolled over a few times but suffered no real damage except ringing ears and a few bruises. Criss hastened over to the men to see if they had been seriously hurt. Grateful for the warning that saved his life, Skipper struck up a conversation with Criss, during which the men developed a mutual respect. Texaco never learned about the meeting. The lost well got written off with income tax deductions, and the incident was forgotten. Skipper and Criss kept in touch over the years doing other jobs together, resulting in this evening's mission.

Initially, they drove around Transtec and surrounding streets, looking for someone who might guard the building. Seeing no one, they parked two blocks away, making their way to the Transtec building by flitting from shadow to shadow, watching for cameras or other means of surveillance. Nothing was visible to the three men as they ultimately converged by the front door of the building at 111 Short Creek Drive.

The guards inside the building were studying hidden infrared cameras, showing the heat signatures of all three men. Correctly assuming that this was merely a reconnaissance mission, the inside guards did little but watch and evaluate the activity going on outside.

Checking just to be sure, Skipper tried opening the door and was not surprised to find it locked. Peeking inside, his crew could see the soaring atrium and beautifully furnished lobby. They were impressed by the building and what they could see of the interior—the three men set about checking for power and telephone lines. While disappointed, it was no surprise that all services to the building were underground. This meant that the only way to discover what happened inside was to break into the structure somehow. After walking around the building, studying the loading doors, windows, and other outside doors, the three men left to discuss their findings and consider their next move.

Skipper would have been mortified to discover that another set of black-clad individuals had watched them circle the building before leaving. This new group had not circled the facility in a vehicle but parked some distance away and crept towards the Transtec building, where they observed Skipper and his crew trying the front door. They remained hidden until Skipper and his men had disappeared into the night before beginning their own surveillance.

***

There were five Navy SEALS in this reconnaissance mission led by Sergeant Leo Wolf; a full-blooded Native American raised on the Pomo reservation in northern California. At five foot eleven inches tall, weighing 240 pounds, Leo was a large man compared to other members of his tribe. Although his size and fierce countenance were intimidating to many, none of that mattered to the other members of his team. That he had earned the right to lead them signified all they needed to know. Specialists in nearly every form of warfare, these warriors were a formidable group. Leo had his team spread out circling the Transtec building, looking for any kind of weakness they could exploit besides gathering basic information about the facility.

Would it be possible to breach the building without doing too much damage? Was there any way through the roof or perhaps an open balcony up on the top floor? Tonight's excursion, just basic reconnaissance. Later, back at their motel, they would compare notes and make plans for tomorrow. Although the hidden cameras had not been spotted, the SEALs, being SEALs, had an uneasy feeling that they were also under observation. Getting inside could prove to be a problem, especially if guards were protecting the secrets.

Inside the building, the guards on duty duly noted this second group of potential invaders, who disappeared after doing their surveillance like the first group.

Shortly after 4:30 a.m., the final group of dark-clad investigators circled the Transtec building. There were only two men in this group; however, the watchers inside, looking at the infrared heat signatures of the men as they moved around the building, could feel the solid negative energy the two men projected. While the first two groups were not there on friendly terms, they appeared businesslike and professional. These two new guys projected danger and utter disregard for human life.

Captain Wilson, the guard leader on duty, remarked to his companion, "Those two men outside could be a real problem. I don't believe they have a moral code. Can you feel it?"

Gerald Haymaker, his companion, nodded as he added, "Yeah. You can just tell by the way they move and the intensity of their stalking that these guys could be trouble."

"Well, we were warned that this was not going to be a picnic," Wilson remarked. "Tomorrow should be an interesting day. And the demonstration the day after might turn out to be a free-for-all."

CHAPTER TWENTY-NINE

Oh Shit. That fucking McCutchen is gonna figure it out. After that big honcho King's visit and then the detective, they're gonna be looking at me for murder, not to mention all the crap I've stolen. Good thing I scored with the phones. After my buy tonight, I'll just head for Mexico. Wonder what that big shiny ball is all about? Can't get it apart and it's heavy for an aluminum ball. Must be stuffed with something. It could be worth a fortune. "Ya, but who ya gonna sell it to? Can't shop it around without somebody figures out I stole the damn thing. Besides, I don't even know what it is."

Okay, so maybe it was stupid taking the damn ball. But it was just lying there in that fancy box. It hasta be valuable. I've never seen anything like it, so it's pretty unique. Better hang onto it for now. It ain't like it's taking up a lot of space. Somethens gotta come up. And besides, I can always dump the damn thing.

Yeah, and we gotta be smart. This car will get me hung. Wonder if ole Hicks is still willing to buy the heap? I could use the money. Luckily, I know where the old man stores his cash. With his money and what I can get for the car, I should make it in Mexico.

Shit.

Mexico.

Hiding out.

God, but I fucked the duck. Stupid to get hooked on that shit. Look what it's gonna cost me. My ole man is jest gonna shit. If the police do not get me, the ole man would most likely kill me, anyway. Good thing I never told him where I went to in Mexico. He and the cops will probably think I'm in Mexico, but they won't have any idea where to look. It's a big country, and I know how to get lost if I need to.

First thing is to dump the ride. Ole McCutchen will have a lookout for it in another hour at most. I'll hide it in my storage unit and give Hicks a call. That should buy me enough time to make my meet tonight and start for the border. I'll have Hicks bring me a banger that nobody will miss and won't attract any attention.

CHAPTER THIRTY

When Josh arrived at the police department, he was surprised to find King sitting across from the detective, engrossed in a serious conversation. The talking stopped as Josh entered the room, and both men rose to greet him, shaking hands.

Eager to learn what was going on regarding the robbery of his D.A.D. model, Josh spoke so quickly that he sputtered as he asked, "Wa..., what's the latest Larry. Any good news?"

"Okay, Josh," McCutchen began. "Slow down. I'm going to fill you in with what we know and what we guess, but we are not sure of anything at this time. You cannot reveal anything we are going to be talking about until we have more information. I assume you find that agreeable?"

"Oh, hell yes. Just tell me what's happening," he said. Sounding somewhat normal, Josh seemed to have regained control of his emotions.

Detective McCutchen began reciting what facts were available. "We currently believe that Marco Cabrini is responsible for the recent rash of robberies and the murder of David Chen. King discovered that all the recent mall robberies were in buildings constructed by the Cabrini's. We both visited the Cabrini offices in Willow Glen, where we discovered Marco had been studying the blueprints for all the older malls built by his father and uncle. Marco saw both of us in the office, and we believe he cottoned to the fact that we were growing suspicious. Since then, he has disappeared. He drives a flaming red Ferrari, which we have listed on an all-points bulletin, but no one has seen the car so far. We suspect he ditched the car to avoid being spotted. That's all we know at this time."

Stunned by the revelation, Josh looked at King to see if he had understood correctly. Marco Cabrini, son of one of Silicon Valley's wealthiest families, was a suspect in several robberies and a murder?

After seeing the confusion on his friend's face, King elaborated.

"There are indications that Marco has been heavily involved in smuggling high-grade cocaine into the valley for some of the biggest names among our movers and shakers. I was made aware of this several months ago, but dismissed it as being unlikely. Just a rumor put out by someone jealous of the Cabrini wealth. After all, Marco is highly paid by his father for basically doing nothing other than being a son. With almost unlimited finances and a flashy car, Marco didn't seem to require any other sources of income."

Josh thought about what he had just heard then asked, "How long has the BOLO for Marco's car been in effect?"

McCutchen looked at his watch before answering.

"We radioed the Be-On-The-Lookout about four hours ago. Every cop and cruiser in Silicon Valley is currently looking for Marco and his Ferrari. We were just discussing this when you arrived. King and I believe he has probably ditched the car someplace. It's just too visible if it's on the street. However, there are plenty of back alleys and remote streets where he could be parked. Eventually, the car will show up."

"I suppose the Cabrini compound and homes are being watched," Josh commented as though stating a fact, although he was asking a question. He didn't want to offend the homicide detective.

McCutchen smiled at the conflicting statement, "Yeah, Josh, even the San Jose Police Department gets it right once in a while."

Chagrinned at his awkward comment and the detective's subtle putdown, Josh hastened to add, "I'm sorry for the offense, Larry. I'm just anxious about my stolen property. Hopefully, the car and Marco will show up soon."

"Yeah, Josh," McCutchen said with a bit of weariness in his voice, "King told me you lost one of your new inventions. We'll keep you in the loop and let you know as soon as something happens."

"Come on Josh," King said, standing up. "I'm ready to leave and let the police department handle the police business. Let's head over to Denny's for a late-night coffee."

Disappointed with what he had heard, but satisfied that everything was being done that could be done, Josh nodded his head as he got up from his chair. After thanking the detective for his briefing, he followed King down the hall towards the front door.

***

On the Pentagon's main concourse close to the Hall of Heroes is the office of Admiral Walter J. Whittaker, Chairman of the Joint Chiefs of Staff, the military's top officer. The admiral's office complex was more like the inside of a mansion than an office building. The foyer was over 2000 square feet, more extensive than many houses. Handwoven Persian rugs were arranged in a giant open square in which several dark brown leather couches were placed. This room often served as an informal gathering for special military ceremonies in which all the various services participated. The far end of the foyer featured an arched entryway to the Admiral's gatekeepers. In most executive offices, this space would be the receptionist or secretary's desk, but here it comprised of four large wooden desks manned by officers from the Air Force, Army, Navy, and Coast Guard. The officer's rank varied from time to time, but never less than the equivalent of an Army Major. Anyone visiting the Admiral had to pass through these gatekeepers. Your business with the Chairman must be of extreme importance to be admitted to the next level of scrutiny.

Beyond the initial gatekeeper was a single large wooden door that opened into the Chairman's private secretary. This was also a large room festooned with rugs and couches. Near a pair of seven-foot hand-carved wooden doors was the secretary's desk, permanently manned by an Army Colonel. Nearby were two smaller desks occupied by assistants to the colonel. Getting by the colonel into the Chairman's office beyond the double doors was even more difficult than passing by the initial gatekeepers. Overseeing the vast military complex of hundreds of thousands of men, billions of dollars of equipment, thousands of contractors, and several simultaneous military excursions around the world required a focus and dedication rare by anyone else. Given the complexity of modern warfare and the divergent societies in which the military operated required today's Chairman to be nearly superhuman.

In contrast to the outside spaces, the Chairman's office was almost diminutive, comprising only 1500 square feet. The four surrounding walls featured original paintings representing engagements by the various military organizations. Black leather couches under the pictures sat on a thick Fereghan Sarouk carpet that covered the floor. An eight-foot redwood burl desk stood against the far wall behind which the Admiral sat on a designer chair made in Italy. In front of the desk, four large soft padded armchairs were arranged in a semicircle. Today these chairs were empty while standing before the desk, Navy SEAL Colonel Tilford was reporting to the Chairman.

"Our guys performed a reconnaissance mission on the Transtec facility in San Jose last evening. The building is a new ten-story glass and steel structure in the heart of San Jose, about a mile from the airport. Although my guy didn't believe anyone was presently housed in the facility, the building appears ready for occupancy. Everything appears new and unused. Security appeared absent. No security cameras, no guards, at least visible from the outside, and no physical barriers. Forced entry, should that be required, would not be a problem. The team will stay on site for further observation and evaluation."

Whittaker received the report in his usual expressionless demeanor.

"I take it then that this Transtec thing might be real."

Without missing a beat, Tilford responded.

"The building is real. My guys tell me the sign outside is a real work of art, all rock and stainless steel. It looked to them like there was serious money involved."

"Thanks, Colonel, keep me informed. I'll let the President know we may be dealing with something that needs to be kept under close observation."

***

Twenty-four hundred miles south, Carlos Barrera was on the telephone with his operative in California. Mateo Ramirez had called with a report of last night's visit to Transtec.

"New building, nobody around," Ramirez reported. "No guards or anything. We could easily break in if the machine is inside."

"Let's just keep watching for now," Carlos responded. "We need to know what we're looking for and where they keep it. Just be sure you get into the demonstration so you can give me a first-hand report on what you see."

"Sure thing, Boss. That will be no problema."

"Just keep it that way."

Barrera couldn't keep a wolfish smile off his face. Owning the world's free energy machine, plus controlling the main oil flow, would make him a big man on the world stage.

CHAPTER THIRTY-ONE

Lillian Dempsey reported to Texaco's Colonel Conrad on last night's adventures in Silicon Valley a few hours later.

"I had some of our representatives in California look at the Transtec thing; you know, the anti-gravity, free energy machine business."

"Oh yeah, that was the wire you read me last night. What's the story, Lillian?"

Rageous was in good form today. Mary Beth's charity event had been a big success, which made for a happy evening. Clearly, the good feelings had continued as the Colonel had a big smile and seemed to be more relaxed than he had been in days.

"Our troubleshooters found the Transtec building in San Jose. They reported it is an expensive big new building with a large permanent rock sign. It looked legitimate. There appears to be real money behind the company, so the odds are they have something to demonstrate in a couple of days. We need to get one of our engineers out there to evaluate the device."

Lillian was dressed in a dark blue designer slenderizing sheath dress that emphasized all of her physical charms. She didn't believe the Colonel would ever cheat on his wife, but it didn't hurt to let him look at what he was missing.

For his part, Rageous, Ray to his friends, was well aware of his assistant's physical charms, which didn't hurt the office atmosphere, but brains and a quick mind were her main appeal to the Texaco Chairman.

"We just hired that new physicist from Cal Poly, didn't we?" Ray asked, leaning back in his chair, enjoying the sculptured view Lillian presented.

Aware that she had the desired effect, Lillian answered, "His name is Quincy Robertson, and we have him training at our San Diego facility. It makes sense for him to drive up to San Jose and see the demonstration. I'm assuming that if these Transtec people are serious, our engineer will be given a chance to examine the machine first-hand."

"Okay, Lillian, make it happen. But have Scott Appleton, our PR guy, go along to assess the company and personnel. I'd like to know what and who we're dealing with."

Slithering a little as she turned to emphasize her curves, Lillian answered as she left the office.

"I'll take care of it, Ray, and I'll keep you posted as always."

CHAPTER THIRTY-TWO

Almaden Storage is nestled in the foothills just off the Almaden Expressway about two miles west of King's house. The storage units are in a shallow hollow that snaked around a low hill, affording privacy to those units at the far deep end. A six-foot tan adobe wall surrounded the ten-acre complex. A heavy metal gate with a combination lock was the only way into and out of the complex for added security. Marco had searched all over the valley for a storage unit that afforded him the privacy required for his illegal activities. Unit 417, a large unit next to the last in the inside row, was where he had spent an uncomfortable night cramped in his Ferrari.

It was after ten o'clock in the morning and Marco was starting to panic when his friend Steve Hicks drove in next to the storage unit in a 1965 Ford Mustang that had seen better days. Steve was the only person Marco trusted with the combination to the front gate. He honked the horn to let Marco know he was there and that no one was around to see inside of the storage unit with the door open. Hearing the horn, Marco opened the door halfway so he could slip out by bending over, but making it difficult for anyone outside to see anything inside, especially with the lights off.

Knowing that his friend had been cooped up in the storage unit most of the night, Steve had brought two large cups of steaming coffee and a couple of sausage-egg McMuffins.

"Oh God, am I happy to see you, Hicks. And you sweetheart, bringing me coffee and breakfast."

"I figured it's the least I can do," Hicks said, handing over a cup of coffee. "After all, you are giving me your car."

"Like hell," Marco replied, almost yelling. "I'm making you a hell-of-a-deal, but it ain't free."

"I know, I know," Steve said quickly, with a brilliant smile. "But forty-thousand is all I can come up with, and if you let me have the car at that price, you are practically giving it to me."

Leaning against the Ford's fender, Marco set his coffee on the hood as he took one of the egg sandwiches from Steve.

"Man, I'm so starved, I could damn near eat the wrapper," he said as he began wolfing down the muffin. "How many miles are left on this wreck I'm leaning on," he asked between bites.

"The engine and drive train are in good shape," Hicks answered. "I just had everything mechanical reworked. The tires are worn, but should be good for eight to ten thousand miles. I haven't gotten around to the interior or exterior bodywork, was leaving that for last. But you wanted a beater, and this is the best I could do on short notice."

"Nah, it's perfect," Marco said. "I just need it for a few thousand miles. Is it legal? I mean, it's got a current license and registration, right?"

Hicks had been eating his sandwich and had to wait a second before responding. "Yeah, it's all current. I brought along the DMV forms so we can legally transfer titles. I'll wait two or three days before giving them to the DMV so that they won't know what car you're driving."

"Oh, that's great," Marco said. "Let's finish these sandwiches and a little coffee, then we'll get down to business. I need to transfer a bunch of stuff into the Mustang. You can help if you got the time."

"I've got nowhere to be," Hicks mumbled, trying to swallow his last bite.

"You know this Ferrari might be a little hot," Marco said. "You'll have a clear legal title, but you'll probably be pulled over pretty quickly. Once they find it isn't me driving and you have a legal title, they'll have to let you go. You can't leave here until I get a good running start, and of course, you do not know where I am, where I'm going, and what I'm driving. I will not be registering the car, at least here in the States, so they won't be able to find out you lied to them. If they ever check with the DMV to see if you have any other cars, you can always tell them that the Mustang was stolen. I doubt though, that they'll check it out."

"Don't worry about me. If I get pulled over, I'll just tell the cops that you showed up at my house and offered to sell me the Ferrari. You knew I wanted the car and said you were leaving town so I could buy it for a reasonable price. That's all I know."

"Sounds good; help me load my stuff into the Mustang," Marco said as he checked to be sure no one was in the area before finishing opening the storage unit door. As they transferred clothes and boxes from the Ferrari to the Mustang, Hicks picked up a heavy, sizeable wooden box. "What's this?" he asked.

"Damned if I know," Marco said, breathing hard. "It was in the electronics shop I boosted. I thought it might be worth something I could sell, but I'm out of time, and I can't figure out anything it could be used for, other than decoration."

"Let me have a look," Hicks said. As he was speaking, he set the box down on the ground and unsnapped the lid. Opening the box, he saw the foam packing and under that the shining silver ball. Neither man noticed the remote tucked in one corner hidden by still more foam.

"It's heavy," Marco said. "Got any idea what it could be?"

"Nah, it's probably a toy or experiment of some kind. Want it in the Mustang?" As he was speaking, Hicks replaced the foam and secured the lid.

"I don't think so," Marco answered. "I can't think of anything it could be used for, and it's damn heavy. Let's just leave it in the storage unit. If you hear about a reward being offered for something like this, you might consider turning it in, but probably not. You don't want to be considered a thief."

"I'm just going to forget I even saw it," Hicks said, returning the box to Marco's storage unit. "It can just sit in here until someday, years from now, the manager cuts off your lock to re-rent the unit."

CHAPTER THIRTY-THREE

Ted, Bill, and Janet were picked up from the secure facility, their home away from home for the evening, and returned to their official lodging at 458 Dilbert Avenue. The enclosed van they hid in looked like an ordinary delivery van for any eyeballs that might be interested. The van was driven to the rear of the house; an area obscured from the street or nearby residences. The three Transtec executives were marched through the house to their regular guards, already waiting on the front steps where they were escorted to the same black Ford Explorers they rode in yesterday for the trip back to the office.

After being escorted through the front doors of Transtec, they were surprised to be met by several new people they had never met. Three ladies introduced themselves to Janet, then followed her to the office, where they began the day's training. Maria, a short, slightly plump Mexican lady, was proficient in almost all office equipment. Holly was a slender blond woman in her early sixties who organized and ran large demonstrations. Maxine, who looked like an army drill sergeant in drag, was there to teach Janet how to handle those individuals who might wish to disrupt the demonstration. There would be guards available to take care of the rough stuff; Janet's job would be to maintain order and decorum commensurate with the demonstration.

Brad Tillman was the quintessential businessman. Tall, in his mid-fifties, he was a professional speaker and company spokesman besides running his own consulting company. His job was to get Ted comfortable addressing a large, raucous audience of curious, skeptical, frightened, angry disbelievers. Vernon McIntire, the dweeb-looking professor in a plaid sports coat with leather elbow patches, sported a bald head and Van Dyke beard. Vernon, a physics teacher at San Jose State University, made sure Ted could pronounce the technical words in the demonstration spiel Gene had written. In addition, it was imperative that Ted talked and acted like he understood the technical terms he would use during the demonstrations conducted by Bill.

The final member of the greeting committee was a nineteen-year-old world-class computer gamer named Henry Rawlings. In looks, he was almost a younger version of Bill, with a long blond ponytail and tattered jeans. It was his job to make Bill proficient in handling the D.A.D. The demonstration required several intricate movements of the machine besides lifting a heavy object. Wild Bill needed to handle the remote controls as though he had designed and built everything himself. He had all day to practice flying the D.A.D. under the tutelage of his youthful instructor.

It wasn't until a lunch break that the three actors were together again in the break room. A large television was turned on, and no sooner had the three hungry trainees delved into their catered sandwiches than the screen came to life with a grinning picture of Gene, their boss.

"Oh, hi gang. Don't let me interrupt your lunch," he said with a big grin, seeing the startled members of his cast putting down their sandwiches. "I can see that you are starved. We'll get together tonight for a recap. I just wanted to see if everything was going okay with your training. Any questions so far?"

Ted looked at his workmates before answering for the group. "I think everything is on track, Boss. It's kind of like one of the speed rehearsals where you learn a new play overnight. I haven't done that for a couple of years, but like riding a bike, you never forget, right?"

"That's exactly the response I was looking for, Ted," Gene replied. "I was afraid that if we spent too much time getting into the roles we're playing, the tension would build, and our nerves would misbehave. This way, we're much too busy to worry about all the various things that might happen."

"We're busy, alright," Bill said. "Henry's got me working up a sweat."

"Sounds good," Gene responded. "How about you Janet, do you feel you're getting the support you need?"

"Oh yes. You've provided some excellent trainers. It's a lot of work and so much to learn, but I think your strategy is excellent. I'm much too busy to have stage fright."

Gene sat in contemplation for a few seconds as he considered what to say next. "I've decided to limit the number of invitations for tomorrow's demonstration to 100 individuals," he announced. "There is too much-unauthorized interest in our activities to invite more trouble."

"Most media outlets will undoubtedly send three people: a photographer, their reporter, and a person with some physics and engineering training. Counting television, newspapers and a couple of magazines, this should be about 45 people. We sent special invitations to OPEC and twenty corporations, but we will limit their participation to two individuals each. These invitees add another 42, leaving us with 13 extra slots. I'm allotting the remaining spaces to various domestic and international government agencies. Janet, I've faxed you an updated invitation list which I would like you to send off just as soon as you finish your lunch. Maria can help with the dissemination. I have already given Captain Wilson a copy of the list naming our invitees."

"You're going to be seeing a lot of activity in the next few hours as security installs the metal detectors and electronic scanning equipment. If there are no questions, I'll talk to you in a few hours. Just remember, have a little fun today and tomorrow. The real danger and problems won't start at the earliest until tomorrow or the day after, which might be optimistic. I expect a few serious attempts to wrest D.A.D. away from us in the next few days, but hopefully, we've planned well and have nothing to fear. Learn your roles, and I'll take care of everything else. Last chance, questions?"

"Yeah," Billy spoke up. "Why is the machine called dad?"

Gene frowned at the question and hesitated before answering. "It isn't, dad; it's D.A.D. and you don't need to know the meaning of the acronym."

The television shut itself off, and the three Transtec executives were left looking at each other, wondering what Gene meant when he said the real danger wouldn't start for another two or three days. What was the threat? And why the considerable secrecy about D.A.D.? Unfortunately, they were about to discover the answer.

CHAPTER THIRTY-FOUR

Losing the spare D.A.D. machine was throwing complications into Josh's otherwise finely tuned plan. Josh had to appear in full makeup as Gene for the Transtec people and their contingent of security personality, plus all the consultants he had hired. In dealing with the police and other locals, there could be no trace of his dual personality. Getting in and out of character was wearing on his nerves.

Dealing with King was a different story. While King was not appraised of the whole production, he knew that his friend Josh was into something pretty heavy and would not have been surprised to come across his friend in his full makeup mode. So far, that had not been necessary, but interfacing with so many different factions was time consuming and hunting for his missing D.A.D. device had not been factored into the plans. Josh wanted to keep King at a distance so King could honestly plead ignorance regarding any of Josh's actions. It looked like he might have to include his friend in the proposed con, and he was not sure that King would agree to participate. King had a lot to lose if his involvement could be proven and not a lot to gain if everything went great.

With four or five hours remaining before visiting with the Transtec people via television, Josh removed his makeup and costume before heading back to the San Jose Police Department. He wanted to get an update on the search for Marco and see if there was anything he could do personally. There was no way that the San Jose Police Department should have access to or even look at the extra D.A.D. machine. After tomorrow's demonstration, the entire world would know precisely what D.A.D. looked like. The San Jose police could not know that Josh had the same machine without knowing that Josh was responsible for the entire con. The only way Josh could keep his identity a secret was to find the missing D.A.D. before the police.

This situation meant walking a very narrow line. Josh had to appear very interested in recovering his stolen property, but there could be no connection to the big Transtec demonstration tomorrow. Somehow, Josh had to be appraised of whatever information the police might have. He also wanted to know where they might search and have the flexibility to move quickly before the police discovered his secret. Managing the search while controlling events at Transtec was taking a toll. Unfortunately, there was no way to postpone or cancel the demonstration at this point without losing everything he had planned for the past thirty years.

Josh was attempting to steal ten billion dollars, but in his mind, the theft was justified. Theoretically, no one was going to die. His theft should pose no hardship on any private individual, and big oil, along with OPEC, had been screwing the American people over for years.

A group of camel herders in the sands of the Middle East had been grafting billions and billions of dollars from the American citizens for over sixty years. American petrol dollars had provided citizens of those countries tax-free living with free housing, medical care, and food for longer than most American citizens had been alive. While Americans had to work and pay for their energy requirements, most OPEC citizens were living fat off American dollars.

What was even more galling, this was all being done with the blessings of big oil and our own government. But, of course, they were getting rich as well, including key leaders of the nation. No, in Josh's mind, when he witnessed the carnage at the Chevron Station in San Francisco during the first significant OPEC oil embargo, everything he was doing in making them pay for their greed was justified. No one individual would be hurt, and those people being conned could afford the loss.

The plan had been in preparation for many years. True, Josh had made a fortune with his inventions, but most of his profits had gone into developing a D.A.D. prototype that could be safely controlled. In addition, years of testing had been required to determine the limits and capabilities of the machine. Then full-scale drawings were prepared to detail the research and development necessary to build a practical flying device capable of hauling people and supplies. Besides the transportation models,

Josh had developed several prototypes capable of providing free electricity. The ten billion dollars was not an arbitrary amount. This was the amount Josh believed would be necessary to deliver free energy to the entire world. The entire ten billion would be spent on R & D with full-size working models to complete the project. This was the dream. Hopefully, the missing D.A.D. would not turn it into a nightmare.

CHAPTER THIRTY-FIVE

The evening session with Gene was conducted after the Transtec people were safely tucked away for the evening. Gene was dressed in his usual natty attire of jeans and a sweatshirt with a heavy dose of theater makeup on his face, including putty, to accentuate his nose and cheeks. It was difficult to tell whether his short blond hair was a wig or just a good dye job, but the smart money was on a wig.

There was a certain strain around the eyes that had not been witnessed before by the three people watching his image on the television. A few worry wrinkles cut into the temples, adding a few years to his normal appearance. The three viewers didn't give his appearance much thought as they were wrapped up in their pre-opening night jitters. What little notice they gave to his appearance was written off as mere anxiety before tomorrow's big show.

"Let's get started," Gene said. "I want to know how you all did today, but this meeting will have to be short tonight. Let's start with Janet. Do you feel you can handle your duties with the crowd tomorrow?"

Janet squirmed in her chair a little as she replied. "I feel comfortable with what I've learned. The main trouble will be those unknown situations that always seem to occur on opening night. If the three of us can improvise fast enough to handle the situation, we should do alright."

"How about you, Ted? Are you ready to wow the audience with your technical wizardry?" Despite his stress, Gene managed a tight little smile.

"Aw shucks, Boss," Ted responded, this time with a genuine smile of his own. "We're going to have one hell-of-a-show tomorrow. You wrote some fancy lines for me to speak. Hopefully, there won't be a lot of Ph.D. physicists in the audience who will want to get extremely technical."

Gene seemed to relax for the first time tonight. "Just remember one thing, Ted. No matter what is said or what questions they might throw at you, your out is to emphasize that you will only answer certain technical questions after selecting the potential buyers. After all, this is a very proprietary device, and you didn't file for a patent for obvious reasons. As soon as you file a patent, the entire world will know your secrets. If they want answers to certain questions, they have to buy D.A.D."

"Okay," Ted replied. "That sounds easy enough. I think that should work well enough tomorrow."

"It's your turn, Wild Bill. Are you able to put D.A.D. through all the maneuvers?" In talking with Bill, Gene seemed to come alive. Obviously, a lot was riding on tomorrow's demonstration, and D.A.D. had to work perfectly to make believers out of a roomful of skeptics.

"Oh yeah," Bill said with enthusiasm. "Don't worry, Boss. We'll have that little silver ball running rings around every skeptic in the audience. Your game kid knows how to make things fun. I'm going to be having a real ball tomorrow. Ted and Janet might be a little uptight and nervous, but I feel great. I can't wait to see everybody's faces when we put D.A.D. through its paces."

"That just great Bill. Although don't get cocky. I want you to have fun and make it interesting, but no show-boating. Remember, this is a serious bunch of witnesses, and we need good publicity. If the world is convinced that we really have a free energy machine, it will make the rest of our little theater production that much easier to sell."

"I got it, Gene. We won't disappoint you tomorrow. You did a good job of casting this little show, and we're prepared to give the performance of our lives. Right, guys?"

"You damn right," Janet said with a look of absolute determination on her face.

Ted sat up straight in his chair, and looking the camera straight on, just as though he was sitting right in front of Gene looking into his eyes, he added his thoughts.

"I have a feeling just how much this means to you, Gene, and we all know how much of your life and soul you have invested in this production; all I can say is that we will give you the best performance of our lives."

"Well, gang, I couldn't ask for anymore. Break a leg tomorrow, but get a good rest tonight. I'll see you in the office in the morning before everything gets started. Oh, and by the way, be prepared; there will probably be a big crowd in front of the doors when you get to Transtec. Your guards are prepared and will see you safely through. Don't stop and chat with anybody on your way inside. You won't know who's who, and not everybody outside is going to get inside. Just be professional and on guard."

"Alright. Thanks, Gene," Ted said, speaking for the group. "We'll see you tomorrow."

***

In a late-night meeting at the White House with the President, Admiral Whittaker and DOD Secretary Bachelor both gave assurances they had personnel lined up to attend the show in San Jose. The U.S. Government did not receive a direct invitation; however, both CBS and CNN had been allotted three visitor invitations and agreed to let the government have one of their open slots. The government employee would have to be admitted as part of the press contingent; but, with one physicist and one military observer from the Air Force, both Admiral Whittaker and Secretary Bachelor were comfortable believing that they would receive the required information.

While he seemed happy with the report, President Carleton was still dissatisfied. "What are we going to do if that damn machine provides free energy? We can't let this technology out in the civilian population. Hell, it would wreak havoc."

"Well," the Admiral responded, "we clearly cannot have that technology in the hands of civilians. Suppose our guys attending the demonstration tomorrow are convinced the machine is real. In that case, we will have to plan on our operatives getting control of the machine and all the documentation. The inventor and other employees of Transtec will have to be silenced. Whether or not we can appeal to their patriotism is to be seen. We can always use the national security tag to claim access to the technology. The people are another problem."

"Dammit, Admiral," the president exploded. "I want a detailed plan to deal with the various possibilities. Who are we going to use? Will the Attorney General be involved? How about using the EPA under some kind of environmental study requirement? Give me something that makes me feel comfortable about what we're going to do."

"Mr. President," Secretary Bachelor interjected, "I'll be happy to work with the Admiral and the JCS to come up with detailed scenarios regarding every conceivable outcome. The demonstration is tomorrow. I expect it will be a few days before there is any serious action. We should have a complete set of options for you by the day after tomorrow. Don't you agree, Admiral?"

"Oh, that should give us enough time. We'll get our planners busy right now, tonight. We have several qualified strategic thinkers throughout the military, and of course the civilian employees," he quickly added to avoid dismissing the president's staff and the thousands of civilian contractors working with the government.

"That's just fine," the President said. "Keep me informed. This meeting is adjourned."

***

Following his video meeting with the Transtec people, Josh visited the San Jose Police Department in their new downtown building only a few blocks from the new steel and glass building housing D.A.D. and a contingent of armed guards. Detective McCutchen had gone home after going over thirty hours without sleep. Several detectives were working with the Chen murder and another group was handling the string of robberies, but no one had any recent news. Marco was still the leading suspect, but he was nowhere to be found.

***

After eleven o'clock p.m., Marco dropped Hicks off at his favorite bar on 12th Street before heading back to Willow Glen and his family's office complex. His father had left for home as expected, and the compound was vacant. Yes, there were video cameras and other security devices, but

Marco still had access and could disable all the alarms. He wasn't worried about the video cameras. He figured everybody knew about him by now, so there was no point in trying to be invisible.

Dario always kept between fifty and a hundred thousand dollars in cash for what he called grease. If he needed an inspector to act quickly on one of his projects, or one of his contractors or subs was not performing up to expectations, a little 'grease' always seemed to get things moving. The money was kept in Dario's desk, which was locked, but since the compound had such a great security system, Dario didn't feel a safe was necessary.

Marco didn't feel bad about breaking into his father's desk and stealing the money. From Marco's viewpoint, the old man had millions and wouldn't miss a few thousand dollars. Besides, he reasoned, if he could talk to his father about his problems, it was more than likely that he would just give Marco the money. His conscience was in overload, anyway; he was beyond the point of clear thinking. After breaking the drawer lock and pocketing the cash, Marco at least reset the security system. You never know what kind of pervert might try to break into the family business.

CHAPTER THIRTY-SIX

August 12th in Silicon Valley started as a thin gray line in the eastern horizon above the Santa Cruz Mountains, slowly turning into a golden orange before the sun crested the hills in a blazing yellow fire. Although early in the morning, the road in front of the Transtec building was already crowded with television vans, cars full of newspaper and radio reporters, plus another fifty vehicles belonging to those hoping to grab a seat for the big demonstration. Vying for a close, upfront seat were representatives from all over the world. At least twenty foreign countries were represented, including Russia, China, and Japan. Not noted for its restraint, Silicon Valley has been the site for hundreds of spectacular new product promotions and company announcements. It can be safely stated that none of the previous events came close to the excitement generated by the promise of *free energy.* People were already lined up in front of the double-wide tall twin glass doors. Those close to the front of the line could see armed guards inside, discouraging anyone from trying to force their way into the building.

A couple of hours later, the caravan carrying the three Transtec executives turned onto Short Creek Drive. Seeing the long line of vans, trucks, and cars plus the mob of people in front of the building caused all three actors to start feeling severe stage fright.

"My God," Ted whispered to no one in a voice that betrayed his feelings. "I'm not sure about this. I sure in hell hope Gene knows what he's doing."

Janet was the first to get control of her feelings. "This day should be exciting. I hope our beloved leader has the event more organized than that crazy scene in front of our doors."

Wild Bill was into his pre-entrance routine. Before going on stage, he withdrew into himself, closing off all external inputs. There is a zone we all have where we can isolate ourselves and focus our thoughts and energy. Once on stage, a consummate actor betrays no hint of the nerves felt only seconds before. Bill was not allowing himself to be drawn into the thoughts and words of his fellow actors. When the time came for him to perform, he would be at his absolute best. Until then, he kept to himself as much as possible.

Gene had already told the drivers of the two Explorers to drive around to the rear entrance by the loading dock. Two vans from Gerald's Catering were parked by the docks, waiting to set up their special morning treats. Along with a selection of Danish rolls, berry and apple turnovers, bear claws, and assorted muffins were large urns of coffee, juice, and cold water. Two guards were outside on the dock, waiting for the three Transtec employees. They all helped the caterers carry trays and urns inside. Gene had spent considerable time investigating the catering companies before settling on Gerald's. Those employees chosen to work the big show had been vetted personally by Gene. Pictures of the ones who would be allowed inside the building had been given to the guards, so no unauthorized person could sneak in uninvited.

On the second floor of the Transtec building, there were two large rooms next to each other. One room was set up with 100 padded steel chairs arranged in five by five configurations with big aisle spaces between each chair grouping. The adjoining room had several tables on which the confections and drinks were placed. Janet supervised the caterers on where to set up and how she wanted the food arranged. Once the tables were to her satisfaction, a guard escorted the catering personnel out of the building with instructions to return in six hours. Janet then worked with the guards regarding instructions for the various passes.

When the invitations were sent out, they were color-coded. A red pass was issued to the oil and energy companies. These formal invitations included representatives from OPEC. Holders of this pass were those designated to be fleeced. Blue passes were issued to major companies in industries that would be most affected by free energy. These companies included primary automobile and electric power distributors. Gene's intent was not to focus on this group for his scam, but he was flexible if it proved to be expedient.

Yellow passes were issued to the media, a not-so-subtle reminder of yellow journalism. Each organization invited to attend the demonstration had been allocated three passes, making this the largest group. A few black passes were given to government agencies, such as the EPA, FAA, foreign governments, plus the Small Business Administration.

Gene knew the military would not be shut out of the demonstration. The DIA, DOD, and JCS would find some way to infiltrate the demonstration to appraise the free energy machine. Gene also believed the U.S. Government and several foreign agencies would be after the technology shortly after the demonstration.

The front row of chairs was reserved for the various technical experts who would have the most significant say regarding D.A.D.'s abilities and authenticity. There was no other restricted seating; however, everyone in attendance was required to wear their passes on a lanyard around their neck so Ted and Bill would know who they addressed during the question phase of the program.

While Janet was busy with the caterers and guards, Ted and Bill were going over the final details for the demonstration. One of the windows in the second-floor demonstration room had been remodeled so that it could be opened from the inside. At one point in the demo, it was essential to synchronize the window's opening with the D.A.D. maneuvers.

Ted and Bill had to be prepared to back each other up as the demonstration proceeded. Gene had planned their respective comments and actions, but specific allowances had to be made for real time. As every actor knows, no matter how well prepared you are for a performance, and regardless of your rehearsals, during the live production, there are always deviations. The actors must ad-lib their lines and movements in harmony with the general theme to make the show successful. It was planning their reactions to these unpredictable program deviations that Ted and Bill were devoting their time.

It was just about showtime. Multiple rehearsals had been completed. The grand opening was about to begin. One can perform all the pre-entrance routines, but controlling stage fright just before the curtain goes up is always a period of high stress. Added to the usual high tension were these little phrases that kept running through both actor's minds. *This could be dangerous. Receipts will not be necessary. You could be killed.*

CHAPTER THIRTY-SEVEN

At exactly 10:00 A.M., the two massive front doors to Transtec were opened by the guards. Many just outside of the doors had been standing in wait for several hours and were eager to get inside and see this fantastic new machine. There was a lot of pushing to get inside, but the guards raised their tactical military-type weapons, blocking the way. When the crowd settled back down, Leon Whittaker, a large dark-skinned guard with a voice like thunder, began explaining the rules to those waiting to enter.

"Listen up, folks," he said in a commanding tone that immediately caught their attention. "Here's how it's gonna be. You will enter one at a time. You must show me your invitation or identification before you will be admitted. Immediately inside of these doors is a metal detector. Anything that looks like a weapon will be confiscated and the bearer will be expelled from the building. Following the metal detector, you will be subject to a pat-down search by another set of guards. Once this has been accomplished, you will be directed to go upstairs, where you will be treated to a special arrangement of pastries and beverages while waiting for everyone to be cleared. Any questions?"

"Yes," spoke up one skinny pock-faced man with long stringy gray hair who looked like a stick scarecrow that once dotted this former garden city, "what about our cameras and equipment?"

"Oh yeah," Leon said in a voice that was almost, but not quite, apologetic. "I forgot. Once inside these doors, your cameras and any other electronic equipment will be handed over to the guards immediately inside. Everything that goes through these doors is going to be inspected. If your equipment checks out, it will be returned. After all, we want you to see and record this once in a lifetime event."

The first person through the door gasped at the splendor. The lobby soared ten stories high, with unique colored artifacts hanging from the ceiling in tiers. The mosaic tiled floor featured butterflies of every color combination found in nature. Mahogany couches were interspersed with soaring palms and giant potted ferns. In the center was a twenty-foot high waterfall that emptied into a large koi pond stocked with fifteen-inch specimens. Soft instrumental light classical music added a touch of opera. A wide circular staircase was at each side of the lobby, ending at a mezzanine fronted by an ornate railing made entirely of rose-colored marble. Standing in awe at the fantastic sights, each entrant had to be prodded by the guards to go through the metal detectors and then be frisked.

At the top of the stairs was one of the most beautiful persons on planet earth, directing everyone to the refreshment room on their right. Wearing a flaming red sheath dress and Jimmy Choo shoes with three-inch high heels, Janet was a vision that complemented the ornate surroundings. Little did anyone know that the rest of the building was practically empty except the lobby and the two rooms set aside for today's demonstration. The guards had a kitchen and a room with cots plus the vault for D.A.D. Otherwise; the building was vacant. Guards were posted in the hallway to make sure there were no visitors in unwanted spaces.

It was nearly eleven o'clock before the 100 invited or allowed guests were all inside. On the outside, several hundred frustrated, angry, shouting men and women threatened to turn the event into an abattoir. Without those two menacing guards at the front doors, the building would have been breached, possibly turning the demonstration into a nightmare. Inside, the excitement was so high you could practically taste it in the air.

When everyone was accounted for, Janet, that vision in scarlet, ushered them into the main demonstration room. Standing before a mahogany podium on a raised stage, Ted was the epitome of a Silicon Valley executive. His fifteen-hundred dollar black Mezlan Bernard shoes were topped by camel-colored Hackett slacks with perfect creases. His cream-colored Patrick James cashmere V-neck sweater was just casual enough to be California svelte without being New York fussy. Tall, good-looking with square-jaw, clean-cut features topped with his 'new' stylish black hair, Ted exuded all the poise and presence of Steve Jobs introducing a new Apple product.

A few feet away, slumped in a heavily padded black armchair, Bill was the exact opposite. Wearing his Wild Bill trademark washed blue jeans and a loose sweatshirt, it was hard to see anything exciting about this derelict-looking man. His attire also comprised simple slip-on moccasins with no socks. A long blond ponytail hung down his back, completing the picture of a sixties hippie who never grew past the protest phase. A couple of feet to Bill's left was a big mahogany box, behind which stood two armed guards. It did not take a genius to know what the box contained. Hidden cameras at both ends of the room provided Gene with real-time images of both his actors and the audience. The show was about to begin. For fifty-three years, Josh Logan had been preparing for this moment. The next hour would determine his future.

CHAPTER THIRTY-EIGHT

Ted tapped the microphone sprouting from the podium, getting everyone's attention while quieting down the room. Looking around the room, Ted could see television cameras in the aisles for each of the major networks plus a couple of local stations who had been invited to keep the San Jose political administrators happy. Several women were in attendance who Ted assumed were reporters, although there were many highly professional females in engineering, physics, and management in today's world.

"Good morning," he said in a southern drawl that could have been Georgia or perhaps Kentucky. "My name is Ted Blankenship, CEO of Transtec International. To my left is our budding genius, Bill Westlake, the inventor and founder of Transtec. He needed someone to run his enterprise and, lucky me, I was chosen." He said this with a big wolf-eating smile. "In the back of the room, that beautiful creature in a vision of red is our girl Friday, Janet Hills, office manager, zookeeper, and overall boss. She looks friendly and sweet, but do nothing to piss her off."

Here Ted paused to catch his breath and relax just a bit. Opening lines are usually the hardest, and once on stage, past that first awkward moment, seasoned actors catch their wind and start sailing on smooth water. Giving his audience a brief smile, Ted began the actual speech.

"First, I would like to welcome everyone to Transtec and our free energy demonstration. Before waking up, Bill," he said with a chuckle, waving over at the reclining figure seemingly half asleep, "to show you what everyone came to see, let me give you a little background and some context. Bill will explain in a simplified scientific way how D.A.D. works, and we will answer questions that do not disclose any proprietary information. I'm sure you already know, D.A.D. is not patented."

This drew a laugh from the audience while Ted gave everyone that knowing smile. The smile that tells everyone we are all big boys here, and we understand how the game is played.

Continuing, Ted said, "When a patent is filed, everyone can get a look at the technology and invention. There is nothing we could do to stop you or anyone else from copying the ideas. Sure, we can file patent infringement lawsuits, and after several years and many millions of dollars later, we might get an award, but first, we must have the millions of dollars to defend the suit. Most of the businesses represented here have the money and lawyers to protect themselves, so you understand we did not file a patent. During our presentation today, we will be as specific as possible, disclosing no proprietary information. That information, gentlemen and ladies, is going to cost TEN. BILLION. DOLLARS."

There was a collective gasp from the audience. This was the first time money had ever been mentioned. Gene had chosen this moment to let everyone know that what they were about to see was extraordinary and not a cheap scientific stunt.

"What you are going to be witnessing today," Ted continued, "is something so revolutionary that it will transform the world beyond anything you can imagine. We know this is true. Consequently, we want to share this free energy with the world in the following manner."

To say that he had everyone's undivided attention would be an understatement. It seemed like hardly anyone was breathing, waiting for the following statement.

Smiling as he continued, Ted said, "Most of you industry people in the audience are in the energy sector in one way or another and will suffer the most from free energy; unless you have something to replace your present income stream. The automobile and aircraft industry will be severely impacted. Then there are the electric power distribution companies and related industries, such as coal mining, wind farms, and geothermal heating. Without a safety net, your companies will all suffer drastically."

As Ted paused, you could see the audience come to grips with the reality of free energy. Most of the attendees came prepared to scoff at Transtec and find out how the hoax worked. The harsh reality of a machine that worked caused those industry people in the audience to feel chills that froze their blood.

"To spread the technology around to various industries," Ted continued, "many of you have been issued a white appointment card with your invitation. Everyone with a white card will be offered a private appointment during the next few days for an exclusive showing with an opportunity to examine D.A.D. up close and personal with your technical representatives. Now here is the important part," Ted paused to make sure he had their attention.

This was unnecessary, as he could not possibly have a more attentive audience. Ted took a drink of water and looked over at Bill during this break, exchanging a brief smile. Just two actors, acknowledging a performance that was going well.

"We will invite ten companies representing various industries to buy an interest in D.A.D. for one billion dollars each. How these companies share the technology is not our concern. Once the ten companies are under contract, they will be given the D.A.D. machine you will see shortly. Accompanying the machine will be one full set of blueprints detailing every component it contains for each of the ten successful buyers. An exchange will take place no later than ten days from now in which each of those companies selected to purchase D.A.D. will deposit one billion dollars in bitcoins in an account to be provided. When all the money has been collected, these ten companies will be given D.A.D. and the blueprints. How these companies work out the details for sharing and evaluating the technology will be up to them. Transtec will have no further interest in what happens after the exchange."

When Ted had finished this speech, a dead silence filled the room while those in attendance tried to wrap their minds around what they had just heard. If this thing were real, life in the future would never be the same. Naturally, every businessman in the audience could visualize the impact of free energy on their business, and each was determined to be one of the ten businesses selected.

One of those selected for the front row raised his hand while speaking at the same time.

"Why ten billion dollars? Why not let everyone who wants to participate get a piece of D.A.D.?"

Fortunately, this was one of the questions Gene had expected and had prepared Ted to answer.

"Bill and I talked this over and thought that any more than ten buyers would make the prospect for a working combine almost impossible. Besides," he continued with a smile, "we decided ten billion would see us through to our old age."

There were a few snickers from the audience, but everyone was still sitting in high expectation of the demonstration that would follow Ted's remarks.

Someone from the government section stood up and asked Ted, "What if a company only wants to put up a few hundred million. Can't you let in more buyers if each one does not have to come up with a full billion dollars?"

Ted answered immediately. "There are plenty of companies that can afford the one billion dollar buy-in. We intend to limit the number of participating companies to ten, as we believe this is enough to introduce the technology to the world. Adding more companies to the initial program just adds more complications in allocating rights. When you consider that every home can have its private energy source, and everyone can travel wherever they want for however long they want at no cost, several industries are involved. Some companies, or several companies worldwide, will make the energy machines for homes, businesses, and the government."

"Other companies will make transportation devices for individuals, families, and even large units that can carry several thousand people. So, choosing only ten companies in various industries makes it easier to allocate rights for territories, individual products, and industries such as energy and transportation. By paying one billion dollars each, the participating companies will all have an equal share in the technology."

The audience was interested in Ted's comments, but he could sense they were growing restless, waiting for the actual show to begin.

Giving his trademark grin, Ted announced, "Let us turn this over to Bill if I can wake him up. He will demonstrate the capabilities of D.A.D. Your technical experts are free to examine the floor, walls, and ceiling for magnets or other electrical devices that could create the illusion of a flying sphere with no apparent motivational power. You notice," he said, pointing to one of the windows, "we have restructured one window to open so that D.A.D. can fly outside where no such artificial propulsion devices could exist."

As Ted was speaking, Bill slowly stood up, then walked over to the box containing D.A.D. With all the panache of a David Copperfield performance, Bill slowly bent down as though what he was about to do was the most outstanding feat in the universe. With all the dramatic flair of a consummate actor, he released the box lid. Once the cover was open, Bill reached in, retrieving something that looked like a violet television remote controller. Brandishing the controller like it was a conductor's baton, Bill looked up at his audience while breaking out in a big smile showing a mouthful of blazing white teeth. Pointing the colorful handheld device at the audience in typical theatrical fashion, Bill touched one of the buttons. The big show was about to begin.

CHAPTER THIRTY-NINE

King met Detective Larry McCutchen at a local Denny's for coffee. While not crazy about their food, King loved their coffee, which he drank while munching on a toasted English muffin. McCutchen wasn't particular about where he ate or the coffee he drank; his crazy schedule didn't allow being real picky. Usually, when he had a few minutes to catch up on a meal or a coffee break, he stopped at the closest place he could find. Tired and irritable, the detective ordered coffee with the Grand Slam Breakfast with scrambled eggs and French toast. When the King was buying, Larry felt free to indulge.

Without waiting for the King to ask his questions, Detective McCutchen started talking as soon as their stunning black waitress in flattering tight jeans was through taking breakfast orders.

Watching the waitress with just a hint of lust as she walked away, Larry said, "Marco is nowhere to be found. A few minutes ago, his Ferrari was picked up over in East San Jose, parked in front of a house up on the hill. It turns out some kid claims he bought the car from Marco last night. He even had a bill of sale. I'm going to question him after this great breakfast you're buying."

"Josh is pretty upset over that invention he believes Marco stole when he robbed the electronics store," King said. "He's tied up this morning and asked me to see if I could help find out the status and hopefully recover the stolen property. I'd like to go with you to see this kid in Marco's car. Afterward, I'd like to go see Dario, Marco's dad."

"Dario might be a little uptight right now," Larry offered. "The last time I talked with him, he seemed mighty upset. Imagine your only son who has everything; stealing and murdering. Dario admitted Marco emptied his petty cash drawer last night. It sounds like his petty cash was like fifty grand or more."

"Some petty cash," King said. "Wonder why he kept such a large amount?"

"Who knows," Larry responded. "He's a big-time operator. Maybe in his business, he needs that much. He won't be a happy camper today. Maybe I should go with you when you see him."

"Sure, let's do it. Right after we see that kid driving Marco's car."

The pretty waitress with the tight pants brought breakfast, interrupting their conversation. With hunger overriding his libido, McCutchen dove into his Grand Slam, hardly even looking at the girl's backside as she walked away. Well, maybe just a tiny peek.

An hour later, King and the detective were at the police department where McCutchen had them bring in Steve Hicks, Marco's friend, for questioning. Steve's bravado vanished quickly when King followed McCutchen into the interview room. Interview rooms are not made to feel homey or comfortable. An interview is a polite way of saying detention. Painted a dirty yellow-green, the windowless walls looked more like a jail cell, although a little larger. In the room's center was the ubiquitous gray metal table with four metal chairs without cushions. The chairs looked like they had been thrown against the wall a few times. The dented walls looked like that was also a possibility. Hicks was in one of the chairs, ostensibly not under arrest; however, the attending officer made it clear that leaving was not an option. Completing the room's décor was the one-way mirror mounted on one wall and a television camera mounted in the corner opposite the chair where Hicks was sitting.

By this time, Marco was nearing or already across the Mexico border. Under stern, no BS questioning by McCutchen, it didn't take Steve Hicks long to realize that giving up his friend was not only wise but probably the only way he was ever going to get out of this dismal, depressing room. Over the next hour, King and McCutchen learned about the car Hicks had traded to Marco. An all-points-bulletin with a be-on-the-lookout for a blue 1965 Ford Mustang with dented fenders was ordered for all of Nevada and California. Hicks steadfastly claimed not to know where Marco was headed, and although neither King nor the detective believed his story, and short of torture, there was no way to discover the truth. They learned about the storage locker in west San Jose, which they planned to visit later in the day. But first, they wanted to talk with Dario, Marco's father, to see if he had any idea where his son might be hiding.

The splendid Cabrini complex had the feeling of a mortuary as King and McCutchen entered the foyer with its splashy fountain. Arlene, the sexy receptionist with a crush on King, was somber, barely acknowledging either King or the detective. Without being prompted, she immediately informed her boss of the two visitors who were immediately granted permission to enter his office.

Although dressed in his usual classy attire reflecting wealth and power, Dario seemed to have aged a dozen years since they last visited. Dark circles under his eyes, combined with deep creases in his forehead and gray cheeks, made him look weary and defeated. His sad countenance and sloping shoulders conveyed the sorrow and despair that only a profoundly wounded parent can express.

In keeping with the melancholy feelings in the office, King was the first to speak in a gentle voice, displaying both his sympathy and affection for Dario.

"Dario, we're sorry to intrude on you at a time like this, but it's imperative for us to locate Marco. Do you have any idea where he might be?"

Waving both hands upward like a child throwing leaves in the wind, Dario said, "Honestly, King, I don't know. He's often talked about Mexico, and he speaks a little Spanish, but he could be anywhere."

Still standing, McCutchen added, "I realize this is a tough situation for you, Mr. Cabrini; please realize that we both feel for your disappointment and sorrow. If, or when, we find Marco, I promise to be as gentle with him as possible."

"I appreciate that, detective," Dario said. "I just can't believe that Marco could have killed that shopkeeper and committed all of those robberies. He had everything. What could be his problem?"

King and McCutchen had both heard Hicks describe Marco's cocaine habit and big-time dealing to the Valley's movers and shakers, but neither man seemed inclined to burden the grieving father with this information. When the time came that Dario needed to know about his son's habits and activities, he would be told. Until then, he had enough grief to deal with at the moment.

"When we find your son, we'll know the answer to your questions, Mr. Cabrini," McCutchen said. "I don't see any reason to bother you any longer. I feel awful about what you must be experiencing. Hopefully, this nightmare will end soon."

"Dario," King said. "I know this sounds trite, but if there is anything I can do for you, you know there is nothing I would not do. Maybe talk to the city about one of your projects or something. Anything. Please, please call me."

"Thanks, King," Dario responded, trying to force a smile on his face, but the eyes wouldn't cooperate. "I appreciate your concern and kind offer, but this is something I'll just have to learn to live with."

"Okay then," McCutchen said as he began turning toward the door. "We'll be leaving. If we learn anything about your son, I'll call you right away."

"Thanks, detective. I will appreciate hearing from you."

"Don't forget," King said as he followed McCutchen towards the door, "let me know if you would like my help. Maybe just have a drink after work or to talk."

"Sure, King," Dario responded, with a glimmer of hope spilling out of his eyes. "A nice bottle of an excellent Italian wine sounds great about now. Perhaps later tonight."

Waving at his friend King and McCutchen left Dario's office, passing Arlene, who never bothered looking up from her desk.

CHAPTER FORTY

The audience sat in stunned silence as a shining silver ball slowly rose out of the wooden box. Those witnessing the ball's levitation couldn't shake the feeling they were seeing some sort of magic show. This was precisely the response Bill was striving to achieve. He was confident that as the show progressed, and it slowly dawned on the audience that they were seeing history being made, it would have a more profound impression than if they started as true believers rather than skeptics.

Bill commanded the ball to circle slowly around the room, just a few feet above the heads. As the ball began circling the room, television and radio reporters started describing events breaking the silence.

"To convince you that this is not a magic show or an illusion," Bill said with a big smile, "I'm going to have one of the guards open the window. D.A.D. will leave the building and travel across the street. Over there, I will have it do several maneuvers that should convince even the most ardent skeptic that this is the real deal."

One of the burly guards went to the window, opening it wide. While Bill controlled the silver ball out of the opening, the audience left their chairs crowding the windows to avoid missing the action. Television cameras had to jostle for position along with everyone else. Once across the street, D.A.D. began a choreographed dance moving up and down, zooming around in circles, bouncing around trees, and buzzing the flower beds. After several minutes of aerobatic maneuvering, Bill set the ball on top of the Transtec sign, making a dramatic scene for the television viewers. Gene wanted everyone to associate the free energy machine with Transtec, and this scene was the culmination of his life's work.

After bringing D.A.D. back into the building, Bill pushed another button, releasing a small trapdoor at the sphere's bottom. A thin titanium string dropped out of the ball. Attached to the end of the line was a one-inch wide hook made of the same metal. The hook looked like one of those big fishing hooks used to catch a marlin. Flying D.A.D. to the back of the room where an extra metal chair had been positioned, Bill had the machine hook the chair, raising it to the ceiling. He then flew the chair around the room before returning it to its original position. While this was going on, Bill began his prepared rap.

"What I'm showing," he said dramatically, flourishing the remote like a conductor's baton, "is that D.A.D. is more than just a pretty bauble. It can lift several times its weight. I would like to direct your attention back to the front of the room," he said, bringing D.A.D. back to his side.

While everyone had been following the ball's flight around the room, dangling the chair from its metal hook, Janet had gone to the front of the room where a large canvas matching the wall in color had been erected. With a magician's flourish matching Bill's, Janet pulled on a rope, dropping the canvas covering. On the wall was a large, almost full-scale drawing depicting the inside of a flying saucer. A happy smiling family was shown relaxing on couches drinking some kind of beverage.

"What you are seeing," Bill explained, "is our concept for future transportation. You notice no one is at a control panel flying the machine. D.A.D. cannot impact another solid three-dimensional object. There are no fears that two machines can ever collide or hit something like a building or mountain. All you have to do to fly D.A.D. is enter the GPS coordinates for the place you want to go in the machine, and it will automatically take you there. Once programmed, you only need to punch one button to fly anywhere you desire or back home. No piloting, no watching out for other vehicles. You just relax and let D.A.D. do the driving."

"Okay," shouted someone from the front row. "How does the damn thing work?"

This was the big moment Gene had been preparing for since his dad had shown the shining silver ball to a small tow-headed boy. Watching from wherever he was, he could not help but smile as Bill, with his casual nonchalance, pointed at the questioner as he responded.

"Weeelllll," he said, drawing out the word as long as possible for dramatic effect. He also recognized that his following few words were being broadcast worldwide to a very interested audience.

"Without violating company proprietary interests, I cannot give you a detailed answer. However, what I can tell you is that this universe is crammed full of incredible energy. All that black empty space we see in the sky or even the surrounding space here in the room is full of energy. Modern physics tells us that everything, even our bodies, or this controller I am holding in my hand, "here he held up the colorful violet remote controller waving it around like someone showing off the crown jewels," is nothing more than an energy field. My initial question to myself was, "How do I make a machine to use all of this energy.'"

There was a stirring in the room as Bill's response, while stimulating thought, also left a lot of questions unanswered.

This unease was expected, so Bill continued, "You all know about gravity. There is no place in this universe where gravity does not exist. However, an even more prevalent energy exists that has far greater power than gravity to move heavenly," here Bill paused with a big smile for dramatic effect, "or even earthly objects."

As though it had a mind of its own, D.A.D. bounced up and down like a yo-yo in agreement. This action resulted in a small nervous laugh from some of the audience members.

"You are all aware of the enormous energy in a single atom," Bill continued. "An atom's energy is pitifully small when compared to the infinite energy in any old space." Bill held his hands up in front of his body, showing the space between his hands. "This space between my hands has enough energy to destroy the earth. Or, it can be used for more practical purposes, as you just witnessed. If you want to know its secrets, it will cost you ten billion dollars," he ended with a huge grin.

"You may also be surprised to learn that ancient peoples, and by ancient, I mean tens of thousands of years ago, knew about this energy and how to harness it for their use. While we cannot be sure about what happened back then, it is speculated by many that these people lost control of their energy devices, which led to their destruction."

People in the audience looked at one another, and whether in confused bewilderment or total disbelief, it was hard to tell. Bill and Ted both just smiled at each other as the audience was slowly coming to grips with the concept of unlimited free energy.

"I can tell you that it was my study of ancient rock carvings left behind by these distant ancestors that led me to discover how humans can harness this fantastic energy for our use without destroying ourselves."

As he was talking, Bill walked across the stage to a table in the corner draped in a black drop cloth. With another of his practiced magician's flourish, Bill whisked the fabric from the table and its contents, displaying a Rube Goldberg contraption. The only recognizable components were a miniature silver ball, like the one hanging in the air close to the table, and a string of light bulbs hanging around the entire device.

"What you are seeing," Bill continued while pointing to the table and its assemblage of components, "is a crude example of a machine to generate electrical power. Many, if not most of you, will presume there is a battery, or a hidden energy source somewhere. I can assure you that such is not the case. After this demonstration is concluded, those specialists with technical expertise are invited to visit this table to verify my statements. In the meantime, please observe the small silver ball over at this side of the generator."

Bill pointed to the tennis-sized ball attached to a lever at the side of the machine. Picking up another remote like the violet model used to control D.A.D., Bill continued his dialogue.

"This little fellow," pointing the remote at the small silver ball, "we call D.A.D.'s son, uses the same technology as the big fellow floating over there," he said, pointing to D.A.D. "We configured an electric generator using only those components available at a local science shop. Little D.A.D. supplies the power to run the generator. Please observe." Bill then punched a button on the second remote, turning the tabletop into a blinding white display.

Bright light temporarily overloaded the television cameras as the operators hastily scrambled to adjust the exposure so the audience could see the brilliant display.

After giving everyone in the audience and those watching television a chance to see the generator in operation, Bill punched a button, turning off the blinding white light.

"What we wanted to show is that D.A.D. is not just a pretty little boy that can fly around in circles, but is truly a free energy device capable of lighting up the entire world."

Most of those in the audience were sitting in stunned disbelief. A few skeptics still would not accept the free energy reality without a more severe and rigorous examination. Sitting in his secure location, viewing the proceedings, Gene could not have been happier. His goal was to show the world free energy, and he had succeeded. As brilliant as this demonstration was proving to be, Gene feared that the real problems were still to come, along with the life-threatening danger he had warned the actors to expect.

As the audience was buzzing with people trying to convince each other that what they had witnessed was real, Bill guided D.A.D. back into its wooden box and then closed the lid.

While the audience was coming to grips with what they had just witnessed, the television and radio reporters excitedly described the preceding events. It was hard to tell which group expressed the most enthusiasm, the audience or media reporters.

As soon as the lid on D.A.D.'s box was secured, the two guards at the demonstration table picked up the box, carrying it out of the room. Two other guards immediately entered the room and took up positions at each end of the table, holding the generator.

"This concludes our demonstration," Bill said as the equipment was leaving the room. "Those interested in viewing our elementary electric generator are welcome to visit its table. Now, if you will kindly give Ted your attention," Bill said, grinning like a schoolboy who had just given his first show and tell as he waved over at Ted still standing behind his podium, "he will answer questions and explain the next procedure."

As Bill was walking across the stage, someone in the second or third set of chairs stood up and began clapping. First another, then another until the entire room was standing clapping with many shouting 'bravo,' just like a real theater audience. Bill could not stop himself from giving a graceful bow, like any leading man going offstage.

Tapping the microphone to get everyone's attention, Ted waited for the crowd to quiet down before beginning the following scripted dialogue.

"We told you at the beginning that D.A.D. was going to be sold for ten billion dollars. After witnessing our little show, I believe everyone will agree that it is practically a steal at this price. In the main lobby downstairs, Janet and her aides will be available to book appointments for those with a white appointment card. Appointments will be for one hour, giving you and your technical representatives plenty of time to make your private evaluation of D.A.D. You may not disassemble the machine or subject it to any x-ray examination. At no time will you be allowed to be alone with D.A.D. Transtec guards and executive personnel will be with you always. You also may not examine the set of blueprints describing D.A.D.'s construction. We would like to conclude the sale one week from today, although we are prepared to extend the time to ten days if necessary, to accommodate the gathering of funds. Just so everybody is aware, this building and D.A.D. will be under constant guard until after the sale."

"What if we don't have a white card and want to be one of the purchasers?" someone yelled.

With a polite smile, Ted answered, "Well, we invited everyone to bid that we thought would help disseminate the technology. If you think you can contribute, please come visit me after we conclude this meeting, and we'll see about adding you to the list."

Once D.A.D. was out of the room, media people started packing up to leave. Announcers were falling all over themselves, seeking adjectives to express their amazement adequately. It might have all been theater, but it had been damn good theater deserving of the highest praise possible.

A couple of small groups gathered at the back of the room in very different conferences. Their interest was in deciding the best way to breach Transtec's defenses. Maybe grab one of the key executives for hostage. Perhaps blow a hole in the building and kill the guards. Grab Bill and subject him to a severe interrogation using the latest chemicals proven to be truth-tellers. And the most dramatic suggestion of all, wait until everyone was in the building, then blow it all to hell, killing everyone inside and destroying that infernal machine.

CHAPTER FORTY-ONE

In Washington, D. C., it was late afternoon on a bright sunny day. However, those assembled in the Lincoln Library at the White House appreciated neither the fantastic weather nor their reason for being cooped up in a room with the President.

When the demonstration started in San Jose, only a few of the President's important people bothered to turn on their televisions. After all, the event was being covered by professionals, and besides, it was more than likely a hoax.

As the show unfolded, telephones began ringing, and by the time Ted concluded the meeting, nearly everyone in the Capital had tuned into the happening. As the show proceeded, the President's Cabinet and advisors began gathering in the library, where DOD Secretary Marcus F. Bachelor broke the silence.

"Well, if that's not the God damnedest thing I've ever seen. What do you think, Admiral?"

Frowning at not liking to be put on the spot, Admiral Whittaker responded, "It looked damn real to me. Hell, we already know about anti-gravity, but this looked like something beyond what we have. Those California boys might be a real pain in the ass."

"Have you heard from your people who attended the meeting?" the President asked.

"Sergeant Wolf called me after the demonstration started," Whittaker replied. "He said it appeared that the machine worked as advertised. The meeting just ended, so I expect him to be calling back in at any moment."

"I had a guy at the meeting," Army General Hutchins added. "He said the same thing. It appears to be real."

"Unlimited, free energy," the President said. "My God. We simply cannot allow that kind of weapon in the hands of our enemies. In the hands of those bastard Russians or those sneaky Chinese, this could be a real casus belli. I expect a recommendation for handling this situation available tomorrow. Meeting adjourned."

***

In the headquarters building at Canaima National Park, Barrera, surrounded by the OPEC oil ministers, punched a remote, killing the television transmission. He was having a hard time keeping a wolfish grin from splitting his face. Things could not have been working out better. Within just a few days, he would control most of the oil in the world besides possessing a free energy machine.

"Well, gentlemen," he nodded to the Keffiyeh-garbed men surrounding the table, "it appears that the free energy machine is real."

"What do you propose doing?" Mohammad bin Salman, the current OPEC chairman from Egypt asked, trying to hide the sneer that was eating at his soul.

"Well, my dear Chairman," Barrera responded with a slight sneer of his own, recognizing the disdain creeping into Salman's voice, "we will just have to capture that machine for ourselves. We will kill those California people familiar with the project and blame it on the Jews." After making this pronouncement, Barrera gave a gracious smile, his chest swelling up, showing how proud he was of his capacity to make the tough decisions.

The oil ministers surrounding the table all nodded as Barrera was making his statement. They especially liked that part about killing the California infidels and blaming it on the Jews.

"Do we have any plans for how to accomplish all of this?" the minister from Iraq asked.

"We have men on the scene to keep us informed about the situation," Barrera replied. "We will all contribute a couple of our most seasoned infiltrators and assassins to help with the job. Let's see who we have available and select the best men and the one to lead the raid."

There was general agreement around the table as the ministers started providing names and resumes of the people they thought should take part.

***

Otto Conrad, old Outrageous, the CEO of Texaco, had been watching a European tennis match on TV when Lilly Dempsey, his assistant, hurried into his office and changed channels on the television without asking for permission. Ray was dressed in his usual light cotton slacks and bright red open-neck dress shirt.

"You've gotta watch this Ray, it's that business in California," she said as she crossed the room and changed channels. She was wearing a beautifully tailored Lilly Pulitzer skirt with a slit up one side topped with a red and white Moda Operandi blouse looking so provocative that the Colonel could not keep his eyes off his sleek-looking assistant. Reluctantly, he focused on the television and the images from California. Bill was flying D.A.D. out of the Transtec window when the new picture caught his attention. Watching the silver ball float out of the window and across the street, Ray asked, "Is this that free energy machine you told me about the other day?"

"Yes, and I heard from Skipper Walls a couple of minutes ago," Lilly responded. "He thinks the machine is real."

"Goddamnit," Ray barked. "We don't need this kind of shit. You better get on the phone Lilly, and round up the gang. Get old Hank at Mobile and Duke over at Chevron. Better call Shell and Exxon while you're at it. Oh, and don't forget Hinksley at British Petroleum. See about setting up a meeting no later than tomorrow afternoon. I don't care where we meet. But since we've already got an investment in this project with some guys on the ground, try to get everybody to come here."

"They probably already know about the free energy machine, Ray," Lilly said. "Is there anything you want them to bring or be prepared to discuss?"

The Colonel scratched his chin while he thought about her question. After a moment, he started thinking out loud. "We must get that machine and silence everybody who knows how it works. Course ya can't say that on the phone, and we do not want a trail that leads back here if something goes wrong. Just tell everyone that we need to strategize and figure out how we're gonna deal with the situation. These are all smart guys. They'll know what's going on. Just tell them to get here, that's all."

"Okay Ray, I'll get right on it. Do you have anything you want me to say to Skipper?"

"Just have him keep an eye on the situation and let us know if anything changes. Maybe you should tell him to prepare a plan to solve our problem," the Colonel replied. "Oh, and ask him to let us know how many people he might want and if he needs someone with special skills. He knows what we're after, right?" he said this last more of a statement than a question.

"Oh yeah, he knows," Lilly smirked as she started for the door. "I made it clear to him right at the start that if this damn machine were real, we would have to get it any way we could."

Watching Lilly leave the room, Ray enjoyed the view while giving her a parting shot. "I always know I can count on you, Lilly. I just want you to understand that I appreciate your work."

Looking back at her boss, Lilly winked as she left the room.

CHAPTER FORTY-TWO

Josh turned off both televisions he had been watching, the ones showing the demonstration at Transtec from both ends of the room. Satisfied that his actors were performing as hoped and expected, he turned his attention back to the missing D.A.D. He needed to find out what King and McCutchen had learned about Marco and the stolen property. After making a few calls, Josh learned both men were on their way back to the San Jose Police Department.

Grabbing his silver-topped cane, he went outside, holding it with both hands. Using his left hand with his right hand on top of the ball, Josh activated the machine inside the ball by pushing a button embedded near the cane's top. Early in his development of D.A.D., Josh discovered that the anti-gravity component of this device made everything within a few feet weightless. Anything in contact with the ball within a ten-foot radius was affected. Long ago, he had learned how to use this miniature version of D.A.D. to travel anywhere, at any time, almost instantaneously. His appearance at the desired location happened so suddenly that even if there were people in the vicinity, no one seemed aware that he had just materialized. Nevertheless he was careful to choose his takeoff and landing spots where he was least likely to be witnessed. In this manner, he had visited Los Angeles and New York to recruit his actors, plus his daily travel around the Valley keeping the big show running.

Landing on a deserted sidewalk around the corner from the ugly windowless gray rectangular box cities almost always built to house their police, Josh quickly turned the corner towards the main entrance. Inside, he was directed to the detective's room along the south wall about halfway down a crowded aisle. The door was open, and King was in an earnest conversation with McCutchen.

King's back was to the door, so McCutchen saw Josh first inviting him into the room.

"Come on in, Josh," he said. "We were just discussing your case."

"Hopefully, you have some good news," Josh replied, entering the room and taking a seat next to King. "How's it going, King?" he asked. "Making any progress on those robberies at your malls?"

"Larry and I just got back from talking with Dario, and we're convinced that he doesn't know where his son is now. We also talked with Hicks, that sleazy friend of Marco's. It turns out he traded cars with Marco so Marco could get out of town without being stopped by the police. We also learned that Marco had a storage unit over in Almaden, close to where I live. We are just waiting for a judge's order to search the unit for stolen property. Hicks didn't seem to think anything of value was left in the unit; Marco fenced all the stuff he robbed to pay his drug debts."

While King was talking, Josh's face revealed hope that his missing unit would be found in the storage unit, and then despair when learning that the unit was probably empty. Still, D.A.D. would not be easy to fence. Since no one knew what it was, at least before today's broadcast, it would be difficult for someone to give a proper appraisal of its value. It might have been left behind since it was heavy, and Marco would not want to lug a heavy silver ball around that he did not know had any value. After thinking it through, Josh decided there might be room for a bit of hope after all.

"Hey Larry," Josh said after thinking about the problem, "if I'm available, could I join you for a look at that storage unit?"

"Sure Josh, love to have you. I don't know when we will be turned loose to break open the lock, but it shouldn't be too much longer. By the way, you look like hell. King tells me you've got some other invention you're working on that's taking up a bunch of time. You need to get some rest, pal."

With a slow, tired grin, Josh responded. "Yeah, I've been putting together some financing for a new project that's taking up a lot of time lately. Having one of my models stolen from the electronics shop hasn't helped. I need that model to close the deal. Anyway, my problem, but thanks for noticing. Hopefully, we can find my missing model, and I'll be able to get some rest."

"The way you look, Josh," King interjected, "if we don't find your model, you might want to invest in a cemetery plot. Larry's right; you really look like hell."

"Hey, not a bad idea, King. Maybe I should buy up a whole square plot, enough to put all three of us in the ground right next to each other." Josh was desperately trying for humor, but it didn't come off.

"No thanks, pal," King said, "I ain't ready for the reaper, and if I was, I'm not sure I'd want to spend eternity lying in the ground next to your wasted body."

"Yeah Josh," Larry added. "Jeez, what a creepy idea. Besides, I think my wife's got a place picked out for our family plot up in Atherton. Right next to Dave Packard. We can't afford to live there, but who said we can't be buried there?"

"I didn't know Atherton had a cemetery," King said with a chuckle. "Those folks have so much money; I figured they just took their bodies with them when they died."

"Look who's talking about folks having money," Larry said. "Hell King, if I had your money, I'd buy the damn cemetery."

"Nah, not enough profit in death to suit me," King replied with a grin.

"If we can forego the pleasures of talking about death and cemetery plots for a bit, how about grabbing something to eat while we're waiting for the warrant?" Josh suggested.

"Yeah, nothing like talking about digging a hole in the ground to build up a man's appetite," King responded.

"I can go for some food," Larry said. "And for damn sure, our friend Josh looks like he needs a carb fix. Let's head over to The Mine Shaft, over by the airport. I haven't had one of their crab sandwiches in a couple of years. I heard King's buying."

"Just like a cop," King said, smiling, "always looking to sponge off the working class."

"Working class, my ass," Larry quipped, grinning like a schoolboy. "Since when does sporting around in a Mercedes convertible constitute work? Besides," he added, "just consider this as an investment in your education, eating with two of the Valley's most popular lunch companions."

They would not have been so confident if they had known what was happening in another part of San Jose; a part almost nobody knows exists.

CHAPTER FORTY-THREE

Bill, who was beginning to have a proprietary interest in D.A.D., supervised the guards who sealed the unit's box before carrying it away to be stored in the vault in the guard's quarters just around the corner. Gene had made it a point for the guards to secure D.A.D. while there were still some people in the room. He wanted everyone to know that the unit was being carefully guarded at all times.

With the main show over, Ted visited the table where Janet was busy scheduling private demonstrations and inspections. Many more people in line demanded a chance to bid on the technology than there were openings on the schedule. Fortunately, the actors had all been carefully prepared for this exact scene by their boss Gene.

Speaking up to get everyone's attention, Ted beamed a big smile while waving an arm at all the people in line. "Gosh folks," he said in the modulated southern drawl he had affected, "it looks like there's a lot more interest in bidding for our little energy machine than we expected. Tell you what I'm gonna do. If you will all give me your business card or contact information, I'll see what we can do to accommodate you with your own private showing. Just give us a day or two to arrange the schedules, and we will get in touch."

While speaking, Ted walked up and down the line, slapping shoulders, patting folks on the back, and shaking hands; all the while smiling, that leading man smile guaranteed to melt the heart of even the most hardened cynic. Motioning to one of the guards standing by, Ted had him come over and help collect business cards. As the cards were being collected, another guard gently urged those in front to exit the building. Everyone was still buzzed by the demonstration and wanted to talk about what they had witnessed. It's common for people who have witnessed a fantastic event to share the experience. People can integrate the entire episode into their psyche by talking about what they saw and how they felt. Most of those fortunate to attend the demonstration wanted to hang around to assimilate the contagious feelings filling the rooms. Some had other thoughts, but they didn't need to hang around after watching D.A.D. put to bed. They had plans to make that did not include a private demonstration.

After the upstairs room was vacated, Bill joined Ted and Janet downstairs in the lobby, where he helped Ted usher people out of the building. With their first big show as a resounding success, he couldn't wait to celebrate. Bill understood with an actor's instinct that his performance at center stage had been a hit. He didn't need to wait for his critic's review to know that the team had performed flawlessly. On the other hand, every time he started feeling good about their performance, part of his mind kept turning over the cautionary words of old Weinberg; *receipts will not be required. It could be very dangerous. You might get killed.*

After everyone had left and the room secured, the three Transtec people were driven by their guards to Hotel Grano de Oro San Jose, a historic downtown establishment featuring the best chef in Silicon Valley. Gene wanted those watching his actors to see that the Transtec people were simply what they appeared to be, company executives celebrating a successful event. This would be the last time they appeared in public, as tomorrow their world would change dramatically.

Bill was still riding high after his successful demonstration, with Ted and Janet feeling much the same way. They all threw themselves into the celebration with enthusiasm. Gene had arranged for a private room, allowing them to let loose, to a certain extent. They had to remain in character, and Gene had warned them to be especially careful with alcohol. Still, it was difficult for the three to show restraint.

Ted was utterly enamored with Janet. She looked stunning in her red sheath and black wig, and her personality was electric. They had all been warned that getting intimate with each other was out of the question, but it took all of Ted's concentration to keep his eyes from exploring the contours of her magnificent body. He was beginning to hate Gene and this whole project. Putting two men, both with an excess of testosterone, in constant contact with a gorgeous, desirable female seemed like punishment.

Their room opened into the main dining hall where a violinist played *The Magic Flute,* a soft romantic Mozart composition. Gene provided a bottle of Dom Perignon, which Bill opened, pouring each of them a brimming glass. Handing a glass to each of his fellow actors, Bill toasted their successful day.

"Here's to us guys," he said with a big grin. "I think we really scored big. I hope the big boss agrees."

"I think he approves," Janet replied. "Otherwise, I don't think we would be here drinking champagne."

Still enamored with Janet, Ted couldn't help himself, "Yeah, and did you see all those guys ogling Janet? I thought a couple of those guys with the funny headdress were going to abduct her for their second or third wife."

Turning just a little red, Janet responded, "They were perfect gentlemen. Well, at least they were gentlemen," she said with a grin.

"Come on, Janet," Bill said, getting into the act. "How many propositions did you get today?"

"Honestly," she said with a sly little smile, "I lost count. I sure never had this kind of treatment before."

It was all Ted could do not to ask Janet for information about her past. Instead, he commented, "Our ole buddy Gene sure knows how to dress a person up," he said ruefully with a dreamy look. "Just look at me. Hell, these shoes alone cost more than I made most months in the past."

"Yeah, I know," quipped Bill with a sardonic grin. "Just look at all the expense Gene went to in outfitting me."

They all laughed as a waitress wheeled in a cart containing their dinners. Grabbing a chair, they all sat down, digging into the best Kobe steak in the world. Specially flown in from Japan, the Kobe beef prepared by de Oro's chefs melted in your mouth. Knowing that this was their last chance to celebrate before the real action started, the three actors took advantage of the opportunity to enjoy themselves. However, in the back of each mind was that little voice warning them that the real danger was still ahead.

You could get killed.

***

After their meal at The Mine Shaft, King drove Josh down the road to Almaden Storage, following McCutchen in his government gray Ford, an LTD Crown Victoria, the elemental detective's car. Larry led them to the locked metal gate, forcing him to get out of his car and go into the office where, flashing his badge, he coaxed the manager into opening the gate. Hicks told them the storage unit number and where it was located, making it an easy drive right next to the door of the unit Marco had rented. There was a bright new Master padlock securing the door, which appeared to have been added recently. King and Larry thought that the unit would have been secured by Hicks and came prepared. The detective removed a large bolt cutter from the trunk of his Ford Vic, which cut through the padlock like a sharp knife slicing a chunk from a brick of cheese.

Josh was excited by the thought that his missing D.A.D. unit might be inside the storage locker. During his intense questioning session, Hicks had alluded to seeing a wooden box that held a shining silver ball. After removing the lock and sliding up the overhead door, all three men stepped into the small storage unit, only to find it totally empty. Three galvanized sheet metal walls with an open rafter ceiling and concrete floor. All the men were looking at was some paper debris and dirt. Josh was devastated but tried to hide his intense disappointment from Larry and the King. McCutchen didn't seem to notice Josh's reaction, but King had known his friend for many years and could tell Josh was having a hard time keeping it together. While he was not sure what kind of problem Josh was having, the King was not stupid.

The big anti-gravity/free energy demonstration happened at his building, a fantastic new facility he had temporarily leased to Transtec. He knew Transtec was just a front for Josh. Several months ago, over a glass of wine at King's spacious home in Almaden, King mentioned the problems he was having with the city and the roadblocks they had constructed, making it difficult to get his occupancy permit. Half seriously, Josh had asked him if it would be possible to use the building for two or three weeks. King, of course, was more than happy to let his friend use the facility. If the city investigated activity in the building, they agreed that the company in residence was there simply to decorate the lobby.

King correctly assumed that Josh was responsible for developing the free energy device called D.A.D. Having watched the demonstration, King was pretty sure his friend was planning on stealing ten billion dollars. Knowing his friend and the money he had made with his inventions, King wondered why Josh wanted so much money. King assumed it was for a noble purpose and wondered what the missing device meant to his friend's plans, but he was not about to ask. There was also no way he would ever betray his friend by revealing his suspicions.

Josh was almost sure King had an awareness about what was going on and had purposefully isolated both himself and King from Transtec so that when shit hit the fan, neither of them would be hit by anything. By then, if everything went according to plan, Josh would be out of the region for an extended period. Like everything else in this grand scheme he had concocted, Josh had prepared the perfect excuse for his absence once the plan had been executed. All he had to do was to be alive in a few days to make it happen.

CHAPTER FORTY-FOUR

Josh changed clothes, donning the Genie costume and makeup before making his late evening call to Ted, Bill, and Janet. Waiting for the call, all three still stuffed from a delectable dinner were relaxing in the living room of their secret house. It was next to midnight when the large television in the room turned on, startling them all into complete wakefulness. It was still a puzzle how Gene could operate their television remotely.

"Good evening, guys," Gene started, "you did a fantastic job today. How was your dinner?"

"Awesome," Bill responded. "I never knew beef could be so tender and flavorful."

Rubbing her stomach with both hands, Janet chimed in, "You really outdid yourself, Boss. That was one heck of a dinner."

"Kind of like the last supper, Gene?" Ted queried.

"Not at all," Gene responded. "Just a reward for a job well done."

Although the banter was lighthearted, underlying the good feelings was a tension they were all feeling.

"Tomorrow, it is going to get mean," Gene said. "We have eight private demonstrations scheduled, and each one is going to be difficult. You can expect them all to bring in extra people. The guards will be able to handle that situation, although you may be asked to intervene. However, the most trouble will be by those posing as city employees, such as building inspectors, fire marshals, security reviews, and so forth. They will all have proper documents including perfectly forged identification badges, business cards, and city-building forms such as zoning regulations and occupancy permits."

"What do we do with these imposters?" Ted asked. "And how can we tell they are imposters?"

"Good question," Gene said. "We can be pretty sure that most will be fake; however, it is entirely possible for the United States Government, possibly someone from the Small Business Administration or another government functionary, to persuade the City of San Jose to do an inspection just to add a little confusion and perhaps give them a chance to slip in as inspectors. They all want to evaluate the Transtec building's security, the situation with our guards, and of course where and how D.A.D. is stored."

"Yeah," Bill said, "but what are we supposed to do with these people?"

"The guards have been trained to deflect all such inquiries under the guise that all official inspections must be pre-approved and properly scheduled. After all, a big company like Transtec cannot expect just to drop everything at a moment's notice to satisfy some bureaucratic whim. The only potential threat will be someone posing as a fire marshal. According to city code, a fire marshal can enter any public building without prior authorization."

"What do we do with those people posing as fire marshals?" Janet asked.

Smiling a little at Janet's persistence and dedication, Gene answered. "It is doubtful that a real fire marshal will come calling. If someone does come posing as a fire marshal, the guards will ask for identification. The guards will then contact the city to verify the person's identity, including physical description. Of course, our lovely government in Washington may request the city to send in a fire marshal, accompanied, of course, by someone the government has chosen to do the actual snooping. In that case, the person must be admitted to do the inspection accompanied by the guards. The inspectors will see everything everyone sees or has seen except for the actual storage vault for D.A.D. That room will be unavailable for inspection as it stores sensitive Transtec proprietary documents and equipment. There will be no reason for a real fire marshal to dispute this claim or force the room to be opened."

"Is all of this subterfuge necessary?" Ted asked.

"Yes," Gene said. "It is all part of a smokescreen. We want everyone to know that D.A.D. is stored in a vault on the second floor of the building. Prohibiting an exploration of the area reinforces this idea. Probably there will be several attempts to breach Transtec's security and enter the building. We don't want to make it easy, but someone may succeed, and we cannot let anyone steal D.A.D."

Scratching his head at this seeming conundrum, Bill asked, "If they do break into the building and eventually the vault, how are we supposed to protect D.A.D.?"

Gene just sat there in his chair for a few seconds with a sad smile on his face before answering. "It's best if you don't know the answer to that question, guys. Trust me, D.A.D. will be safe."

There was another pause, leaving the three Transtec people squirming in their seats.

Finally, Gene continued with that same sad smile on his face. "You may remember I told you all that this project could be dangerous."

Sensing that they were about to receive some bad news, all three reluctantly nodded their heads.

"Well," Gene continued, "in case one or more of you are captured and asked where D.A.D. is being stored, it is better that you not know."

"Shit!" Ted exploded. "You mean tortured. Wouldn't it be better if we could give up the machine rather than get killed?"

"Better for you certainly," Gene responded mordantly. "But not for D.A.D. I will simply not allow any enemy forces to get control of the technology. Anyone who tries to steal D.A.D. is an enemy."

Seeing the shock and realization hit his actors, Gene was quick to continue. "Look, you are all under twenty-four hour protection. Your location is a tight secret. A lot of preparation has gone into creating a safe environment for you always. Before anyone can get to your physical presence, they will have to kill or incapacitate your guards. While that is highly unlikely, we cannot discount the possibility. Hence, you will not be aware of D.A.D.'s existence except when Bill is running a demonstration and our prospective buyers are examining the device."

The three actors sat stunned. They had all been told by their agent, old Weinberg, that it could be dangerous; they just had not processed the information until now.

True to his iconic character, Bill couldn't resist a little gimcrackery. "Is it too late to back out now, Boss?" he asked with all the sangfroid of someone perceived as the world's most intelligent man.

Bill's crack broke up the tension with a light chuckle from his two partners. Gene didn't laugh, but he was smiling with his reply.

"Sure, just forget about the million bucks that's yours in a few more days."

This brought a small whimsical smile to the three faces, but not one of them could stop the little refrain from circling in their brain.

"*You could be killed.*"

CHAPTER FORTY-FIVE

A dark tactical military van loaded with advanced surveillance equipment drove slowly past Transtec at 11:45 in the evening. It included thermal imaging scanners to see bodies and hot spots inside the building, infrared scanners to reveal hidden hot spots, Big Ears capable of hearing a leaf fall from a tree three hundred feet away, or conversations inside buildings and telescopic imaging with 10X magnifying power.

Sergeant Leo Wolf, the Pomo Indian Navy SEAL, seated in front of five imaging monitors, oversaw this intelligence-gathering operation. His four other team members were dedicated to analyzing the surveillance information. Tonight's exercise was strictly intelligence gathering. After studying the results from this excursion, decisions would be made in Washington regarding their next assignment. Sergeant Wolf and his team could not have been happier. Transtec was simply a new office building with a few hired guards. For an experienced, well-trained SEAL team, getting inside and neutralizing their pathetic security attempts would be easier than taking a cold shower.

Skipper Walls, the Texaco troubleshooter, and his helpers circled the Transtec building thirty minutes after the military finished their survey. Skipper was driving a dark blue Chevrolet Suburban with blacked-out windows. His two comrades were in the back, which had been reconfigured with swivel chairs in front of video monitors. With Texaco's money, Skipper had purchased black market surveillance equipment like that employed by the SEAL team, except most of his equipment was of Israeli or Russian manufacture. He would also wait for instructions regarding his following action. Unlike the Navy SEALs, Skipper was not that optimistic about breaching the Transtec security. He had been doing this sort of work for many years and was impressed with the way Transtec was being guarded. Getting inside and obtaining D.A.D. would not be easy. He could see no way to accomplish this goal without a significant loss of life on both sides. He was also confident that Texaco would order him to proceed. Running possible scenarios over in his mind, Skipper was trying to figure out how many men he would need and how quickly he could find enough qualified to do the job.

OPEC's designated operative Mateo Ramirez, chosen by Jose Barrera, was not interested in surveillance equipment; he just used his eyes and those of his companion, Juan Martinez. Juan had been in the states illegally for most of his 28 years. As a boy of six, he came up from Mexico with his father to help in the Gringo fields picking tomatoes, but hated the work and was soon part of a teenage gang working as mules ferrying marijuana for the Mexicali drug cartel. Juan was highly intelligent and rose quickly in the cartel, becoming a transporter at sixteen.

Transporters imported not only drugs such as marijuana and cocaine but illegals wanting to cross the border. Juan never grew taller than five feet eight inches and weighed less than one hundred and forty pounds, but he was considered the most vicious operative in California. Without a conscience, his brutality and inhumane treatment of errant mules or thieves became legendary. At twenty, he caught the attention of Mateo, who introduced him to another organization intent on penetrating the United States, OPEC. Together, the team of Ramirez and Martinez roamed around the country, intimidating anyone in the oil industry who dared to oppose the oil cartel. The money was great, and Juan didn't have to watch his back for those who wanted his position. In the drug business, there was always someone who wanted your job. The most uneducated, poor village rats used by the drug cartel as mules and enforcers were always looking for a way to advance. Killing bosses to take their positions was a way of life, and Juan was happy to trade that life for his job with Mateo.

As they crept past the Transtec building in the early morning hours, they were part of a slow-moving convoy. Short Creek Drive had become the most famous road in San Jose. Vans, cars, pickups, and even motorcycles were slowly cruising past the new steel and glass structure as though it was the most exciting building in the world. While it was impossible to view the passengers in this caravan, it was a good bet that many of the vehicles contained operatives from foreign countries. The difference between Mateo's slow drive with Juan and those other vehicles was that Mateo had only one interest. Where to place the bombs to destroy the building and everything it contained? Barrera wanted D.A.D. for the cartel, but if it couldn't be obtained, he sure as hell didn't want anyone else to possess the key to free energy. That would destroy all his plans. While Mateo drove their vintage 1976 Cadillac slowly past the building, Juan had a Bosch and Lomb telescope glued to his right eye, looking for a vulnerable spot where a bomb would do the most damage. He spotted several likely locations that he memorized for later use if it became necessary. Neither man paid attention to the other traffic coasting along the street. If anyone got in their way, both men were experienced at eliminating competition.

***

Admiral Whittaker, Chairman of the JCS, was waiting in his pentagon office for the early morning report from Sergeant Leo Wolf, his San Jose reconnaissance team leader. It was three-thirty in the morning when the telephone ringing jangled his nerves. He had been dozing while sitting in his chair when the sudden, startling sound caused him to almost fall on the floor. Cursing himself for being so careless, the Admiral punched a button, putting the caller on his speakerphone.

"What did you discover tonight, Sergeant?" he snarled, still recovering from his abrupt awakening.

"There are sixteen guards inside. They seem never to leave the building. Another four guards are always with the three Transtec employees. It has been determined that there are only three employees in the entire company. We know where these three people live in a house about two miles away. Their guards pick them up in the morning and drop them back home after work. The Transtec people never seem to leave their home once the guards have dropped them off. No one seems to guard them in the evening. Our heat sensors show only three people in their house and the sixteen guards in the company building. Getting to the inventor and the other two Transtec people will not be a problem. Getting inside the Transtec building and retrieving the free energy machine will be more difficult and probably cannot be done without disposing of the guards. We are looking at ways to incapacitate them, perhaps with some nerve gas or sleep agent. This may not be possible because they are always spread out through the building. We may have to eliminate them to secure the machine."

***

Otto Conrad down in Texas was wide awake when Skipper Walls called in with his report. While Otto had great faith in Lilly, the seriousness of the D.A.D. threat, especially after Skipper's last report about possibly needing to kill several people, made him take a personal interest. His office, high atop the tallest building in Houston, looked out over a sleeping city with its millions of lights. Most of the lights were white or yellow, but there were enough red, blue, and green lights to make it look like some gigantic decorated Christmas tree. Some were blinking, others were flashing red to warn aircraft to stay away, and others were rotating with a broad beam that would sweep around the city in one-minute circles. There were also three high-power beams of light aimed at the sky advertising the location of a big sales event, perhaps a grand opening or a going-out-of-business sale in a city that never sleeps. Otto had been looking at the panorama of lights when his telephone alerted him to Skipper's call.

"What's the latest story, Skip?" he asked. There was never a greeting with Conrad, even if he thought the caller was his beloved wife.

"It's just like we figured, Chief; the building is loaded with armed guards, all carrying automatic rifles plus handguns. You might find it interesting to know that this place is getting more attention than Disneyland. We parked out of sight down the street behind another building, and in one hour, we counted forty-five slow drive-bys, many of them vans loaded with surveillance equipment."

"Were you able to determine who any of these other players are?" Otto asked.

"The only vehicle that stood out carried a couple of Middle Eastern men that were possibly Egyptian or some other Arab country. You can bet that OPEC is very interested in D.A.D. Most of the vehicles had dark windows, so we couldn't see who was inside, but we noticed many diplomatic license plates. There probably isn't a major country in the world that is not interested in having a free energy machine or determined that no one else has one."

After thinking about Skipper's report for a couple of moments, Conrad asked, "When are we scheduled for our private demonstration, Skip?"

"We have tomorrow afternoon at three o'clock for our one-hour evaluation."

"Let's see what you find out tomorrow then," Conrad replied. "If this machine is real, we're going to have to act fast. Based on your report, we don't have any time to mess around with all the interest this has generated. Call me tomorrow when you're through with your final assessment. I'll have some fellows here work up a few scenarios for breaching their security and grabbing the machine. We'll talk about this tomorrow."

"OK, Chief. Talk to you tomorrow." Neither man said goodbye.

***

Carlos Barrera was in bed with two of the beautiful consorts he had hired to entertain the oil ministers when his phone interrupted his fun. Sweating from the strenuous workout being provided, the phone slipped out of his hands as he reached to silence the sharp twilling sound made by the phone's ringer.

"Damn, damn," he gasped slightly out of breath while falling out of bed, grabbing for the elusive instrument.

"Give me your report," he demanded, still short of breath. There was no need to inquire who was calling. No one on earth who knew him would call at this hour except for his operative in San Jose.

In San Jose, Mateo Ramirez grinned into the telephone as he correctly guessed the reason for his boss's shortness of breath. "It's just like we thought, Boss, the entire world is interested in this free energy machine. Our private demonstration will be in two days. We'll be able to make a better determination of our alternatives for stealing the machine after that. Based on all the interest, we should be prepared to move quickly. Can you provide me with some help?"

Regaining his composure, Venezuela's most dangerous man responded. "Help is already on the way. By tomorrow, you will have ten highly trained men skilled at killing. Have a plan for me right after your private showing. I want that machine, and we will let nobody stand in the way. Do you understand?"

"Got it, Boss. Is it alright if we just blow up the whole damn building and destroy everything inside?"

Barrera frowned into the telephone. "Look, we would rather have the machine, but if we cannot get it for our use, it would be wise to destroy it so no one else can have it either. This means, of course, that you have to kill all those who know how it works. However, it would be far more profitable if we could get the machine. There will be a big bonus for you if that is possible."

"Got it, Boss. I'll see what we can do. It should be possible to get the machine with all those men you are sending, but it will mean killing many people. It would be nice if we could blame it on the Israelis."

"That sounds like an excellent idea, Mateo. Let's see if we can make it happen. Call me as soon as your demonstration is over."

"Okay, Boss," Mateo said. "Talk to you soon."

***

It would not have surprised Josh Logan, twisting and turning in bed with his dark demonic dreams, to know that similar conversations were being held worldwide. Venezuela was not the only country interested in blaming the Israelis for killing all the Transtec people and guards; several other countries also thought killing the Transtec people and blaming Israel would be a good idea. However, many favored blaming the Russians or Chinese, while some wanted to blame Japan or North Korea. They all agreed that aggressive action was required, and the sooner, the better.

CHAPTER FORTY-SIX

August 13th began with another beautiful sunny day in what used to be the garden city of California. Underneath all that concrete and road tar sat some of the most fertile soil in the world. Occasionally, you would find a small garden plot in somebody's backyard, growing the most incredible vegetables and fruit imaginable. Such a garden plot was behind the house on Dilbert Avenue, which was the reputed home for the Transtec people. Unfortunately, the ground was fallow and soon to be covered over by a new condominium. None of this was on the minds of Ted, Bill and Janet as they were shuffled from one set of black Explorers from behind the garden fence to another pair of black Explorers waiting in the garage.

The three were still in shock after their early morning briefing from Gene. He sent them a video showing the interest being paid to the Transtec building on Short Creek Drive. As they watched the video, it became increasingly clear how much attention the world paid to their free energy machine. While they could not see the inhabitants of the vehicles, the dark surveillance vans were proof enough that many people were trying desperately to discover a way to penetrate the building and steal D.A.D. Gene also made it abundantly clear that some would not stop at anything to get their hands on this technology. If that meant killing the Transtec people and all the guards, then so be it. The reality of the situation scared the hell out of all three actors, but Gene assured them that their safety was the number one priority on his shortlist of concerns. While he did not discount the possibility of an earlier action, he believed no one would attempt anything drastic until after all the private demonstrations today and tomorrow.

Back at Transtec, Ted asked Janet to review the list of demonstrations scheduled for today. Gene had Janet plan sixteen private demonstrations in a specific order. None of the actors were sure which ten of the sixteen attendees were the targets for his big con, but they could all guess, and knowing Gene's feelings about the oil industry, they could be pretty sure about their choices. In response to Ted's request, Janet opened a folder and handed both Ted and Bill a copy of the itinerary for the next two days.

Wednesday, August 13th

8:00 A.M.General Motors
9:00 A.M.ExxonMobil Oil Company
10:00 A.M.Citco Oil Company
11:00 A.M.Ford Motor Company
1:00 P.M.Royal Dutch Shell Oil Company
2:00 P.M.Rosneft (Russia's Oil Company)
3:00 P.M.Texaco Oil Company
4:00 P.M.OPEC Oil Cartel Ministers

Thursday, August 14th

8:00 A.M.BP British Petroleum
9:00 A.M.Chevron Oil Company
10:00 A.M.National Iranian Oil Company
11:00 A.M.Saudi Aramco Oil Company
1:00 P.M.PDVSA Venezuela Oil Company
2:00 P.M.PetroChina Oil
3:00 P/M.ADNOC Abu Dhabi Nat Oil Co. United Arab Emirates
4:00 P.M.Iraqi Oil Ministry

"I wonder which ten our boss is going to steal his billions from," Bill asked, not really expecting an answer.

"I can guess along with you two," Ted responded. "I just hope to hell we're a long way away when they find out they were scammed."

"That's what Gene promised," Janet added. There was a hint of hope and a lot of fear in her voice.

"By the way. How is it going to be a scam when we know the machine works and Gene has promised to deliver the working model plus a full set of blueprints to the lucky ten bidders?"

"We haven't been told that information, probably for our own good," Ted responded. "Okay, troops," he continued, "it's just about showtime. I sure hope these guards know what they're doing."

Just then, Captain Arnold Wilson, who commanded the guards, strolled up looking confident and prepared. His very presence seemed to provide reassurance to the three actors.

"You guys ready for the big show," Wilson asked with a knowing grin splitting his chiseled face.

"You bet, General," quipped Bill, with a big grin and never at a loss for words.

"Thanks for the promotion, Bill, but you can merely bow and genuflect without all the words if you would rather," Wilson said with an even bigger grin.

Seeing that he had their undivided attention, the Captain began giving instructions. "Okay, here's how I'd like to play it today. Janet will stay here in the foyer with the guards at the door. Her job is to make sure that the correct representatives are here for their appointment. We can expect several attempts at gate crashing, but we only want to let in those with scheduled appointments. Everyone else wanting into the building will have to wait for their appointment. At no time are we going to allow over one group of people in the building at a time. There will be four guards here at the front door to enforce this rule."

Seeing that the Transtec people were paying close attention, Wilson continued, "I would like Ted to spend his time between the lobby and the demonstration room, if that is okay with you, Ted. You can greet your guests, then escort them up to the demonstration. Bill will be in the demonstration room at all times with D.A.D. With him will be four guards always watching over the demonstrations and the machine."

"Gene instructed me to allow the inspectors access to D.A.D., but they are never, under any circumstances, to be left alone with the machine. Bill can explain the controls and let them play with the device, but we cannot allow them to fly it outside where some confederates might be waiting. Ted can stick around for the demonstrations and answer questions before escorting his guests back to the lobby. Our guards will monitor every move made by those we let into the building. Every single person entering this building will be subjected to a full-body scan and pat down. Any inspection device or tool they want to bring in will also be inspected. Anything the least bit suspicious will not be allowed past the inspection station. Questions?"

Ted, Bill and Janet looked at each other to see if anyone had something to ask or say. After a moment's hesitation, Bill asked, "What will you be doing, Captain?"

"Oh, thanks, Bill. I should have said I'm going to be roaming around inside and outside, looking for problems. Our guards are all well trained, and they each have their assignments. I do not expect any real trouble today or tomorrow, especially during the day, but it won't hurt to keep a close watch on what might be going on. We expect an assault during the next few days and possibly several attempts. You guys don't have to worry," he said, nodding at the three actors. "We will let nothing happen while you are here, and as you know, Gene has provided excellent protection, plus your nighttime residence is known only to your guards."

"What about the people staying in our house on Dilbert?" Janet asked.

"They are highly trained military professionals. It is even probable that an attempt will be made to kidnap them by people thinking you three are in the house. I can assure you, anyone foolish enough to make that attempt will be very sorry."

As he spoke, there was a note of pride in his voice, almost like he knew what would happen and could predict the outcome.

Looking out of the window, Ted could see a crowd milling around on the lawn and sidewalk in front of the front doors. Recognizing the three people from General Motors who had attended the demonstration yesterday, he announced, "Looks like it's showtime people. GM is here."

With trepidation and a fearful heart, Janet left the group to be with the guards at the front doors. Ted reluctantly followed behind. In both of their minds was old Abe's warning, *you could be killed.*

CHAPTER FORTY-SEVEN

Accompanied by guards, Bill's trip upstairs to the second-floor demonstration room was monitored by Josh watching from his secret location. For the next two days, he would be glued to the television monitors, watching every move made by his team of actors and their visitors. Everything he had planned and worked for during the past twenty years was now in the endgame.

Were his actors good enough to pull it off? Could he provide protection when the action got rough? Were his plans to secure D.A.D. failsafe? Josh was almost positive there would be several attempts to steal D.A.D. He was also confident that he could prevent that from happening; however, even if some group stole his model, it would not do them any good. However, if his baby got robbed, that would ruin his plans. No model, no sale. Without D.A.D., he could not collect the ten billion dollars which were needed for his next project.

Anxious about the private demonstrations that were about to start, Josh could not stop himself from worrying about the other missing anti-gravity model that had been stolen from Valley Electronics. Even if everything else was successful, losing his other D.A.D. would be catastrophic. He was getting to the age where he could not afford to give up another five or six years of building another model. He had to do every bit of the detailed construction by himself. The inner workings of D.A.D. were so complex, with such extremely tight tolerances, that it took hundreds of hours to make some parts. Josh wanted to be alive to see his father's dream completed, which meant recovering the lost model. After the day's demonstration activities, he would be forced to spend his evenings working with King and McCutchen to locate the missing machine. Fortunately, Bill and the General Motors team entered the demonstration room, pushing his attention back to the present.

Josh had a direct line to the Transtec building and could contact his team any time he wished; however, it would be difficult, if not impossible, to contact them without blowing his cover. The Transtec team was supposed to be in total control of the entire situation. A call from Josh, or Gene, as they believed him to be, might expose the fact that there was another player in this drama, causing suspicions to arise. It might not end the show, but afterward, it would give those seeking revenge another person to hunt. If another person were suspected of having a hand in the robbery, there would be every effort in the world made to discover his identity. This might focus attention on King, who owned the building. Josh was not worried about being identified or caught, but he did not want to put his friend in an uncompromising position.

Josh watched as the guards brought D.A.D.'s box into the room. Bill carefully opened the box, exposing the shining silver ball. The General Motor's team hovered around the box, straining for the best view. After the three men from GM had finished examining the machine sitting in its box, using the remote, Bill caused D.A.D. to levitate slowly. Stopping the shimmering silver ball at eye level, Bill let the GM team examine it for several minutes. They used stethoscopes to listen for sounds it might be making. Electronic equipment was used to look for hidden magnets or some kind of electro-magnetic device using a hidden energy source inside the room. Once the team was satisfied that no games were being played, Bill had Isaac Holmgren, the team leader, hold out his hands. Warning him that the ball was hefty, Bill gently settled D.A.D. into the palms of both hands. As the total weight of the ball became apparent, Holmgren grunted with the effort straining to hold the ball without dropping it on the floor. He need not have worried. Bill was standing by with his finger on the remote in case the ball slipped through Holmgren's fingers.

The GM team measured the ball's circumference then weighed it on a scale they had brought. They did not trust Transtec to provide them with the proper equipment. Opening the trap door and releasing the hooked cable, Bill demonstrated D.A.D.'s ability to lift various objects around the room. After all the tests and demonstrations were completed, GM wanted to see the inside of the ball.

Bill firmly rejected this request, backed up by Ted, who had joined the group. The guards were standing by in case the scene became ugly, but GM backed down, recognizing the futility of their request. They had not expected Transtec to let them have an inside peek, but it never hurt to ask. Satisfied that the free energy device was precisely as advertised, GM reluctantly followed Ted as he escorted them back downstairs. Fascinated by the machine, they would have loved to stay and play for the rest of the day. When pressed for information relative to purchasing a share of D.A.D., Ted told GM he would not decide on the buyers until all his prospective buyers examined the product.

Pleased by how the examination progressed, Josh watched GM leave the room. They were not one of the companies that Josh wanted to steal from. If he was ready to release D.A.D. into the world, GM would be one of the companies chosen to take part. Perhaps at a future date, they would be given their chance. In the meantime, Josh had no desire to defraud GM out of a billion dollars. Exxon/Mobile scheduled for the next demonstration was another matter entirely.

The scene outside of Transtec's front doors was one of complete chaos. Besides those scheduled for appointments to test D.A.D., there were hundreds more clamoring for entrance. Media of all types, radio, television, newspapers, magazines, and freelance journalists, were mixed with representatives of governments from around the world. In addition, there were representatives from every company around the globe, all wanting a piece of the action. Slithering around in this sea of madness were the teams looking for some way to breach Transtec's security. The mob provided all the cover needed for a close-up examination of the building and the guards controlling the situation.

Watching the outside scene from hidden cameras, Josh could not help but smile as he watched what happened when one of the bad guys ran into another bad guy from another team. People in their line of work give off specific vibrations recognizable by everyone else in their profession.

Bumping into someone not from their group, these special operators tried to determine who the competition was and what kind of qualifications they might possess. Foremost in the minds of each operative who happened to have one of these meetings was how difficult it would be to take out the other person. Such occurrences were evident to anyone looking for them, and Josh was looking. He had the same questions. How difficult was it going to be to take care of these guys?

CHAPTER FORTY-EIGHT

Every individual uniquely responds to poverty. Some are strengthened using self-discipline and positive affirmations. Others become helpless when faced with a lack of life's necessities when there is no end to their misery in sight. Those who use dire circumstances to explore alternative life avenues often excel far beyond those born with silver spoons. Then there are the Howard Trent's of the world, more recently known as William or Billy Westlake.

Being a starving actor is no myth. For every actor able to make even a modest income from their passion, thousands are perennially hungry, hustling anything possible for their next meal. Being poor, struggling to exist is a way of life. For many who find themselves in this situation, people like Howard, hustling becomes their way of life, even when there is no longer a need for this behavior. Playing the role of William "Wild Bill" Westlake was providing him with all he had ever asked for in life, playing a significant role in a costly production.

Besides that, he was soon to receive a million dollars. But the thought that Gene would collect ten billion dollars was stuck in his mind. The hustler in him could just not stop looking for a way to get a more significant portion of all that money. While his fellow actors, conscious of the fact that they needed to be sharp in the days ahead, were trying to clear their minds and relax, Billy's mind kept churning out idea after idea after idea. Different ways he might grab a few extra million, or heck, maybe even a billion. So what if he betrayed Gene and his fellow actors? He didn't owe them anything. He would do the job he was being paid to do. If he could get a little bonus, what difference would it make? Surely Gene could afford to give up a few million or more. He just might have to make a deal with one of those oil companies, or maybe one of the companies Gene was not interested in scamming. He just needed to figure out how to do it without getting caught.

***

Josh was trying to get a hold of King or Detective McCutchen when his other telephone rang. This was a private line he had installed just for this operation, so he had to know it was someone from his team; he just couldn't imagine what could have prompted the call. Hopefully, it was not bad news.

"This is Gene; who's calling, please?"

"Hi Gene, this is Ted. Is it okay to talk on this line?"

"Oh hi, sure Ted, what's on your mind?"

"I just got a call from Lincoln Strong, the CEO for General Motors. GM wants to be one of the players. He wants to give us a billion dollars for a share of D.A.D. He even said GM is prepared to provide us with the full ten billion dollars. What do I tell him?"

Josh had to think for a minute. It had never entered his mind that someone would volunteer to join the D.A.D. sweepstakes this early in the game. He had always thought that it would take a little more persuasion to get buyers to commit a billion dollars for a ten percent share in free energy. That GM wanted in after today's demonstration for their investigators changed everything.

"What did you tell Mr. Strong, Ted?"

"I thanked him for his offer and told him that until we could identify all ten participants, it would be premature to confirm acceptance. All ten buyers had to be aware of each other and be willing to work together. I told him we wanted representation from many industries."

"Wow, that's good thinking, Ted. What was his reaction to your statement?"

"He said that he totally understood, and GM was willing to work with all the partners purchasing the other nine shares of D.A.D."

"When is he expecting a firm answer?"

"I told him that we had several more private demonstrations scheduled for tomorrow and would give him an answer just as soon as they were completed and we had firm offers for the remaining shares."

"Okay, that's good." Josh paused for a minute, collecting his thoughts before continuing. "Keep up the good work, Ted. I want Exxon/Mobile to be one of the ten participants. Let's give them one-hell-of-a show."

"Got it, Boss. We will do our best."

"I know you will. I have complete confidence in you and your team. Thanks for the call, Ted. We will talk later."

"Sure thing. Bye for now."

Josh replaced the telephone on its hook while deep in thought. GM could afford to lose a billion dollars without jeopardizing the company or their future, and maybe it would be a good idea to let them purchase an interest in D.A.D. In a few years, when he had a fully operational model, GM would be a prime candidate to build the transportation modules. Perhaps, at that time, he could make them a special deal based on their early participation in the model. They would be angry at having been duped earlier, but after seeing the full-scale model and being given a chance to have exclusive North American rights, Josh expected their anger to disappear quickly. It was now time to watch the Exxon/Mobile show.

Ted had called Gene from his private office at Transtec. He was feeling euphoric after talking with the boss. Gene's compliments and confidence in his actions provided an extra quickness to his step, more control of his thoughts, and more assurance in his actions. After completing the call, he went downstairs to usher in Exxon/Mobile.

When Ted reached the lobby, he found Janet in a heated conversation with a tall man in a dark suit. The man wore his long brown hair tied back in a ponytail, emphasizing a sharp aquiline nose. His angry black eyes were focused on Janet, who remained calm and possessed despite the negative energy thrown her way. Seeing Ted approach, she smiled and turning to face him, she said, "Oh hi Ted, you're just in time. This gentleman, Mr. Olaf Gunderson, is from Exxon/Mobile and insists on having four people in his party to investigate D.A.D. I've explained that we only allow three individuals at a time into the demonstration room, but he keeps demanding that we allow him one more investigator. Can you help?"

Ted smiled his million-dollar smile and, holding out his hand, he said, "Hello, Mr. Gunderson, I'm Ted Blankenship, the CEO. Welcome to Transtec."

Seeing the smiling company big-shot holding out his hand, Olaf had no choice but to grasp it in a brief shake. "Thank God," he said in clipped tones, barely able to suppress his anger. "Somebody to provide a little sanity. I've explained to this young lady that we simply have to have our chemical engineer along to help with our examination."

Still smiling, Ted answered the angry representative from Exxon/Mobile. "I believe we explained during our public demonstration that every group invited for a private demonstration could only use three investigators. This limitation has to do with D.A.D.'s security. I'm sure you understand," he said with the million-dollar smile firmly in place. "But I'll make you a special offer. Suppose, after the demonstration with your chosen three individuals, you still feel that you need an extra person to validate D.A.D.'s characteristics. In that case, we'll let them attend the demonstration with another company. Several companies are only using two evaluators, and I'm sure one of them would welcome your fourth person to help them with their evaluation. Would that work for you?"

Confronted with the smiling, confident CEO of Transtec and being made a reasonable offer, Gunderson had no argument to make. The serious-looking, fully armed Transtec guards, standing by to enforce company policy, confirmed the notion that his request for a fourth person would not be honored.

Unsmiling, but with less anger in his eyes, Gunderson responded, "I guess that will have to do."

"Great," Ted said. "Let's get your guys and head upstairs. D.A.D.'s waiting."

Gene watched the private demonstration for Exxon/Mobile with only partial concentration. He now had confidence in his actors, and his mind kept wandering to the missing model. Where was it? Was McCutchen making any progress in locating the loot stolen from the electronics store? What could he do to help with the investigation? Where was Marco? Would King help find the thief and the stolen property? King had many contacts in the valley not associated with the law. His strip malls and many tenants, building projects, and political connections brought him into contact with a diverse assortment of individuals. Gene was sure that King was making the rounds looking for leads. After all, it was his buildings that the thief had targeted. True, Marco was the prime suspect, and he was in the world someplace, but there had to be others in the loop. Marco had to fence the stolen goods, and Josh already knew that Marco used the storage facility to house the stolen goods until they could be sold. Somebody must know something. Maybe one of King's contacts could help.

Billy ran the demonstration for Exxon/Mobile with increasing confidence in his ability to maneuver D.A.D. at will. He could make the little silver ball dance. While he let the oil company representatives play with the machine, part of his mind was occupied with the question of how he could exploit his knowledge for a few extra million dollars. What would Exxon pay to learn that they were being scammed? How could he convince them it was a scam? Gene had told his team that they would deliver the model and a complete set of drawings to the purchasing cartel. Where was the fraud?

The model worked. He was positive that the model incorporated the secrets of free energy, as Gene advertised. What Gene had not shared with his team was how the scam worked. Unless he could figure that out, it might be impossible to convince anyone that they were going to be robbed. Then there was the other issue. If he could persuade Exxon or somebody that they were about to be taken to the cleaners, what would that do to Gene and his fellow actors? The aggrieved party would certainly back out of the deal and pull the rest of the participants along with them. There would be no big payday for Gene, and his fellow actors would not get their million dollars. How did he feel about that? Well, it hurt a little, but the thought of several million dollars in his pocket salved the conscience. Hell, he didn't owe them anything. Okay, Gene had been generous, but then he played the long con and had no choice if he wanted to succeed. He hadn't planned on having a thief as one of his actors.

CHAPTER FORTY-NINE

While the scene inside of Transtec was orderly and went according to the script, the outside scene was a different matter. Journalists and reporters alike characterized the atmosphere as electric. Chaos, confusion, excitement, and fear permeated the streets and grounds around the building. There were television vans, reporters from every kind of mass media, journalists from around the world, and curiosity seekers jamming every square inch for several blocks around the free energy world headquarters. The San Jose police were over-matched in trying to control the crowd, but the Transtec guards hired by Gene maintained a strict no-trespass rule within twenty feet of the building. The fully equipped guards had both hands on semi-automatic rifles crossed in front of their bodies. They patrolled the open space between the crowd out front and the building proper. Anybody attempting to enter the open space was ushered back, and if they offered any resistance, the guards were quick to exert whatever force was required to assure compliance with their requests. After a few bloody faces and a couple of broken arms, the crowd learned not to test the guards. They were on private property; the people were told that trespassing would not be tolerated, and the police could not intervene since it was on private property. Besides, they had their hands full with the crowds filling the surrounding streets and grounds. This chaotic activity was very welcome to a few select individuals who used the cover to study every move made by the guards and police. It was good to know the opposition.

Josh watched the chaotic scene outside of Transtec on several monitors, each one showing the street and grounds around the building from a different perspective. On another large monitor, he was watching the Exxon/Mobile demonstration. Like GM earlier and subsequent visitors, Exxon tried to get Bill to open the window so they could fly D.A.D. outside of the building. Unable to convince the Tanstec executive to open the window, the Exxon evaluator flying D.A.D. aimed the silver ball flying at full speed towards the window to break through the glass. Bill and Ted thought that somewhere in the chaos outside, a group of men waited to snag the machine once it cleared the building. What those inside discovered was a fact Bill had discussed the day before. The anti-gravity machine could not collide with another solid object. D.A.D. was sent speeding towards the window by the Exxon operator, but at the very last second, it stopped barely a few centimeters from hitting the glass. After attempting to steal the free energy machine, Bill had Ted and the guards escort the three Exxon/Mobile evaluators outside.

Nothing that was happening outside or inside was a surprise to Josh. The circus outside of Transtec might have been a little more exaggerated than he had expected, but things were happening according to his script. He was pleased with the way his actors were performing. Now, if only he could recover his missing machine. Time was running out.

***

President Carleton was conducting a meeting with those cabinet members working on the free energy project. Besides those in attendance for his previous briefings, the President had invited Susan Whitebridge, his attorney general, to attend.

"Well, Susan, what have you decided. Can we grab this blasted machine under the guise of national security?"

"Mr. President, according to existing statutes, HR 717 and HR 893, passed by the house in 1968 and ratified by the Senate, to declare an object or an event a threat to national security, there must be a clear and present danger. It is difficult to see how a free energy machine could be classified a threat."

"Goddamnit, Susan, we need to get control of this technology. Isn't there some legal way we can force Transtec to hand over their machine and papers?"

"As you well know, Mr. President, the law is often what we declare it to be. Should we decide it is in the best interests of the American people for the U.S. government to take control of free energy, who is there to argue?"

Marcus Bachelor, Secretary of the DOD, could not help but comment, "It's kind of like that old joke, we just do what we want, and if there is any push back from the media or our corporate allies, we ask for forgiveness."

With angry eyes and a stern look on his face, President Carleton said, "All I want to know is if we confiscate this machine, are we going to be risking any kind of impeachable offense?"

"No, Mr. President," Attorney General Whitebridge said, "You could get a lot of criticism from a variety of sources, but there is nothing impeachable for an act performed in the best interest of the American people."

"What about it Admiral?" the President asked of his JCS Chairman. "Are we ready to storm the building and grab the machine?"

"Right now, Mr. President, the scene out in San Jose is very messy. There are hundreds of media types from all over the world. I'm talking television, newspapers, magazines, radio, and freelancers, all looking for a story while monitoring the activity taking place at Transtec. Every company taking part in a private showing is surrounded by the media as soon as they leave the building. They all report the same thing. This free energy machine is real. It works as advertised. Our problem is the hundreds of witnesses surrounding the building if we should try to enter forcibly. The Transtec guards are very proficient, well-trained, and heavily armed. There is no way we can force our way inside without a full-scale assault involving dozens of well-trained military personnel. And even then, there would be many casualties, all documented by the press. We should wait for a better opportunity."

"What are you suggesting, Admiral?" the President asked.

"At night, the media personnel leave the area. There are only a few stragglers in the street, probably other operatives, looking for the same opening that we want. If we make a nighttime raid, there will still be casualties, but the media will not be there to record the event."

"How many casualties are we talking about, Admiral?" asked Secretary Bachelor.

"Right now, we are estimating about twenty-six dead and another couple of dozen injuries. We can expect to lose at least ten soldiers while killing all sixteen guards. These numbers do not include the Transtec civilians, who are also slated for removal. Their elimination should not be a problem. However, we do not know where they go after leaving work. We thought they lived in a private house in San Jose, but we determined plants occupied the house in question. We need to follow the three Transtec people to their final location before acting. It is also possible that guards surround them. This is still to be determined."

"Well hell," the President grunted. "With all the international interest in this free energy crap, anything we do could be casus belli. Admiral, we need to find some way to grab that machine and make it look like another party is responsible. Can you do that?"

"I will have one or two options available for your review within twelve hours, Mr. President," the Admiral responded.

With a grim smile on his face, President Carleton called the meeting to an end. "We'll meet in the morning to go over your plans, Admiral," he said on the way out of the door.

Those left sitting around the table after the President left the room looked at each other with a foreboding feeling. The thought of killing innocent citizens was not something pleasant to contemplate. With great consternation, they finally pushed back their chairs and left the room with a heavy countenance.

CHAPTER FIFTY

The first long day of private demonstrations was finished, but Josh's phone link to Transtec kept ringing every few minutes. Relaxing in his favorite brown recliner, Josh was sipping on a Jack Daniels over crushed ice, trying to plan his next moves, but the telephone kept interrupting his thoughts. It was Ted who kept calling. Every participant but one in the private demonstrations was willing to pay a billion dollars for their ten percent cut of free energy. The OPEC cartel, the last demonstration of the day, had not yet joined in the chorus. Josh was surprised so many were willing to commit immediately after their private demonstration. He was not surprised that OPEC had not already joined the others in offering to buy into the project. Josh was unaware of the oil minister's meeting in Venezuela; however, he knew that getting consensus from all the members would take a little time. OPEC was one of the main targets for his big scam, and he was determined to make sure they would take part. He would wait for them to signal an interest before closing the trap.

Satisfied that his actors were safe for the evening and the building secured, Josh tried contacting King. He tried three different numbers before catching King in his car.

"This is King." After another long, fruitless day trying to find Marco and Josh's stolen silver ball, King was tired, hungry, and a little short on temperament.

"King, this is Josh. I'm sure you're probably as tired as I am, but I was hoping you might have a little good news."

"Sorry, old friend. Nothing new."

The short report presented in King's flat, unemotional voice further deepened Josh's growing depression. Without his backup ball, there was no way he could complete the scam. There was no way out of completing the sale of his working model. He could still sell D.A.D. and collect ten billion dollars, but several years would be lost; time Josh did not have to lose.

"Damn," he groaned. "I was hoping for good news."

King, hearing the depression in his friend's voice, had to find some way to help, despite his own fatigue.

"Hey, Josh, why don't we invite Larry to meet us at Joe's for dinner. Haven't had their special for a couple of years, and I know Larry likes their lasagna."

Josh was not stupid and recognized his friend's attempt to help. Still, he was hungry, and maybe Larry could provide some encouragement.

"Sounds good King. I'll head over there now. Are you going to invite Larry, or do you want me to call?"

"Why don't you call, Josh. I'm driving. Easier for you."

"Sure, no problem. I'll still meet you at Joe's, even if Larry is tied up or something."

"Okay, see you there." King's termination was as abrupt as his greeting. Seldom a hello or goodbye.

Josh was very familiar with his friend's terse phone conversation habits and never gave it a thought. Instead, he simply dialed the number for Larry's portable phone. Just finishing another miserable day with no positive developments in any of his cases, the detective was more than happy to have Josh or King buy his dinner. Hell, practically all his time was spent working their cases. The tail he had following Hicks was about to deliver some exciting news.

CHAPTER FIFTY-ONE

What used to be the Garden City lay sprawled between the San Francisco Bay to the north and Coyote Creek to the south, part of the greater Almaden Valley. The western boundary included much of the Santa Cruz Mountains where King lived, leaving only the eastern border. The eastern foothills forming this border are practically the unwanted stepchild of greater San Jose. Dry with little water, this part of the city was late in developing. Hidden behind the low-lying eastern foothills were some of the city's more exciting and dangerous sites. Home to motorcycle gangs, drug dealers, and other criminal elements, they were primarily unnoticed by the general San Jose population. It helped prove the old adage, *out of sight, out of mind.* Hidden away up there in hidden valleys are large private estates surrounded by high, thick walls.

High on these East San Jose hills overlooking the city is a large red two-story brick house. The house was built by Leonard Dippo nearly a hundred years ago. The Dippo's owned three of the four large packing companies shipping garden produce all over America. Their old orchards, farms, and gardens are history; paved over by roads, covered by apartment houses, home to condominiums and housing tracts, and large commercial projects, including high technology campuses.

The Dippo house, surrounded by two acres of lawn and privacy hedges over eight feet high, is unknown today. The present owner, a fat Armenian named Amaras, was the fence most thieves, including Marco and Hicks, used to dispose of their ill-gotten wares. Amaras was a second-generation Armenian from a long line of smugglers. His parents immigrated to the land of the free when a truckload of illegal arms being transported from Turkey to Iraq was captured. Knowing their crew would turn them in with the threat of being tortured, they fled their country for the safety of America.

Amaras had wispy gray hair worn in a bad comb-over. With a bulbous nose blossoming under strabismus eyes, he was hard to look at without wincing, but free coke and alcohol made his swinger's pad a popular gathering place for those seeking amour-propre through sex. His around-the-clock swinger parties served as the ideal environment to offload the hot items provided by an army of thieves. The perpetual swinger's party is always attracting couples interested in trying out the swinging scene for themselves. The free coke helps get them addicted, adding to a market serviced by Mario and his buddies.

Amaras opened the house and grounds for his merry band of thieves under the pretext that conviviality leads to a more harmonious relationship. The truth is, Amaras wanted to monitor his thieves, but more importantly, he did not want them going elsewhere with their stolen goods. By opening his house and liquor cabinet, he hoped to keep them all in the fold. All the free sex they could handle didn't hurt either.

In one corner of the large lot, under cover of giant redwoods, was a large sixteen-person hot tub. The large tub was the primary meet and grope location for the swingers. Amaras's free drugs and liquor seemed to attract swingers like flies to a fresh cow pie.

Hicks was not a swinger in the true sense since he had no wife or steady girlfriend, but that did not keep him from enjoying the scenery and occasional sex partner. He was soaking in the sight of a terrific blonde woman who looked a lot like a naked Anita Ekberg when Amaras touched him on the shoulder, inviting him inside for a conference.

"Let us go have a little private chat," he mumbled quietly.

Hicks tried hard not to let his host's misdirected eyes cause him discomfort. While he owed Amaras for taking any stolen goods which he paid for in immediate cash, it was still hard for Hicks to be comfortable in the fat man's presence.

"Sure," he said reluctantly, taking his eyes off the statuesque blonde as he rose dripping from the tub. "Let me grab a towel."

After getting inside, Amaras found a quiet corner free from a pair of lovers before speaking again.

"Are you sure you know nothing about that silver ball you gave me yesterday?"

"No, honestly," Hicks responded. "I couldn't find any way to open up the ball. I don't know what it does. I told you, my friend stole it from an empty electronics shop."

"Well, I can't pay you for something that doesn't seem to have any value. You might as well throw it in the trash. I don't want it here anymore."

"I thought maybe you could figure out what it was for," Hicks whined. "I was hoping for at least a hundred bucks."

"You must be out of your mind, Hicks. Why would I pay you a hundred dollars for something that does nothing, and we don't even know what it is? For all we know, it is just some pretty bauble somebody made for their kids. That your friend found it in that electronics store that was practically empty tells us a lot. If it had any value, do you think they would have left it in the building when they moved all the rest of their valuable stuff to their new location?"

"Yeah, I see your point," Hicks conceded. "Okay, I'll dump it in the trash."

Amaras retrieved the handsome box from a nearby cabinet, grunting from the effort as he handed the heavy burden over to Hicks. "Go put this in your car," he said. "I don't want it in the house anymore."

It was a point of pride with Amaras that he had never been associated with any of the stolen property that passed through his hands. When he bought something from one of his thieves, he already knew exactly where he could dispose of it and at what price. He rarely held onto any of the stolen merchandise for more than a few hours. Living in the shadows, he was constantly wary of the police showing up at his door, looking for stolen goods. There was always the chance that one of his thieves got sloppy and led the police right to his door.

Hicks took the box outside and put it back into the trunk of the Ferrari he had got in the trade with Marco, still unaware of the control mechanism hidden in one corner of the box behind the foam lining.

Unfortunately for Amaras, hosting a perpetual sex party replete with drugs and alcohol left little time for television. Besides, his eye condition gave him a headache if he watched television for more than a few minutes. Hicks never watched television, so neither man was aware of the drama unfolding on the streets of downtown San Jose. If only they could know that this seemingly worthless silver ball was worth a fortune.

CHAPTER FIFTY-TWO

Original Joe's, a San Francisco Italian restaurant, became famous for a scrambled egg dish with spinach, garlic, onions, mushrooms, and ground beef. According to the story, the restaurant was a favorite late dinner spot for theater patrons after leaving the last show. On one bustling night, a group of actors coming late after removing their makeup and visiting backstage with fans were told that the restaurant was out of their favorite dishes. Hungry, the desperate actors begged Joe to fix them something. Anything. Reluctantly, management agreed and just threw everything left in the kitchen into a scrambled egg dish. It was an instant hit and has been a staple at all the Joe's in the Bay Area ever since.

Sitting in a back booth at the San Jose version of Joe's, Josh enjoyed his comfort food. That is what he thought about the famous dish. Tired, upset, and worried, Joe's special seemed just the thing to help lift his spirits. King, who had initially suggested the restaurant and Joe's special, feasted on veal parmesan while Larry was busy devouring a plate of lasagna. It did not hurt that King had ordered two bottles of 1968 BV Cabernet, one of the classics. The 1968 vintage rivaled anything produced by the famous Rothchild vintages that sold for over four hundred dollars a bottle.

"Damn nice of you to buy me dinner, King," Larry said between bites. "Thanks."

Reluctant to bring up the subject of his missing silver ball, Josh finally had to ask the detective about progress on finding his lost property.

"Larry, do you have any news about the property stolen from Valley Electronics?"

"I'm sorry, Josh," McCutchen said between bites. "Nothing new." Clearing his mouth, the detective took a long drink of wine before continuing. "What is it about that property of yours that has your shorts all tied up in a knot? We are looking hard for any clue what Marco did with the stuff he stole, but unless something breaks, all we have is Hicks, and so far, he has been of little help."

Gulping for air, Josh was at a loss for words. What could he say to the detective without admitting to the big fraud he was about to commit? There was no way the detective could stand by while he stole ten billion dollars from the wealthiest oil companies in the world.

"My dad was an inventor, Larry. Most of his inventions were impractical, but he had several that helped change the world. For instance, he invented swim flippers. He sent his drawings and claims to the Patent Office in Washington, D.C. The Patent Office gave the drawings to the Navy, who classified them Top Secret. This happened at the beginning of World War II, and Navy swimmers were the first to use flippers on their feet. After the war, the Navy declassified the drawings, giving anybody interested the opportunity to exploit the idea."

King always suspected that his friend had some interesting stories about his background that had never been shared. The news about his father's inventions did not come as a surprise.

"Didn't your dad get anything from the Patent Office in compensation or rights?" McCutchen asked. "And what has this to do with your missing property?"

"No," Josh said. "All the Patent Office did was send my dad a letter telling him that the government had classified his idea for swim flippers."

"Damn," King said. "No compensation. That's tough."

"Yeah," Josh responded. "But to answer Larry's actual question, I have to tell another story. Dad also invented the posthole digger. You know, that auger you see the telephone company using to dig holes for a new pole. Anyway, my dad was disappointed with the Patent Office, so he sent his post hole digger drawings and ideas to John Deere. He was a big fan of their tractors and thought the post hole digger would be a great complement to the tractors and could be operated from the power takeoff unit at the rear of the tractor. John Deere wrote back telling my dad that his idea was impractical and they had no interest. The next year, John Deere came out with the world's first post-hole digger. Surprisingly, it looked exactly like my dad's drawings."

"Alright," an exasperated McCutchen said between bites of his lasagna, "what does this have to do with your missing property?"

"Hang on, Larry," Josh said patiently, "I am getting there."

"While I was still a small boy, my dad created something really great. Not trusting the Patent Office and not sure who he could turn to for help since John Deere screwed him over the posthole digger, Dad put his invention in a box he gave to me. His instructions were to use it when the time was right. The time is now, and that is in the box stolen from Valley Electronics."

"Oh God, Josh. Sorry, I've been such an ass," the detective said. His countenance reflected a man troubled by the story he had just heard and the shared pain of such a significant loss. Josh was not a close friend, but they were on friendly terms, and Larry had great respect for the inventor and his contributions to society at large.

King sat stoically in his seat, almost afraid to breathe. He was confident he knew what was in the missing box. Having watched the television production showing D.A.D. to the world and having Josh's description of his lost property, King was sure Josh was missing another free energy machine. Why the second machine was so important, King could only guess. He assumed Josh was afraid of his invention in the wrong hands; someone else could profit from his hard work, leaving him out in the cold. Whatever the truth, he would not betray his friend by letting on what he suspected. But if it was a free energy machine, King could only guess as to its potential value.

"We have one thin lead we can follow up on," McCutchen said, hoping to leave Josh with something positive. "It isn't much," he added, not wanting to build up too much hope. "For several months, we have been watching a man over in the hills of East San Jose, who we suspect is a fence for a lot of the thieves in the area. He has a big house on a large secluded lot where a perpetual swinger's party is in progress. We believe he is the fence Marco used or at least one of his fences. At any rate, we've been holding off on any kind of raid because it doesn't appear that he keeps any of the stolen merchandise at his home. We still do not know what he does with the stolen goods he buys. We keep trying to catch him with one of his thieves making a sale, but we have come up empty so far. Maybe it's time to pay a visit and rattle his cage."

"Man, I sure hope it pans out, Larry," Josh said, desperation twisting his face into a grimace where he meant to smile. "I'm running out of time."

"We'll keep on it, Josh, until we find your missing ball," King said. Chances are Marco didn't have a clue about what he stole. It might be tough to fence. He probably ditched it someplace. We just have to track his movements to see where he might have left it."

Josh recognized that both of his friends were trying to help, and his downer attitude needed to change. "Thanks, guys; I know you're doing all you can. Just please, let me know the second you know anything." This time he managed a genuine smile, although it was weak and barely reached his eyes.

CHAPTER FIFTY-THREE

August evenings in San Jose can be cool but pleasant, and the evening of the 13th was no exception.

Late evenings warrant a sweater or light jacket, allowing the five men in dark jackets strolling down the sidewalk along Short Creek Drive to appear as simply ordinary citizens enjoying a late evening stroll. Unless you were very observant, you would not notice their jackets were specially tailored to conceal firearms under both arms. Their mission tonight was to make an accurate assessment of the force that would be required to storm Transtec's building and grab the free energy machine. The Admiral did not want a confrontation at this point, but he wanted more information about Transtec's security.

The team was not looking for action; their primary goal was to evaluate the guards' response to their presence, not start a war. Knowing several other potential bad guys were interested in the same thing, they came prepared just in case one or more of these groups caused them a problem.

Creeping down the service driveway behind the Transtec building were three more dark-clad individuals carrying duffel bags full of Semtex high explosives besides the assault rifles held in their opposite hands. They used the shadows cast by old eucalyptus trees the developers left standing when designing the business park. Slinking from one deep shadow to the next, these three dark figures were slowly converging on the back of the building. Their goal was also to explore Transtec's security. Of course, if the opportunity presented itself, they wouldn't mind snatching the damn thing and running. They planned to stash the explosives in a convenient place to bring down the building if that was the plan.

Slinking down Short Creek Drive from the direction opposite the five SEALs were four more sinister-looking men carrying rifles in dark clothing. The street was quiet, and they thought to sneak in without being noticed. The rifles they carried were the latest style G36 from Heckler and Koch. These rifles are gas operated with the standard 30-round detachable box magazine. With folding stocks and the convenient carrying handle, the rifles could be mistaken for simple gardening tools, especially in the dark with sparsely spaced streetlights. Although, why anyone would carry garden tools in a commercial district would be equally suspicious at this time of night. Short Creek Drive curves around from the south towards the east, making the two sneaking groups of men temporarily unaware of each other, although that was about to change.

Believing that penetration of the building was possible, even likely, Josh had stationed eight of his guards outside shortly after dark, one at each corner and another guard along each wall. The first sign of trouble was when the two groups of men walking down Short Creek Drive noticed each other. The men with the classic H&K rifles were at a disadvantage as they needed to ready their guns for action. The five men they faced simply reached inside their jackets, pulling out matching Heckler and Koch MK 23 Model O pistols. The semi-automatic pistols chambered for 45 ACP were equipped with laser aiming modules featuring an ambidextrous safety and magazine release. People familiar with firearms knew better than to start a war against this firepower.

Sergeant Wolf's SEAL team was under no illusions about the four men they faced or their intentions. With red laser dots centered between their eyes, Skipper Walls and his three helpers stood by helplessly as the SEALs relieved them of their rifles and pistols. The SEALs quickly incapacitated the four Texaco operatives, leaving them lying on the sidewalk bound up in zip ties. If a police cruiser happened to drive by at this late hour, it could be a problem, but Sergeant Wolf felt that speed was more important than taking the time to hide the four men now lying in restraints. Unbeknownst to both groups were the Transtec guards standing in the shadows observing the entire confrontation.

The SEAL team re-holstered their weapons as they turned, facing the Transtec building. The building was dark, with only a lobby light shining through the tall cut glass windows on either side of the wide double doors. While no one was visible, it was only prudent to assume there would be a guard in the lobby. Sergeant Wolf signaled for his men to spread out as they walked towards the building. When they were fifty feet from the entrance to the doors spread out across the entire front of the building, blazing lights came on, rendering the SEALs temporarily blind. Three Transtec guards stepped from the shadows, screaming at the five interlopers to throw down their guns and raise their hands. Each guard was carrying a fully automatic Heckler and Koch UMPs, a weapon that was also a SEAL favorite.

The three Transtec guards had their rifles pointed at the SEALs and fingers on the triggers. Sergeant Wolf and his team were temporarily blinded by the lights and, recognizing that any move would be disastrous, immediately threw up his hands, calling a halt to his troops. His men likewise thrust their hands high in the air.

Creeping around the side, Mateo Ramirez, OPEC's team leader, and his two side-kicks, Juan Martinez and Andres Orta had neared the front of Transtec's building without becoming aware of the guards hiding at each corner or the one standing behind a recently planted six-foot Blue Point Juniper. As Mateo and friends neared the back of Transtec, they saw the front corner guard suddenly step out with his automatic weapon pointed at some other men fifty feet away. They raised their guns, preparing to fire, when the other two guards on that side of the building stepped from the shadows shouting, **"Throw down your weapons and raise your hands-NOW."**

Hearing the yells, six other guards came sprinting from their hiding places, helping to surround both groups of men. It was not a good night for those seeking to steal into Transtec or destroy the building. Captain Wilson had been one of the outside guards this evening. After relieving the would-be thieves of their weapons and explosives, he released them and the four Texaco operatives lying in the street with a warning to steer clear of Transtec. He had considered calling in the local police, and the men would undoubtedly spend time in jail under several charges. Still, ultimately, their employers would just find another team to replace the ones in jail. It was only by the grace of God that the evening had not turned into a bloodbath on both sides, but perhaps next time, and Wilson was pretty sure there would be the next time. The three groups of humbled men slunk away in the same directions from which they arrived.

CHAPTER FIFTY-FOUR

President Carleton's early morning six A.M. status meeting was not going well. Admiral Whittaker had just informed those assembled of the SEAL team's ignominious failure. Being sent packing with their spirits dragging, not to mention being caught doing the President's work, was almost more than the most powerful man in the world could handle. At least with any amount of grace.

"Goddamnit Admiral," the President stormed, "what kind of amateur hour are you running out there? I know California is home to a bunch of left-wing nuts, but good God man, do your boys have to act like the locals?"

Calling them *your boys* instead of *our boys* left no doubt in anyone's mind that the President would let no one in his administration off the hook for failure.

Red in the face and squirming from the President's rebuke, Whittaker was slow to respond. "Sorry, Mr. President. Our boys were not expecting the competition to be so aggressive and got distracted. It won't happen again."

The President continued the meeting in a stern, take no prisoner attitude, not the least bit mollified. "What the hell do you propose next? We cannot let the damn Russians or Chinese get their hands on that technology. Not to mention those fucking OPEC bastards." His usual Oxford English decorum turned into backroom bar gutter talk when the President was upset, reminiscent of his Louisiana swamp background.

"Hell, Mr. President," DOD secretary Marcus Bachelor chimed in, "our SEALs are the best-trained people on earth. Let's give them another chance to continue with the mission. There are still a few days left before the sale is completed."

Susan Whitebridge, the Attorney General, spoke up for the first time. "If I might suggest, Mr. President, perhaps it might be safer and less messy to wait until the sale is completed. With any luck, we could be one of the ten buyers, and if not, we will at least know the final ten winners. Wouldn't it be easier to grab the machine from the winners after the transfer? After all, it's going to take those ten winners time to get organized and replace Transtec's security measures."

"Susan makes sense," Bachelor hastily jumped in, saving the still flustered JCS Chairman the need to respond. "We can have the SEALs monitor the situation looking for an opportunity to move in if an opportunity presents itself, but snatching D.A.D. right after the transfer might be a lot easier and possibly with significantly fewer casualties. We can always pick up the Transtec people later."

Running fingers through his dyed dark-brown hair, President Carleton sat still for a moment with a scowl plastered on his face before asking, "What's your thoughts on this suggestion, Whit?" the President asked using his nickname for the Chairman.

"Well," the Chairman started his reply, still trying to process the latest developments, "Transtec seems to be guarded by well-trained operatives. Storming the building when we're not sure the device is stored there overnight is a risky proposition. Even in the best scenario, I imagine grabbing the device inside Transtec's building would be very costly in terms of human life, not to mention the negative publicity. I think Susan's idea has a lot of merit. I suggest we follow Marcus's suggestion to monitor the situation and make contingency plans to snatch the machine after the transfer."

Still displeased, the President abruptly stood up, signifying an end to the meeting. "Okay Admiral, keep me informed."

***

Down in Texas, the Colonel was angrier than a bull being chased by horseflies. "Lillian, how in the hell did a bunch of fucking rent-a-cops drive our boys off the scene?"

That he said Lillian instead of Lilly was a sure sign the boss was out for bear. Knowing there was no answer to the Colonel's question that would be satisfactory, the lovely assistant just kept quiet, letting the big boy vent. When he said Lillian, there was no use talking until he was through with his tirade.

"I mean Jesus Horatio Christ, aren't we paying those miserable bastards enough money to get the job done right? God almighty, I feel like hiring somebody to kill the whole damn bunch and start over."

Sweating from overexertion, Ray wiped the sweat from his brow using the sleeve of his five-hundred-dollar Hawes and Curtis silk shirt. "Goddamnit, Lilly, what do we do now?"

Using her pet name was a sign the storm was nearly over, and it was safe to speak again.

"I don't think we can fault Skipper too much for what happened in San Jose, Ray. I walked him through the entire situation, and it appears to have been just bad luck that two other parties had the same idea at the same time. I know it sucks, but you know as well as I do that sometimes shit just happens."

Lillian rarely used words like shit, but a little profanity always seemed to help calm him down when the Colonel was riding a mad-on.

"So," the Colonel continued, "the Transtec guards just let our guys walk with no questions?"

"That's what Skipper reported," she responded, relieved that the Colonel was calming down. "Skipper believes that since they were dealing with three different groups of men, the Transtec guards just didn't want to be bothered with the hassle of getting the cops involved. It kind of makes sense. Knowing that interested parties were actively seeking to steal the device for themselves, Transtec probably didn't think it was worthwhile to take these men off the street. Other men would just replace them."

"You're probably right, as usual Lilly. Any suggestions for how we proceed?"

"We have to be one of the ten buyers chosen by Transtec. Then we just deal with the other nine buyers. There should be a lot of opportunities after the sale is completed when we can walk away with the whole thing. Other buyers may have the same idea, so we just have to be smarter. I think Skipper wants a chance to redeem himself, so I say let's just have him monitor the situation and start making plans for a snatch down the road someplace."

"I think we have a good chance of being one of the successful buyers," Ray said in a much calmer voice. "That would make our chance to get ahold of the machine a little easier, but just in case, we need to be prepared if we don't get selected. Have Skipper make plans for both situations, and by God, he better not fail again."

Lilly was relieved to see the Colonel settle back into his seat in a more relaxed manner. "You bet, Ray. I'm sure Skipper wants a chance to prove himself again. I'll get ahold of him right away."

***

Mohammad bin Salman, the man with an evil eye and current head of OPEC, was happy to see that fat bastard Barrera sweating. It was an open secret that Barrera was trying to oust him from the leadership, and that big fiasco in San Jose, California, had weakened his position considerably. Feeling full of himself, Barrera had only recently been swaggering around the big conference table brimming with confidence, assuring all the various oil ministers how great their collective power would be once they secured the free energy device. The San Jose setback weakened his standing in the cartel.

With a sly grin twisting his scarred face, Salman asked his host, "What now, Barrera? What's your next glorious plan to please Allah?"

Even though his guts were churning with hatred for the miserable Egyptian, Barrera managed a weak smile. "These things happen sometimes. Allah will see the righteousness of our cause and bless our good fortune soon. It is only just that we possess the free energy machine as today we provide most of the world's energy."

"That is all so much foolish talk, hoping Allah will bless your miserable plans," sneered Salman. "Just what do you propose we do now, Mr. Minister?" he asked disdainfully.

Feeling the grip on his desire for leadership of OPEC and ultimately the world slipping, Barrera knew he had to act quickly to salvage the situation."What happened in San Jose was simply unfortunate timing. Perhaps Allah was simply testing us to see if we were committed to world dominance. I can assure you that this free energy machine will be ours..., or nobodies. We now have twenty highly trained saboteurs on-site. Mateo, whom you all know, has assured me he has the situation in hand. When the final ten buyers have been selected, Mateo will be on hand to verify that the machine is transferred to the buyers. We intend to be one of those buyers. Whatever the situation, it will be up to Mateo and his team to either terminate the entire group or steal the device. We would like to have the machine, but it is better for it to be destroyed rather than to remain in the hands of infidels."

Normally Barrera would not stoop to using religious words or symbology, but, being desperate and knowing how the other oil ministers paid lip service if not complete fidelity to Islam, he will forego his own preferences. Straining to remain cordial, Barrera forced a smile while concluding, "As you know, we were given our private briefing yesterday, and I was assured by our team leader that if we make an offer to be one of the buyers, it will be very well received. In fact, he was almost assured that we would be one of the successful buyers. After today, we will know our position and can make plans accordingly. I'm certain that Allah will bless our endeavor."

With a smirk on his face, Salman concluded the meeting.

CHAPTER FIFTY-FIVE

Hicks reluctantly left the swinger's party in a foul mood. Not only could he not fence that ball thingy, but it was stolen, and now it was in his car. Unfortunately, Hicks was in Marco's car, which the cops were looking for all the time. He couldn't decide what speed to drive coming off the San Jose east foothills. If he went too fast and got pulled over, the cops were sure to search his car again, and if they discovered the ball, his days of freedom were over for the time being. If he drove slowly, he would spend more time on the streets and there was a better chance of running into a patrol car. He couldn't wait to dump the jinxed box, but where? He could probably lift it into a dumpster, although the damn thing was heavy, and it would be difficult. If someone saw him dumping the box, they would check it out, and his new ride was guaranteed to garner attention by pointing the finger directly at him.

Although it was chilly and the windows were down, he was sweating like a high school boy about to ask a girl out for his first date to the junior prom. Ultimately, he decided to take the box and ball back to Marco's storage unit. The cops had already checked it out and unfortunately, he had taken the ball to see about fencing it to Amaras. If he had left the damn thing there, the cops would have it by now, and its theft would be blamed on Marco. If the cops came back for another check, they would know that he had possession of the ball and its theft could be blamed on him. At least, by putting it in the storage unit, it wouldn't be in his car, and he could worry about getting rid of the damn problem tomorrow.

Driving up to the storage unit, he remembered the lock. The cops had busted the new lock he installed just yesterday, and he didn't have a spare. It was late at night or rather early in the morning, and the chances of somebody checking out storage units before sunrise tomorrow were slim to none. He would dump the box for now and decide what to do tomorrow. He began wondering if he had made a devil's deal, his soul, for Marco's car.

***

Hicks wasn't the only one sweating. Although it was early in the A.M., all three actors were wide awake. Lisa was wondering if the million dollars were worth the grief. She was getting a sense of the real danger, and they still had several days to go before the show closed for good. Gene, Abe, whatever the hell was his real name, was showing obvious stress. She had no way of knowing that Josh's strain was almost entirely because of his missing D.A.D. While he was always in perfect makeup, this could not hide the fatigue and worry in his eyes, which every trained actor knows to look for during a production. Whether her co-performers were aware of Gene's condition, she didn't know. She was reluctant to discuss this, as she didn't need her fellow actor's fears added to her own.

Joseph (also known as Ted) was sweating in his room for an entirely different reason. He couldn't keep the image of his sexy co-star out of his mind. As he experienced her, Janet was simply the most desirable creature he had ever worked with, and that was saying a lot. That she was also a very talented actress and extremely intelligent only added to his desires. He remembered Gene's directive about prying into each other's true identity. There had to be a way. Yeah, he got the danger and risk thing, but once this was over, why couldn't he meet Janet in some far-off location where nobody knew them, and they could get to know one another? Where was the risk in that? He kept twisting and squirming in his bed, trying to find some way of making this proposition to Janet without blowing their cover. Ole Gene was keeping a mighty close watch on things, and if he even hinted at these thoughts, he could only imagine the shit storm that would ensue. Still, there had to be some way.

Bill's problem was trying to control his greed. Ten billion dollars and all he would get was one stinking million. Who was taking all the risks out here, anyway? Shouldn't the risk-takers get a more significant share? Of course, he had no intention of getting more money for his co-stars; if they got screwed, it was no sweat off his skin. It was inconvenient to put them into the risk box while trying to figure out his own scam. Gene had his scam exceptionally well organized; still there had to be some way to muscle in, or better yet, sneak in the back door and help himself to a few of those billions. The problem was, he couldn't figure out a way of blowing the scam without losing the whole thing. If he could just figure out the nature of Gene's fraud. That D.A.D. worked, there was no doubt. And the buyers were to get the same machine he was showing, yet he could not come up with any scenario that would enable Gene to pull off a scam. Gene got the money. The buyers got the machine. Where's the fraud? Arrgg. I got to get some sleep. Tomorrow's going to be another hectic day.

Maybe something will come up that will give him some ideas.

CHAPTER FIFTY-SIX

The sunrise of August 14th in Silicon Valley was a beautiful vision if you happened to be up at that time of the morning. The day started with a thin orange line on the horizon turning to a red band, then a brilliant golden sky as the sun crested the eastern mountains. This was the final day for private D.A.D. demonstrations and the guards at Transtec were already prepping for a raucous day of visitors, both outside on the street and in the demonstration room. Everyone in the world is interested in free energy, and some would go to any extreme to gain control of the floating silver ball.

Gene had spent many hours with the guards, preparing them for what he assumed would happen. He expected several attempts by many organizations and governments to steal D.A.D. Gene did not expect anyone to destroy the entire building, killing everyone inside to prevent free energy from becoming a reality. When his guards found the backpacks loaded with Semtex, he realized his assumptions were misguided. His guards and actors were in much more severe danger than he had expected. This realization, along with the fear that his second D.A.D. model may not be found, resulted in another long sleepless night trying to find a solution for his problems.

Flying his magic cane to the backside of Transtec in the early morning hours for a meeting with his guards, Gene ignored the glorious sunrise. Not even mother nature could ease the pain in his soul. If players in this drama were willing to destroy buildings and lives, he worried about his ability to control the situation and keep everyone alive. He had to make sure his guards were aware of the danger and had plans to avoid disaster. D.A.D. could be surreptitiously moved during the night, but this would not solve the human problem. Gene was not prepared to lose one life for his dream.

*****

Washington, DC 9:30 A.M.

The President was huddled with his team of advisors plus several cabinet members in the cabinet room just a few steps from the oval office. This meeting was more relaxed than their previous gatherings as the President merely wanted a quick review of their status. While waiting for the Navy lieutenants to finish serving coffee to his guests, the President told a story about a female constituent when he was the governor of Illinois. At a fundraiser, this woman came up to the then governor requesting an autograph for her daughter. The woman was well endowed in the chest department and wore a low-cut blouse showing a lot of cleavage. She had a pen with a flip-up cover for the tip, and when the woman flipped up the top, it went flying in the air, landing between her breasts. The President said that as the tip went flying up; he tried to grab it out of the air, only to end up snagging the woman's blouse, pulling it down, exposing her breasts. As he told the story, a chuckle emerged while relating how embarrassed he felt.

His captive audience appreciated the President's attempt to lighten the mood, and all gave the obligatory chuckle at the appropriate moment. When the lieutenants finished serving coffee, the President waited until they left the room before beginning the meeting.

"Today we find out who the buyers are, isn't that right?" President Carleton addressed the question to his Secretary of the DOD, Marcos Bachelor.

"It is our understanding that today is the last round of guests invited for demonstrations. After they finish with this group of potential investors, the company has indicated that they will announce the ten parties from whom they will accept the one billion dollars buy-in. We expect that announcement today, but it could be tomorrow."

"Are we all set up to intercept the machine if our partner is not one of the selected buyers?" The President's question was asked with a stern voice. He didn't like what they were planning on doing and used his tone to mask any feelings he might have regarding their proposed actions.

It was Army General Hutchins who answered. "Yes, Mr. President. We have several teams in place. Depending on circumstances and who ends up with the machine, one team is prepared to intercept what we expect will be a convoy and retrieve the machine and any blueprints. We hope to do this without loss of life, but again, circumstances will dictate our actions."

"And the other teams?" the President asked, attempting to keep any emotion from his question.

"Well, yes. Another team will shadow the three Transtec principals, ready to take them out as soon as they leave the building for the final time. The team may wait until the principals have returned to their homes before executing the final takedown to minimize any adverse fallout from the public and the news people. We plan on making them disappear like they took the ten billion dollars and ran."

The General didn't seem to share the President's disdain for this unpleasant task. Perhaps he was too used to giving orders which undoubtedly would lead to the loss of life for many individuals. What are three more when added to what must be hundreds in his past? What if they were civilians and citizens? They shouldn't be messing around with national security.

The President couldn't help the scowl that creased his face. He knew if his office was ever associated with the actions they were considering, his tenure as a leader of the free world would end.

Observing the President's scowl and understanding the reason, General Hutchins continued, eager to put an end to the misery.

"One final team will sweep Transtec headquarters for any miscellaneous paperwork that might have significance. After that, they will visit their house to remove any incriminating or valuable information."

"Keep me informed. I want to know the minute we have secured the device. I don't care what time it is tonight or in the morning."

Although he thought their actions would cause at least three deaths and perhaps many more, the President left no doubt that he favored their plans. Free energy was just too precious to allow in the hands of the public. Why hell, if people had machines to fly anywhere they wanted to go at any time, borders would no longer have any meaning. National security would be a joke. No. It must not be allowed to happen.

***

Venezuela 10:30 A.M.

Although the official OPEC meetings had ended, the oil ministers from each country never left the palatial accommodations provided by Barrera. All were gathered around the large table, eager to hear the latest regarding their plans to steal D.A.D. or destroy it along with everything and everybody associated with the evil device. Once again Carlos was center stage and while everybody was looking to him for answers, Salman could only sit and seethe at the attention given to the man who wanted to be his replacement.

Banging on the table with his beefy fist Carlos called the meeting to order.

"As our dear chairman has already told you," Carlos couldn't help but give the seething Salman a smirking smile, "our men in San Jose were found placing the explosives that would have destroyed the building and all evidence of the free energy device. Yesterday was our day to examine the free energy device, and our agents reported the device is real and works as we witnessed on television. We simply cannot allow this machine into the world. It would destroy all of our economies and possibly our nations. Fortunately, over the past two days, we have assembled enough trained agents on-site to eliminate the other buyers and all the Transtec personnel. Transtec guards have prevented our attempts to destroy their building, but as soon as they release the machine to the purchasers and it is being transferred, we will act. There will be a significant explosion and battle the likes of which the evil empire has never witnessed. And the best part is, we can blame it all on the pig Israelis.

***

San Jose, California 9:15 A.M.

Josh was watching his actors preparing for their final day's guests to arrive and their examinations of D.A.D. when his private phone made an annoying noise. His ring tone was The Vienna Waltz, which he usually found pleasing, but at this moment, as his team began their final act, it was a nuisance. Glancing to see who was calling, he noticed it was Detective McCutchen calling. Hoping to get information regarding his missing machine, he answered the call.

"Good morning Larry, do you have some good news for me?" Josh didn't believe in crossing his fingers while wishing for good luck, but his anticipation still made him squirm in his seat.

"No such luck Josh. I was hoping you could meet with King and me for a late breakfast." The detective's tone was severe, and while it sounded like an invitation, it came across as an order.

Josh suddenly had a lump in his throat. Larry's voice was not encouraging. "I'm kind of busy right now, Detective," Josh said with what sounded like a squawk. "Can we make it some other time?"

"It's pretty serious, Josh. We really need to talk." The detective was not taking no for an answer.

"Okay, I get the message." Josh was resigned to meet and to find out about the big mystery. He had to trust that his players would continue their performance without the director's observation. So far, they had been performing flawlessly. His big concern was what would happen afterward. He had to orchestrate the final selection of buyers. Hopefully, this meeting with Larry and King would not take long. "Where do you want to meet?"

"There's a Denny's over on First Street, not too far from your Transtec building. See you there in twenty minutes." The invitation did now allow for any dissent.

"I know the place. See you there." Josh could not imagine why the detective called and insisted on this meeting. Could the police know about the scam? Were they aware of his plans? Larry disconnected the call without saying goodbye. Not a good sign.

CHAPTER FIFTY-SEVEN

When Josh got to Denny's, he saw King's Mercedes already parked and assumed the Crown Victoria was McCutchen's ride next to it. Sure enough, just as he entered the front door, he spotted both men huddled together in a back booth, away from any curious ears.

"Hi guys," Josh mumbled, unsure exactly what this hastily called meeting was all about. It couldn't be good news. If Larry had found his missing D.A.D., he would have said so over the phone.

"Good morning Josh," King said. The detective remained silent with a scowl on his face.

"Okay, Larry. What's the big deal, interrupting my morning with such a demanding invitation?"

Josh had barely asked before a cheerful lady in a Denny's tee-shirt came by to take their orders. In her mid-forties, a plump, smiling lady with black hair in a butch cut stood with pen and pad in hand, waiting for them to order. He assumed that either King or the detective had asked her to wait for their missing party.

"Just coffee for me," King ordered. The other two men ordered the same. The smiling waitress frowned as it looked like the big spenders would not order food, meaning her tip would be negligible.

Eager to get this meeting over with so he could get back to observing the day's demonstrations, Josh probed the detective again. "What's up Larry?"

Without bothering to hide his displeasure, the detective started talking. "I watched the news last night Josh. I know what you're doing in King's new office building. Leaving all the implications of free energy aside, for now, Short Creek Drive almost looks like a war zone."

God. If you only knew, Josh thought to himself, biting his tongue before actually saying the words out loud.

Larry continued with the scowl firmly in place. "The San Jose police are stretched to the max trying to maintain some kind of order while trying to keep traffic moving. Why in the hell did you not give us some warning, and for Christ's sake, why didn't you have your fucking demonstration somewhere outside of a busy city?" The detective was almost frothing at the mouth as he finished speaking.

Josh looked over at King who simply nodded, such as to say, well Josh, this is your mess; it's up to you to clean it up.

Without hesitation or the least bit intimidated, Josh answered. "Look, Larry. I did not know it would get this out of hand. Sure, I expected some interest. After all, free energy is a big deal. I even expected some attempts to steal the technology, but this," he said, waving his hand towards the street outside as though this was where all the commotion was taking place, "is totally beyond anything I expected when I asked King to let me use his building for a few days."

"And that's another thing," McCutchen barked, "that building has not been cleared for occupancy. What in the hell were you thinking?" As he talked, the detective was getting angry and red in the face.

Not in the habit of backing down from a fight, Josh spoke up as soon as Larry stopped talking. "Go to hell detective. I don't need your goddamned barking and snapping like a rabid dog or a jilted lover. King did not know what I planned for his building. We entered into a legal contract to finish out the foyer and some interior offices. That work was completed last week. I needed a respectable building for my demonstrations and King's building is exactly what I needed. The damn building is not occupied, merely used for a demonstration. The City is free to inspect at any time and validate our improvements."

King and McCutchen both sat stunned at Josh's outburst.

Before he continued, the waitress brought their coffees. Sensing the table's mood, she quickly deposited the cups and saucers and left without a word.

"And let me talk to you about free energy." As he spoke, missionary zeal took over his voice and countenance. "This will change the world. Yes, I know the vast majority of the world's economies float on energy. Entire industries are built around the use of energy. Automobiles, planes, electricity, natural gas and so forth. I imagine seven or eight out of every ten jobs in the developed world are energy-related. This still leaves out about a third of the world struggling to live day to day without energy of any kind. Free energy can lift these countries into the modern age given a chance. Yes, millions of jobs and industries will be eliminated, but new jobs will replace them. Companies making wind turbines, solar panels and other types of energy production can easily retool to manufacture free energy devices to run houses, companies, apartment buildings, hotels, etc. Automobiles, trucks, trains, and planes will all need to be reconfigured to use free energy. Ultimately, there will be more jobs, better jobs, servicing the free energy sector than working in the existing energy sector. In addition, free energy does not add pollution to the air, water and earth. Many powerful governments and energy corporations are determined to see that free energy never becomes a reality, including our government. I am raising ten billion dollars so that I can simultaneously introduce thousands of free energy devices around the world sometime soon with no government control or interference from existing businesses."

Josh took a moment to take a sip of his coffee delivered earlier that was growing cold.

"The biggest hurdle is the governments. With a free energy vehicle capable of traveling anywhere in the world, the borders of countries will suddenly have no meaning. There isn't a government on the planet that is not opposed to this development."

"Now hopefully, you can understand why I had to get this demonstration out to the public and why I am holding demonstrations to select ten companies who will each give me one billion dollars to own an interest in my machine. I will not divulge the rest of my plans; just rest assured that I think I know what I'm doing."

Here, Josh managed a slight smile. "Maybe that's a little optimistic since there are some serious people out there on Short Creek Drive more than willing to put a bullet through my head. Fortunately, none of those players have the slightest knowledge of my existence. The two of you are the only people in the world who know who I am. Not even the players posing as Transtec employees know who I am. I guess you could say my life is in your hands."

King and Larry both sat in stunned silence. Neither had expected to hear Josh unload his burden. It was the detective who finally broke the silence.

"I'm guessing that missing ball is another free energy machine?"

"Yes," Josh responded softly with all the fire out of his voice. "Now you understand why it is so important that we find it to keep it out of the wrong hands."

"You know Larry," King spoke up for the first time. "We should find that Hicks fellow and wring the little bastard's neck. He has to know more than he's been telling."

"Look," Josh spoke again. "I'm sorry for the mess I've made. I'll be out of here in three days or less. King's beautiful new building will be vacated along with anything having to do with Transtec. If there is any chance of recovering the other device, it will help me rest a lot easier."

"I'm sorry Josh," McCutchen said. "I did not know what you were dealing with. I'll take King's suggestion and go wring Hicks's neck. We'll find your missing ball. If there is anything I can do to help, let me know."

"There is one thing," Josh said with a little more life. "I'm worried that after I transfer the machine to the selected buyers, there will be a massive attempt by many organizations, including our government, to make a grab or destroy the machine and everybody associated with Transtec. I have my people covered, but I'm concerned about the convoy of vehicles carrying the machine. A police escort out of town would be much appreciated."

Both King and the detective nodded as though understanding the real danger Josh was describing. It was Larry who finally broke the silence. "I'll see what I can do Josh. I don't handle traffic, but I will talk with the traffic department. Can you give us a heads up when you expect to make the exchange?"

"I'll try, Detective," Josh answered with a brief smile. "Now, if you gentlemen will excuse me, I need to get back to Transtec. Today is our final big day."

Josh got up from the booth and started walking out. "I'll let you know what we find after talking with Hicks," the detective said to Josh's disappearing back.

"Well," King said with a grin. "I guess our coffee break is over."

CHAPTER FIFTY-EIGHT

East San Jose Foothills-mid morning

Amaras, in blue cotton pajama bottoms, sat outside of his swinger's pad in a lounge chair drinking a brandy-enhanced coffee enjoying the morning sun on his fat face when two naked couples walked by discussing a free energy machine they had seen on television. Intrigued, Amaras stopped the foursome and asked what they were talking about.

A tall skinny man named Brad recognized their host and stopped to explain the television demonstration they had all watched. The couples were divided on whether the machine was real or a hoax. When Brad described the floating silver ball and how it danced around the room, Amaras became highly interested.

"Can you show that to me on the TV?" Amaras asked Brad.

"I'm sure the television station has archived the demonstration footage. It seems to be the only thing people are talking about. Let's go look at your television setup and see if I can find the TV station's stored footage."

Amaras led the way inside his mansion to the oversized living room where three different couples were lying on cushions engaged in various forms of sex. Ignoring the sweating swingers, Brad went over to the television and found the remote control. In just a few moments, he had KGO's archived footage of the demonstration playing on the screen. The sudden shift in noise from soothing background music to the harsh voice of a TV commentator interrupted the couples intertwined in their drug-enhanced sex.

When Amaras saw the floating ball, he dropped his coffee drink in shock. To think he had a free energy machine in his grasp only a few hours ago almost made him sick. He had to find that idiot Hicks and hope the stupid thief hadn't thrown their fortune away in some remote trash heap. In his mind, it was now his fortune. After all, Hicks had brought it to him. He just needed to find the little bastard and have it brought back. Grabbing the phone from his pajama pocket, he found Hicks's number and punched the keys. With any luck, the loser would answer right away. The call went to voicemail and Amaras left a plea for Hicks to call him back as soon as possible.

***

Los Mochis, Mexico-mid morning

Marco was sitting in a dingy waterfront bar named Estrella De La Manana (morning star), nursing a hangover, when the bartender turned the channel of his television to a local Spanish-speaking television station. An old General Electric fourteen-inch set hung above the bar between racks of half-washed glasses and dust-covered liquor bottles. A scarred wooden bar featuring cigarette burns and spilled beer stains ran down one side of the room with ten tall, rickety three-legged stools resembling tall milking stools shoved haphazardly under the bar's overhang. Fifteen dirty tables with side chairs filled the rest of the room. Two locals wearing faded, wrinkled clothes were sitting at one of the tables nursing tequila hangovers. There wasn't much interest on the television for the half-alive gringo until a flickering image caught his eyes. A television anchor speaking Spanish was describing a free energy machine floating on the picture tube. Marco had difficulty understanding the language, but the image was more than enough to identify the silver ball he had so negligently discarded.

Did he dare call Hicks? No one was supposed to know where he was located, and back in the U.S., he was wanted for murder. Still, that damn ball represented a fortune, and he had the thing in his hands just a couple of days ago. Hell, with that thing back in his hands, he could make a fortune. Show up his old man in the money department. He wondered what in the hell Hicks had done with the damn thing? Could it still be in his storage locker? Did he dare go back to San Jose and check it out?

By now, everybody would know he had split for Mexico. He could probably sneak back into the States with nobody knowing if he wasn't stopped at the border. If he timed his crossing just right, say after a bullfight when all the gringos were heading back home, he could probably skate right through without being stopped. Hopefully, that piece of a shit car he was driving would make it back to the States. Downing the rest of his hair-of-the-dog morning cocktail, he burped loudly as he left the bar, leaving no doubt about what he thought about the slime pit.

***

San Jose, California-almost noon

Josh hurried back to his hidden command center to catch up with his actors and their last day of demonstrations. He was just in time to watch Ted and Bill shepherd Saudi Aramco Oil out of the demonstration room while Bill secured D.A.D. back into its carrying case. After watching to make sure the two guards responsible for the safety of his machine were taking their duties seriously, he switched monitors to see his three actors congregate in their main office.

The monitor in the office was left on continuously, so all Josh had to do was start talking to grab his actor's attention.

"Good morning, gang. Sorry to check in so late. How're the demonstrations coming, Ted?"

"We've had a good morning," Ted responded with a grin. "Our guards are doing a phenomenal job keeping everybody organized and behaving. We had a few troublemakers trying to jump the line, but they got sorted out quickly. Got a question Boss."

"Sure, Ted, what is it?" Josh was having a difficult time concentrating on his players. His mind kept wandering to his missing machine. Hopefully, Larry and King could help him recover it before someone else figured out what it was and what it could be worth. With all the television exposure over the past couple of days, there couldn't be ten people in the developed world unaware of his floating silver ball.

"We just finished our demonstrations for Iran and Saudi Arabia. I was wondering why we're giving separate demonstrations to five of the fifteen members of OPEC?"

"That's a good question, Ted. Our most important OPEC demonstration was yesterday afternoon. I chose to include five of its biggest oil producers in private demonstrations today to sow disharmony among the members and to confuse the other bidders."

"Are we still planning on announcing those companies chosen to take part in buying D.A.D.?" This was from Janet as she was reading over the schedule.

"Right. Well, I'm glad you brought that up, Janet. As the three of you know, today wraps up most of the difficult work. Before discussing the next step, I need to reissue warnings concerning your safety. You have all witnessed the madhouse outside on the lawns and streets. Unfortunately, among those crowds, individuals from many countries and companies are eager to see you all dead and D.A.D. buried and forgotten. Your safety is my main concern, but you must follow directions perfectly from this point forward. Even the slightest deviation could cost you and your fellow actors your lives. Before continuing, have you adhered to our agreement not to divulge your real name and home with your fellow actors? This question is vitally important, and I want to hear each one of you respond to the question. You first Janet."

"Not me Gene. Sure, we've kidded around some getting to know each other, but as far as I know, neither of these outlaws know my real name or where I call home?" Janet looked especially fetching today in another striking blue Yves Saint Laurent dress.

"What about you, Ted?" Gene could sense a slight hesitation before getting an answer.

"Yeah. I've kept the bargain, but I don't see the big deal. I want to stay in contact with my other cast members, but as of now, I'm sure no one but you knows my real name."

"Ted, I cannot get into all the reasons; however, I promise you that during the next two days, you will come to respect this warning. Let me repeat; no one must know who you are. Within just a few short hours, there will be a significant worldwide search for each of you, with a substantial price tag on your head. If you have followed my instructions, I will see that you have disappeared and will be safe. Within a short time, you will be free to resume your former lives or continue living under yet another false identity, albeit very different from anything related to your former or present persona. Okay, Bill, what about you?"

Bill choked for whatever reason. Was it just last night he laid awake trying to figure out how to screw Gene and both of his fellow actors? Somehow, Gene's stern warning finally brought home the seriousness of their situation. He had witnessed the insanity outside and did not doubt Gene's assessment of their danger. It suddenly dawned on him that he was playing a different role than the one he thought he was playing. The reason he was being offered one million dollars for a few weeks work finally made sense.

Receipts will not be required.

You could be killed.

"Sure Gene. Like Ted, I've been curious but have managed to contain myself. Nobody here knows my real name or where I live." *Not that I have any place I call home,* he said to himself.

"Okay, that's very good. Now, in the bottom left-hand drawer of your desk, you will find a list of those companies we will offer to sell a share of D.A.D. It will be up to Ted to contact each buyer personally tonight and extend the invitation. I do not expect anyone to refuse to take part, but if there is some reluctance by one or more parties, I will provide another name."

"Now Janet. At the bottom of the page is a numbered Bitcoin account. I expect each buyer to deposit one billion dollars worth of Bitcoins into this numbered account. You will be able to go online with the email address provided to verify the deposit. I expect every deposit tomorrow at the close of business. Ted and Bill will hand over D.A.D. and the blueprints to whoever the buyers designate. I expect to have all ten buyers present when the machine is released to them. I'm sure there will be a significant convoy out in front of Transtec to haul away their purchase. Now, while the guards are busy helping get the machine out of the building, the three of you will disappear out the back of Transtec into three different vehicles. If all goes well, you will never see each other again. I'll be with each one of you later in the day with final preparations and instructions, plus, of course, your million-dollar payment. You can elect to take your earnings in either U.S. currency or your own Bitcoin account. Think about what you want and let me know tomorrow."

The three actors sat stunned. There is almost always a little nostalgia and sorrow when a production closes. When the final curtain drops, there is a sense of relief, but it is the rare actor who doesn't experience a sense of loss. Never again will they play this role with these actors. Besides feeling the curtain about to drop one last time, all three players were sobered by the thought of the danger Gene had just suggested they might be expecting. While he said nothing particularly worrisome, it was all the precautions and maneuvering he described that brought home the absolute terror.

You could be killed.

Janet was no longer feeling sanguine about facing danger. The two men tried to shrug off the feelings of terror freezing their bones, but their weak smiles belied their true thoughts. It was time to finish the day's demonstrations and call the winners.

Josh sat back and tried to relax. He wasn't worried about the final four demonstrations. There was only the PetroChina Oil Company left to whom he was going to offer a piece of D.A.D. The other three demonstrations were simply for show. If only he could recover that damn missing device. Time to call Larry and see if he was making any progress. Josh knew he was bothering the detective more than he should; it was just that he had so much riding on finding the damn missing ball.

Before contacting the detective, Josh took a final look at the commotion outside on the street. As the concept, or in most cases the threat of free energy, swept the world, players on both sides of the issue could barely tolerate each other. It was all the San Jose police could do to prevent a full-scale riot. Motorcycle cops in full battle gear were continually driving up and down Short Creek Drive, keeping the peace. Foot patrolmen were busy separating threatening groups every few minutes. Watching the scene on the street, Josh could only hope the peace lasted another two days. He was concerned the buyers might face significant trouble once D.A.D. left his building, but then, he planned on taking them for a billion dollars each, so he couldn't worry about their ultimate safety.

CHAPTER FIFTY-NINE

Steve Hicks remained hidden in a cheap Milpitas motel a few blocks east of the 680 freeway. He was confident the police were looking for him and Marco's Ferrari which was stashed behind the run-down building. The noisy phone ringing startled him, interrupting his pity party. The twittering phone produced an unusual ring he thought was cool. He was even more startled to hear Marco answer his brief "Hello."

"Hicks, you still have my silver ball?" He sounded desperate.

"Yeah, I put it back in your storage locker. Why are you asking?" Hicks couldn't understand this sudden interest in that damned ball. Even that disgusting pig, Amaras, refused to have anything to do with the box and its contents.

"That isn't important right now. I'm coming back, and I want to make damn sure that ball is back in storage when I get there. I'll call you when I get back. It should take me about ten hours."

"Do you want me to meet you at the storage locker?"

"Yeah. See you soon." Marco disconnected without saying goodbye.

Hicks was left wondering what in the hell was going on. Why this sudden interest in that damn ball? Marco must have learned something down in Mexico, but what could he have found out down there? At any rate, he had his own problems trying to stay under the radar of the local cops. They were aware of his association with Marco and that Marco was a thief and a murderer. So far, they couldn't prove he was a thief, but Marco's red Ferrari was definitely being watched, and he didn't dare go anywhere near the storage unit for fear they would follow him and discover he was hiding the stolen ball. Best to wait for Marco and try to slip in without being noticed.

***

After hearing the stories about Josh's father and knowing the truth about what was happening in King's new building, McCutchen decided he needed to get serious about finding Josh's missing free energy machine. If the device fell into the wrong hands, it could wreak havoc in so many ways. While finding the missing machine would not help him find Marco and close his murder case, it would make him feel better about his cavalier attitude and treatment of Josh. Without totally understanding what Josh was going through, he could see the strain the man was under when they had their breakfast meeting. The detective believed in his mind that Hicks was the key. He had to know where the ball was located. They all thought Marco had stolen the ball when he looted the electronics store, and Hick's confessed to seeing the ball at some point. He just needed to find the shifty thief and make him talk. With Hicks driving around in Marco's car, he should be easy to find.

***

Amaras phoned Hicks again with the same result. The little bastard just wouldn't answer his phone. He was standing on his property in a small gap between oleander plants used for privacy along the highway. He could see most of San Jose and up the peninsula to Palo Alto on a clear day from this position. Looking over the town, Amaras wondered where Hicks was hiding. He never wanted to get too close to the thieves who stole the property he fenced in case they were caught. With little association, he could always claim deniability. If he ever visited the residence of one of his thieves and someone saw him, the police would eventually discover that fact, and his claims wouldn't mean anything. Hicks spent a lot of time socializing with some swingers. Maybe one of them would know where he lived. It wouldn't hurt to ask. He thought they all wanted to keep him happy, keep the drinks and drugs flowing; somehow, he needed to find the creepy little shit.

***

After he met with Larry and Josh, King decided to visit Dario. The man was hurting, knowing that his son was not only a thief but a cold-blooded killer. The father would be grieving and reluctant to talk, but he and King went way back, and he might know something. Out of respect for Dario's position and influence, the police probably didn't ask to search Marco's room, but there was a chance his father had explored his son's room to see if he could find out where his son was hiding.

Arlene was at her desk as usual, but when King entered, she didn't try flirting. There was a hushed tone in the big outer office like you find in a funeral home. It wasn't the solemn quietness one feels in one of those large, old cathedrals. In those massive soaring churches, there is a serene, peaceful feeling. Here it felt like someone had died. No greeting smiles, and Arlene spoke in a quiet, subdued voice.

"You want to see Dario?" It was hard to hear her voice over the tranquil, murmuring fountain.

"Yes, if he isn't swamped." King also spoke softly, feeling like he was intruding on private office grief.

Acting as if she was telling company secrets, Arlene almost whispered, "He just sits at his big desk looking out the window at his Zen garden. He rarely moves all day."

When she didn't move to announce his presence or ask if he could enter, King said, "Would you mind asking him if he could spare a minute for me?"

Embarrassed at her inattentiveness, she pushed the button on her intercom and announced, "Mr. Cabrini, the King would like to see you for a minute if you can spare the time."

She usually called him Dario or Boss. The Mr. Cabrini bit was a sign the office was sick.

King walked into the spacious office and saw a defeated man. Dark circles under baggy red eyes and messy hair sticking out in all directions were signs of a man in deep pain. When King walked into his office, Dario sat slumped in his custom-built Lifeform chair and didn't rise or say a greeting, just gave a weak wave towards one of the sitting chairs fronting the desk.

King was reluctant to speak and intrude on his friend's grief, but Dario seemed unwilling to break the building silence between the two men. Perhaps he was immune to any kind of social interaction. Ultimately, it was King who broke the silence.

"I'm awfully sorry about Marco. I wish I could help, Dario."

Dario merely waved his hand, as though dismissing the thought.

"I know the police have left you alone," King began, "but I need to find Marco for another reason. I wonder if maybe you searched his room to see if you could find any information relating to his whereabouts?"

Dario sat still unmoving until King began wondering if he had been understood or even heard. When King was about to say something else, Dario broke his silence. In a soft, grief burdened voice, Dario finally answered.

"I know many people are looking for my son for several reasons, none of which was good. Why do you want to find Marco?"

This wasn't a question King was expecting, but he was happy to answer. "He stole something valuable from a friend of mine. It is unlikely that Marco has any idea what he stole or if what he has in his possession is of any value. There is also the possibility that he dumped this object in the trash someplace. We just want the object back if Marco knows where it is located. I have no desire to catch Marco or assist the police. I'm just helping a friend. Much as I would help you if you ever needed my services."

Yeah, King knew he was kissing ass with that last statement, but he didn't think it would hurt to remind Dario they were friends and colleagues.

"His mother and I searched his room. We found several pamphlets about Mexico, which I am sure is where he is located. Unfortunately, there was nothing about any specific place. I'm sorry I can't be more help, King."

Despite his grief, King believed Dario wished he could have been more helpful.

Standing to leave, King waved to Dario to remain seated, "Thanks anyway, Dario. I'm sorry for the intrusion. You know I have the utmost respect and warm feelings regarding you and your family. If I can help, all you have to do is say the word. And that invitation for a drink, or hell, even a whole bottle is still on the table."

Dario merely waved as King left the office. Feeling like he had pissed on a church wall someplace, King drove away, wishing he had never gone to visit his friend.

While he didn't know Josh's schedule, he believed that the time was getting short for something significant to happen. He just hoped his new building survived whatever the hell was happening. Much of his money was riding on the structure, and he wasn't sure how much damage his insurance would cover.

CHAPTER SIXTY

Josh decided to forgo trying to track down McCutchen. Instead, he watched the remaining demonstrations by Ted and Bill. Particular attention was paid to the reaction of the PetroChina Oil personnel in an attempt to gauge their enthusiasm. Like the other invitees, their excitement was contagious; although being Chinese, they tried to remain inscrutable. But, in this instance, even the stoic Orientals found it difficult to contain their enthusiasm.

After the final demonstration to the Iraqi Oil Ministry, Josh called his actors together in their office.

"Janet, did you find the list of those companies we wish to extend an offer to purchase D.A.D.?"

Picking up the list and holding it in front of herself so Gene could see the list for himself, she answered, "You bet Boss, it's right here."

"Great, now I want Ted to call the ten companies we have selected for our initial offering. Once Ted has placed the call, I want Janet to send out the following email to all ten companies."

GREETINGS. YOU HAVE BEEN CHOSEN TO HAVE THE OPPORTUNITY TO BE ONE OF THE TEN D.A.D. BUYERS. THIS OFFER IS MADE WITH THE FOLLOWING CONDITIONS:

1. YOU WILL DEPOSIT ONE BILLION DOLLARS INTO THE FOLLOWING BITCOIN ACCOUNT BY 10:00 A.M. LOCAL TIME THE DAY AFTER TOMORROW, AUGUST 16TH. #A38ZF00894-X4PF.

2. THE FOLLOWING IS A LIST OF ALL TEN PROSPECTIVE BUYERS.
GENERAL MOTORS CORPORATION
EXXONMOBIL OIL CORPORATION
ROYAL DUTCH SHELL OIL COMPANY
ROSNEFT (Russian Oil Company)
PDVSA VENEZUELA OIL COMPANY
THE TEXAS CO (Formerly Texaco-Subsidiary of Chevron Company)
PETROCHINA OIL
SAUDI ARAMCO OIL COMPANY
CHEVRON OIL COMPANY
ABU DHABI NATIONAL OIL COMPANY (United Arab Emirates)

3. IT IS YOUR RESPONSIBILITY TO COORDINATE THE PURCHASE AND CONTROL OF D.A.D. WITH THE OTHER BUYERS.

4. ONCE WE HAVE DETERMINED THAT THE FULL TEN BILLION DOLLARS HAS BEEN SUCCESSFULLY TRANSFERRED TO THE ABOVE ACCOUNT, D.A.D. WILL BE RELEASED TO YOUR DESIGNATED CONTROLLER ALONG WITH ONE FULL SET OF DESIGN SCHEMATICS.

5. TRANSTEC GUARDS WILL SEE TO IT THAT YOU ARE SAFELY ESCORTED TO YOUR TRANSPORTATION VEHICLES. AT THAT POINT THE SAFETY AND TRANSPORTATION BECOME YOUR RESPONSIBILITY.

6. IF YOU WISH TO BE ONE OF THE TEN BUYERS, PLEASE RESPOND TO THIS EMAIL WITHIN 24 HOURS.

7. CONTACT INFORMATION FOR ALL PROSPECTIVE BUYERS IS ATTACHED TO THIS EMAIL FOR YOUR CONVENIENCE.

Theodore Blankenship–President
TRANSTECNOLOGIES INTERNATIONAL LTD.

"You have all done a remarkable job, and I applaud you for your performances. You are almost home free. Tomorrow, your only duties are to make a superficial appearance at Transtec to show your faces. I will let you know if the buyers want to take part and respond to Ted's email. I do not expect any company to decline our invitation. In which case, the day after tomorrow at the designated time, Ted and Bill will oversee the transfer of D.A.D. to the buyers. Once the machine is out of Transtec, your jobs are finished. Tomorrow I will go over your final appearances, what you are to do, and finally, your disappearances. It is most important for the three of you to remain out of sight from this point forward unless at Transtec surrounded by guards. Your safe escorts tonight are ready as soon as Ted has completed his calls. Oh, before I forget, from now on, you will all be staying at separate locations. Before this, you will have several stops. You are not to telephone each other or PLACE any other call. Questions?"

The three team members looked at each other in horror. The looks on their faces reflected significant question marks.

What had just happened? This is some serious shit. What do we do?

Janet was thinking, '*you could get killed.*' My God, ***this is real***.

Ted had a stunned look that suggested he experienced real pain upon realizing what they were facing.

While expressing shock, Bill's face showed the fear of a guilty conscience upon learning his planned deception would have guaranteed his death, and the threat of death was still frighteningly real.

Seeing the stunned looks on his actors' faces and recognizing his big blunder too late, Gene hastily said, "Oh my God. I'm so sorry for my clumsy announcement. No, I do not know of any specific threats against you at this point. I am simply instituting one of our programmed changes in our patterns, adding another layer of safety for you."

Believing he should make some kind of response, and considering himself the CEO, Ted said, "You told us there was danger involved. You warned us we might be killed. I guess up to now, I just never thought of that as a real possibility. Maybe one chance in a million kind of thing."

"That's what I thought as well," chirped Janet who was relieved at being able to let it out.

Bill was silent, making both Ted and Janet give him a look, suggesting he should say something. Seeing their faces, Bill spoke up, "I was having too much fun playing to give it any thought." At least that was the truth. Keeping his black thoughts to himself, and hoping it didn't show in his face, he continued, "Like Ted and Janet, I didn't give the danger part much thought." That part wasn't the whole truth. He thought how the long con he had considered posed a significantly greater danger.

"Okay," Gene continued, "your safety has been my primary consideration, even more important to me than the success of my plans to raise money." His audience could read his sincerity. Yet being actors, they had to wonder if this was real? That he had employed several levels of protection for them suggested it might be real.

They listened as their boss continued, knowing exactly what they were thinking, "We always expected there to be resistance on many levels to prevent free energy from becoming a reality. There are some powerful organizations plotting against our success. Keeping you safe is paramount to our mutual interests. Unless you are alive to continue our little drama, the show ends. So, you do understand that my concerns for your safety are real. Yes?"

All three actors nodded, still in shock from their realization of how real the danger had become.

"You will leave Transtec as usual with the same guards driving you to the house on Dilbert. There you will separate, each going with a different set of guards to other locations. You and your guards will play an elaborate game of Monte Carlo, the famous shell game. Where are the Transtec people? With any luck, you will never be found. I'll be in touch with each one of you later tonight. Just two more days and the show closes for good. I am sure it is unnecessary to stress how important it is for you to play your roles as though you do not know the danger you are facing."

"Is this ruse necessary?" Ted inquired.

"Perhaps not," Gene responded with a forced grin, "but I am not willing to take any chances."

Bill was the first one to rouse from their fear-induced inertia. "Okay, Ted," he implored, waving over to the desk, "make the damn calls so we can get out of here."

Moving over to the desk and telephone, Ted managed a weak smile. "Yes, sir, Mr. Westlake, would you hold my hand in case I get stage fright?"

Unwilling to be left out, Janet chirped in, "I'll sit on your lap if it helps." She knew her effect on the star-struck actor and couldn't help but play a little scene, hoping to relieve the tension.

"It looks like you're okay for the time being. I'll sign off for now and check with you all later. Good luck with the calls, Ted." The screen went dark. It felt like the curtains were being drawn across the stage. The three actors were left alone to complete their day's chores.

CHAPTER SIXTY-ONE

It was getting late in the evening, and the President was relaxing with a couple of fingers of bourbon in a Waterford crystal cocktail glass when his private phone buzzed. With a scowl at being disturbed yet intrigued by who would call him, the President picked up the phone with his left hand, keeping the bourbon in his closed right fist. "Carleton."

"Sorry to bother you at this late hour, Mr. President," the President recognized the voice of Lincoln Strong, CEO of General Motors, "but I thought you would like to know that we have been invited to spend a billion dollars to purchase a one-tenth interest in free energy."

That got the President's attention, bringing full alertness to his slumping frame. He even set the bourbon down on the polished end table next to his recliner.

"My God, Lincoln, that's excellent news. You obviously are going to participate?" While sounding like a question, it was more of a statement.

"Well, Mr. President, we will buy into the machine. As of now, I don't know the other buyers, but we should have no trouble exercising control over them. Especially if your participation with the military escort is in order."

"I'll brief my cabinet and security advisor as soon as we finish with our call. Our support is guaranteed. Do you know when you will take charge of the device?"

"I'm pretty sure it is the day after tomorrow. Transtec is expecting our response tomorrow. Money is to be in their possession no later than ten A.M. the day after. If they have ten players with each one depositing as required by ten A.M. day after tomorrow, that is when the transfer is to take place."

"I'll have Secretary Bachelor get ahold of you tomorrow to finalize the military escort. Given the nature of this device and the obvious interest, you should have no trouble asserting authority over its transportation with a show of force if necessary."

"Are we still to take the device to the Alameda Naval Base?" The Alameda Naval Base was just a few miles north of San Jose. Strong wasn't happy letting the military take control of D.A.D., but as long as the damn thing never saw the light of day, he would be satisfied.

"Yes, the military police with you will know where to go. You may have to remain with the unit all the way to the storage depot with the other buyers; however, once there, we will take total charge of the unit. I don't expect any real resistance as the other buyers probably are not interested in seeing free energy unleashed in the world."

"You're probably right, Mr. President. We'll expect your remuneration soon."

"You and everybody else," the President said with a laugh. "Getting their money back and the device disposed of should make them all happy."

"I'm sure you're right. Good night, Mr. President." The call ended without the President returning a farewell wish.

CHAPTER SIXTY-TWO

It was nearly midnight in Canaima National Park. The OPEC oil ministers were all being happily entertained by escorts, compliments of Barrera, when their assistants knocked at each door, calling them to assemble in the main conference room. Unhappy at being disturbed but excited to see what was worth interrupting their pleasure, they hastily donned robes and keffiyehs before hurrying to the meeting.

Carlos was in a euphoric mood. Everything he had so carefully planned for was coming to pass. Allah was providing him with the glorious opportunity to assume control of OPEC and dominate the world oil market.

The bedraggled oil ministers staggered into the conference room, flopping down in the chairs surrounding the big round table. Their assistants stood behind their masters, looking unhappy and every bit as harried. Carlos Barrera, with a wolfish grin plastered on his jowls, and Mohammad Bin Salman, with a glaring hate-filled scowl, were the only two people who looked fully alive.

Barrera, not the seething Salman, took control of the meeting. "Now that you are all gathered, I wanted to share the good news and agree on our next moves. Tonight, five of our members received an offer to purchase a one-tenth interest in the free energy machine. With only ten total buyers, that allows our organization to purchase a fifty percent interest. We will have the biggest share of the machine giving us control. We can transport the machine to our headquarters in Vienna or dispose of it in California. I cannot imagine any of the other buyers having an interest in seeing the free energy machine developed, but we need to be prepared in case one or more want to duplicate the machine for their own reasons."

Unwilling to sit by and let that fat upstart hog the show, Mohammad rose and addressed the group. "Let's not get too hasty in calling for the machine's destruction. Perhaps we could use the machine for our benefit. With unlimited free energy, we could drill for new oil endlessly, power our refining plants and perhaps even use it to drive our tankers."

"Even if we keep the machine or make copies, there is still the issue of those Transtec people." Barrera could not let Salman take back control of the meeting.

"And we cannot control the other five buyers if they should also want a duplicate. If we could keep the machine for ourselves, that would be one thing, but having it out in the hands of other companies makes me uncomfortable."

"Of course, we cannot let anyone else have the machine," thundered Salman. "And we need to take care of those Transtec people."

"We have a team on-site to deal with the Transtec employees," replied Carlos, unwilling to yield the floor. "Some of our people will take possession of the machine, and others will see to the disposal of those Transtec infidels."

"Does anyone have a problem with the purchase of one billion dollars worth of Bitcoins?" asked the Saudi oil minister.

Carlos seemed confused at first; then, his mind kicked in. "Besides you, there are the Iranians, the Emirates, ourselves, and Iraq. No one has expressed any trouble in purchasing the coins. We have until the day after tomorrow to purchase coins in the proscribed account."

"Do we have any plans for recovering our five billion dollars?" asked the Abu Dhabi oil minister.

"Unfortunately, once the money goes into Bitcoins, there is no way to trace the funds. We can try to shift the coins to our account, but I'm afraid the Transtec people will have the money programmed to be redeposited into another account immediately. Perhaps we can try to capture this Blankenship guy, their CEO, and torture the account information from him." Barrera didn't seem too confident in this plan, nor did he care. His country's loss of one billion dollars, while painful, was not an issue.

Angry and frustrated at being left out of the conversation, Mohammed asked, "What are your plans if one of the other buyers wants a duplicate machine, Mr. Minister?"

Not the least bit intimidated, Carlos answered, "I'm afraid the only solution is to destroy the machine and all relevant paperwork such as the schematics. We all agreed initially that destroying the machine and killing the people was in our best interests."

"There could be a battle with the other buyers for control of the machine," Mohammed countered, "and there may be more than one company who would like to own a duplicate. What do you plan, Minister?" Mohammed asked with a sneer on the word minister. "Kill all the other buyers? I'm sure they will have their security forces to help take control of the machine."

For the first time, Barrera seemed unsure. "We will get a list of the other buyers as soon as all ten companies have agreed to take part. Once we have that list, our people can feel out the other buyers for their plans and thoughts regarding the machine. We can then evaluate our position and make final decisions."

Barrera purposefully had not answered the chairman and felt weak in the position he had been forced to hold, yet his answer stood for now. Tomorrow, he would have to deal with whatever the situation dictated. That damned Salman just would not give up easily.

CHAPTER SIXTY-THREE

Josh wanted to contact Larry for an update about his missing machine, but he had another job more important. A promise was made to his actors concerning their safety, and that indeed was his primary concern. Wearing his Gene costume with reluctance and a heavy heart, he found his way to Marriott's Residence Inn by Milpitas. Riding the elevator, he found his way to room 423 on the fourth floor. Rapping on the door, he stood in front of the peephole so the occupant could get a good look at his face.

Opening the door, Janet gasped, then almost shouted, "Gene, what brings you to my fine dwelling?"

Holding his cane and top hat in one hand, plus an ugly vinyl airline carry-on in the other, he asked, "Can I come in?"

"Oh geez, I'm sorry. Yes. Please come in." Wearing only a robe, she was nervous about seeing their boss in person. "I was not expecting visitors," she stammered.

"Relax, my dear. I thought it was time for us to meet again."

Janet was confused for a moment, then the sight of the cane kicked in, and she cried out, "Abe, is that you?"

"I'm afraid that is another of my personas, Janet. I'm only sorry we could not meet as we truly are. But in the theater, nothing is as it seems. Right?"

"I guess that's true," she responded. "You never truly know anyone else." As she said this, a look of sadness covered her face.

"Let's sit down for a few moments while I explain my visit. Is that alright?"

"Certainly. Shall we sit on the couch?"

"That would be just fine," Josh answered with a smile.

"Janet, this may sound unusual, but I would like you to go into the bathroom and completely undress. Take your suitcase. Take off every stitch of clothing, including undergarments and jewelry. Take any other clothes you may have with you and any other items you brought into this room, such as your telephone. In this carry-on is a large bag with a thin metal lining. Put everything you own into this bag, including your suitcase and any bathroom items. When you are finished, I want every item you brought with you into this room put into that bag. Inside of the carry-on, you will also find a completely new wardrobe from the inside out, including new shoes. And a makeup kit. Please dress in those clothes. Close the bag with your old clothing and belongings plus your suitcase and leave it all in the bathroom. Turn on the shower, then come back out here bringing the makeup kit and carry-on with you."

Janet started to ask a question, but Gene held his finger to his lips, indicating silence, do not speak. Confused, but seeing that Gene was serious, she took the carry-on into the bathroom, then came back out to collect those items she had been using from her suitcase, such as some hand lotion.

Janet took only five minutes when the shower came on, and she came back into the main room wearing a chambermaid smock with black stockings. She was holding onto the carry-on and makeup kit.

"Did you fold over the top of the bag with your old belongings?" Gene inquired, just to be sure.

"Yes. Would you mind telling me what is going on?" She was scared, nervous, confused, and seemed ready to cry.

Taking her hands in his with a gentle smile and voice, Gene said, "It's time for Janet to disappear. You have been in contact with several groups of people in the past few days. It is possible, although doubtful that someone may have placed a microdot transmitter someplace on your clothing or other possessions, but I am taking no chances."

"What is going to happen to me?" she asked tearfully.

"Hopefully, nothing but good things from this moment on," Gene answered with as much reassurance as he could project, given the circumstances. "I didn't dare say that Janet was going to disappear when I first entered the room if there was the slightest chance that someone might be listening. The shower in the bathroom should prevent anyone from hearing us in case we missed something."

"Do you think that is possible?" she asked with a little more composure.

"It's improbable, but it is possible. No reason to take any chances. That bag in the bathroom with the metal liner acts like a Faraday cage blocking any transmission."

"Okay. It all makes sense now," she responded, sounding relieved.

Pulling a package from inside of his jacket, Gene opened an envelope showing Janet the contents. "Here are two passports. The top one is in your original name, Lisa Ogden," he said, handing her the stack.

"But I never had a passport," she protested.

"You do now. It's real and legal, but you can't use it yet."

"Why did you give it to me then?" she asked, confused.

"It's for later. The second passport is for your new identity, Melinda Alverez. Take a look. That is what the makeup kit is for. When you leave here in a few minutes, you will look like Melinda Alverez, hotel chambermaid."

"Really Gene. A chambermaid?" The unhappy look on her face belied the tears she had so recently shed.

"It's the best way for you to leave the hotel undetected. While it is highly unlikely that anyone has followed you to this hotel, but just in case, when you leave as a chambermaid, no one will pay you the slightest attention."

Seeing that this was an argument she would not win, Janet glanced at the second passport. "Well, she is kinda cute."

"I considered making you into an old hag," he responded with a grin, "but I didn't want to put up with what I am sure would have been a big fight."

"You got that right, buster," she replied with a grin of her own.

"Okay," Gene continued, "You have a black wig with long straight hair. In the makeup kit, you will find a liquid skin tone to color your face and hands. Add more depth and length to your eyebrows, a little putty on your nose and chin. Well, you've got the picture on your passport. Just match it."

"I'll never know how you get a passport already made that looks like the person you want me to become. Is this passport even real?"

"Yes. Although the name Melinda Alverez is fabricated. Behind the passports, you will find real credit cards and a valid driver's license, all in the correct name and five thousand dollars in cash. The last item is a plane ticket for Miss Alverez to visit the island of St. Lucia in the Caribbean."

"Does this mean I am not returning to Transtec?" She sounded wistful and disappointed.

"Yes, my dear. Your character has left the stage. There are no more scenes for Janet Hills to play."

"But I didn't get to say goodbye," she protested.

"That is on purpose. I'm afraid our CEO has strong feelings for you, and this way, there is no temptation to stay in touch."

"Yes, you are correct. I sensed the same thing. Perhaps it is just as well."

"Alright, Melinda, get going with the makeup. There is a mirror inside the cover of the kit. While you are putting the finishing touches on your new character, I'll go over the plans and your itinerary."

While Lisa was warming up the makeup putty in her hands, Gene began his final instructions.

"The credit cards are primarily for show. There are a few hundred dollars on them for an emergency. Your real passport as Lisa Ogden already has an entrance stamp for St. Lucia. That is for your exit and return to the States, should that be your desire. On the back page of this passport is a sticky note with your Bitcoin account number. Your account contains one million dollars of Bitcoins. You can access this account in almost any place in the civilized world. Guard this number with your life. You lose it; you lose your acting payment. You can change the number anytime you want, and you can convert the coins to cash in nearly any country's currency anytime you desire."

Working with the makeup kit, changing her face to match the passport, Lisa asked, "How long do I remain Melinda?"

"That's a good question. You will enter St. Lucia tomorrow afternoon. I'm afraid there will be a couple of plane changes. Your entire itinerary is just inside your airline ticket folder. In St. Lucia, you are booked into another Marriott as Melinda Alverez. Your carry-on should match the chambermaid, Melinda. Your room reservation number is also in your itinerary package. Once in St. Lucia, you will stay in the Marriott as Melinda Alverez for as long as you desire. However, I recommend you don't play the chambermaid for too long. At some point in time, the authorities will start looking at plane reservations by single women around the time of your disappearance."

"When you get tired of playing the chambermaid, you will check out of the Marriott. You can do that from your room with no need to visit the front desk. Remove your wig and makeup in the room, changing back to Lisa Ogden. Put everything belonging to Melinda in a trash bag, which you will take with you. Burn the Melinda passport and driver's license. Cut up and destroy the credit cards. When all traces of Melinda have disappeared, you will leave the room as your old self, Lisa Ogden. Take the trash bag containing all the Melinda clothing and anything you may have purchased that reflects Melinda with you when you leave the room. Have the taxi drop you off at one of the public parks next to the ocean and stuff your Melinda bag into one of the public trash containers. At this point, you are Lisa Ogden with a million-dollar account and are free to resume your old life. Just be careful, if you continue with your acting career, to avoid any role resembling Janet Hills."

"Wow," a startled cry from Lisa, now looking like Melinda. "It sounds like you have thought of everything."

"I have attempted to do just that. However, I may have missed some detail. You will have to be careful as you leave here to watch for any unusual interest in you, besides the obvious male gawking at a pretty lady." This was said with a beaming smile.

Finished with her transformation from Janet Hills to Melinda Alverez, Lisa turned on her chair and asked, "Well, how do I look?"

"Absolutely perfect, Melinda." Looking at the watch on his wrist while standing up, Gene said, "You have ten minutes to catch your ride to the airport. An Uber driver with a new black Toyota Camry will drive into the portico loading zone, looking for you. His name is Oscar. Uber has already been paid, and the driver will take you to the Oakland airport. He knows your name as Miss Alverez, and should he ever be asked, all he can say is that he picked up a chambermaid and took her to the airport. If he is the chatty kind and wants to talk, you are on your way to Houston to spend time with your ailing mother."

Standing up and closing the lid to the makeup case, Lisa began getting ready to leave the room. "Anything else, Gene?" she asked, reluctant to say goodbye.

"One final word of caution. Be careful with your passports. Put the Lisa Ogden passport someplace safe until after you are in St. Lucia."

Gene seemed at a loss for the words to say farewell. He had put a lot into creating Janet Hills and had a real kinship with the young lady playing the role. With a lump in his throat, he finally said goodbye without sounding like a barking frog. Hugging the girl now called Melinda, he managed, "Good luck, my dear. Thanks for playing the role beautifully."

Unable to speak, Melinda shuffled to the door dragging her carry-on. Gene followed, opening the door for her to leave. Without a backward glance which would have brought tears, Lisa Ogden left Josh's life. Josh went into the bathroom to turn off the shower and collect the remnants of Janet Hills life for disposal at a distant dumpster.

One down, two to go. Hopefully, they would leave the stage with the same easy exit.

CHAPTER SIXTY-FOUR

Bill and Ted were both at Transtec early the next day. There was still a mob crowding Short Creek Drive and the building's front lawns with television vans blocking the road. The two men were driven around to the back and escorted into the building by their usual guards. They had barely reached the office when the phone started ringing. Before nine o'clock, Ted had spoken to all ten companies offered a chance to purchase D.A.D. Every single company committed to depositing one billion dollars in Bitcoins into the company account before 10 A.M. tomorrow. As each company offered a chance to buy an interest in D.A.D. agreed to the purchase price and deposit terms, they were provided with a list of all ten buyers and contact information to coordinate their delivery plans. Gene seemed confident in all ten companies accepting his purchase offer, so there was no hesitation in providing the list to the very first company to commit.

Ted initiated a video call to Gene, but there was no answer. Ted asked Bill if he had any idea what had happened to Janet. The three had split up last night as described by Gene, but this morning it was just him and Bill. Bill said he did not know. They both wondered what had happened to their friend and were afraid for her well-being. Hopefully, Gene could provide some information when he made contact. With nothing to do and all day to do it, the two actors sat in the office playing solitaire with the computer.

In Washington, D.C., the President and his national security advisor were huddled with the Secretary of Defense and other select cabinet officers discussing how they would take control of the free energy machine while putting the three Transtec officers behind bars someplace where they would disappear permanently. When the Secretary's aide entered with the list of all ten buyers, the meeting disintegrated into chaos.

"**What the fuck**!" thundered President Carleton in an unusual profanity-laced statement. "Those goddamned Russians and Chinese are going to be buyers?" Turning to his security advisor, the President ordered, "Get the entire cabinet here immediately, and the Chairman of the JCS."

Down in Venezuela, Carlos was on the phone with Mateo in San Jose, who wanted another hundred fighters to overwhelm any opposition to his controlling the energy machine for the cartel. Carlos thought a hundred was overkill, promising fifty by the day's end. With fifteen countries comprising OPEC, getting fifty fighters, even with short notice, should not be a problem. He was worried that with the Russians, the Chinese, and the U.S. all interested parties, gaining control could be a problem. Hell, if he had to, he would have Mateo bomb the whole fucking crowd. As long as the machine and those Transtec people disappeared, he didn't care who else got caught in the crossfire just as long as they could make it look like the work of those Israeli pigs.

Colonel Conrad in Houston had learned that General Motors was one of the successful buyers for a position in the damn free energy machine. The Colonel felt GM was in the pockets of the Feds and was not sure what to do about the situation. That the U.S. Government already had a free energy device was an open secret in some circles, and its determination to keep this technology out of the free market was also well known in those same circles. The Colonel's plight was, what could or should he do, if anything?

Keeping free energy out of the energy market was also his goal. He thought it might be in his and Texaco's best interest to advise Skipper Walls to stand back and simply monitor the situation. If it looked like the government would take control, just stand by and let it happen. If someone else got into the act, that would be a different story. That the Soviets and Chinese were buyers made him glad the government was playing a hand. He also knew that many companies and other countries would like to own the technology to develop it. The Colonel considered it his job to prevent that from happening. If the U.S. government did the job, so much the better.

The buzz down on the street in front of Transtec included the ten names of those companies invited to purchase D.A.D. Representatives of the chosen companies were eagerly being sought for comments regarding their plans. The scene was a messy, chaotic nightmare for the San Jose police trying to maintain order. The doors to Transtec remained locked, with several guards carrying automatic rifles visible just inside the windows. Within a few hours, everybody knew Chevron was going to be represented by the United States Government. That the Russians and Chinese were also involved gave rise to some fascinating speculation. Many expected fireworks. Few thought there would be a peaceful transition from Transtec to the buyers tomorrow.

Josh received an early morning call from Larry advising him the highway patrol reported seeing Marco's Ferrari heading down Interstate 880 towards San Jose. It was assumed that Hicks was driving and Larry wanted him followed, hoping he would lead them back to his storage locker and Josh's missing ball. Larry advised Josh to get down to the police headquarters and wait for a ride. A few hours later, he was still waiting for the promised ride with no word from Larry. Worried about Ted and Bill back at Transtec, Josh called to get an update. Informed that all ten buyers had elected to take part came as no big surprise. He told the boys to hang tough for a few hours, and he would call with more instructions.

Before Josh could hang up, Ted asked, "Where's Janet? She didn't come in today."

"Janet's role ended, and she exited stage left. Janet is headed back to her old life as promised."

"But we never got to strike the set and say goodbye," Bill sniped.

"The set only comes down when the show is over, and we still have another grand performance. One more big scene. These scenes do not include Janet, who also wanted to say goodbye to her fellow actors, but that was impractical for safety reasons. My job is to see you all home safely. Please, no more questions. I'll talk to you later."

This time he did manage to end the call before either man could respond.

The scene at the police department was a madhouse with officers rushing around shouting orders and jumping into cars; tires squealing as they drove away. Josh had not been told that Marco had been spotted lurking around the storage shed as though waiting for someone, presumably Hicks. When Hicks got out of his car to open the security gate at the storage lockers, he was immediately surrounded by the San Jose

Police Department, who cuffed him before placing him in the back of one of the cruisers. Ten police officers led by Detective McCutchen crept up the roadway towards the back of the storage lot where Marco's storage locker was hidden from view.

Marco sensed that something was wrong and, catching sight of a policeman sneaking up towards his position, took off running up the rocky mountainside. The officer, seeing Marco take off, shouted to his colleagues and took off in pursuit. It took another twenty minutes before Marco was captured and returned to the storage locker. Meanwhile, McCutchen had retrieved the locker key from Hicks and opened the storage locker, finding the only object present inside a box containing Josh's missing ball.

An hour later, Josh was still at the police department when Larry drove up, motioning for the angry, frustrated man to join him. When Josh saw what was inside the trunk of the detective's vehicle, he instantly became all smiles. All was forgiven.

"I never opened the box Josh, but it's heavy, and I assume this is what you have been searching for."

Josh opened the box and took a peek inside. Everything looked exactly like it was supposed to look, so he quickly closed the lid and, with a big smile, went over and gave the startled detective a gigantic hug.

"I don't know how to thank you, Larry. You couldn't know how much this means. Please extend my thanks to everyone on your team who helped recover this for me."

With a big smile of his own, Larry responded, "You know Josh, let's leave that box in my trunk, and I'll give you a ride back to Transtec. I'm sure trying to carry that box around while flying your silly cane would not be comfortable."

With a chagrined look on his face at being caught, Josh had to ask, "How did you figure it out?"

With a wink as he headed to the driver's seat, Larry answered, "You do know Josh, I am a detective. Right?"

CHAPTER SIXTY-FIVE

Ted and Bill were subjected to the same security arrangements as the night before. Driven to their supposed residence, they hustled separately to many locations before ending up in far different locations. Ted was in a hotel near the San Francisco airport while Bill enjoyed a night in Berkeley.

While trying to read *State of Fear*, a Michael Crichton novel, Ted found himself continually interrupted by the thought that the dangers being faced by the book's protagonists seemed to reflect the risks in his own life. All the efforts being made by Gene for his safety were making him uneasy. Were these precautions really necessary? He had observed the madhouse in the streets and lawns surrounding their office building, but he had not felt physically threatened. To avoid causing stress in his actor's lives, Gene had shared few of the late-night problems his guards had encountered. Still, the negative vibrations found a way of seeping into the walls, causing Ted to feel uneasy. He was on his way to the mini-bar in his hotel room to grab a beer when there was a knock on his door.

Peeping through the eye-hole, he saw a smiling Gene in the flesh. Excited to meet his boss in person, he couldn't wait to open the door.

"Hello Ted, mind if I come in?" Gene looked happier and more relaxed than Ted could remember.

"Wah-wah, well hell yes," he stammered, waving his guest inside.

"This is just a courtesy call to make sure you are comfortable," Gene fibbed. He was concerned about his actor's comfort, but the real reason for his visit was much darker.

"Come in and sit down," Ted offered. "Can I get you something to drink? I was just about to have a beer."

Gene was about to refuse, then changed his mind. Maybe having a drink together would make his job a little easier. "Sure Ted, whatever you are having."

Opening the mini-bar, Ted announced, "It looks like Anchor Steam is the beer of choice. Is that okay with you?"

While living in San Francisco for much of his life, Josh had never tried Anchor Steam beer. Not a big beer drinker, preferring scotch, he had undoubtedly heard of America's first craft beer. "Sure, let's give it a try Ted."

Ted grabbed a couple of beers from the bar and some glasses from a small table holding a coffee maker and a selection of morning coffee mini packs. Ever the thoughtful company CEO, he opened the beers, pouring some into each glass before handing Gene a glass of beer and the nearly empty beer can.

After Ted was seated, Gene held his beer up, tilting it towards his young actor. "Cheers Ted, here's to a job well done."

"Cheers, Boss. We couldn't have done it without you," a smirking grin plastered on his face. Such a fatuous, ridiculous, funny statement needed no answer, nor was one expected.

Gene took a sip of the beer then set it on the coffee table in front of the couch where he was sitting. Ted lounged in a padded armchair next to the sofa.

"How are you getting along, Ted? Comfortable here?" Both questions were merely a way for Gene to get comfortable with himself. His visit here was serious, and he needed to achieve a relaxed feeling between himself and Ted before continuing.

"Okay, I guess," he responded with more of a genuine smile this time. "All of this moving around, changing rooms and rides is wearing, but I'm sure necessary for our safety."

"We don't want to take any chances with your lives. Speaking of which, I'm glad you mentioned safety. I do want to discuss tomorrow's plans with you." Gene had a serious look on his face, which immediately wiped the smile from Ted's.

"Aren't we safe?" Ted asked, as though such an idea had never entered his mind.

"Oh, you're perfectly safe where we are tonight," Gene answered, with a stern look on his face. "It's tomorrow I want to talk about."

"What about tomorrow," Ted asked, seeing the severe look on Gene's face. He even forgot about the beer he was holding in his hand.

"Tomorrow is the culmination of all that we have been working towards these past few days. Tomorrow, the curtain closes for good on our little drama. We just need to spend a few minutes talking about taking down the set when the curtain drops."

This was the kind of language Ted understood. It was also the reason Gene continually used theater language when talking with his actors. Gene purposely used theater language to make his cast as comfortable as possible.

"I'm sure you are aware of a high interest in free energy and the mob hysteria it is causing." Gene was speaking calmly and deliberately, not wanting to spook his company's CEO.

"Yeah, it's kind of hard to miss. The show out front of Transtec is about all there is on the local news."

"When we deliver D.A.D. to the buyers tomorrow, there may be trouble," Gene told a now serious listener.

"What kind of trouble are we expecting?" a now worried actor asked.

"I don't expect too much trouble when we transfer the machine to the buyers; it's your safety that is of concern." Gene paused for a second to let those words sink in before continuing.

"The transfer may be messy. Everybody will want control. OPEC has five buyers, and I'm sure they will feel entitled to take control. The other buyers will feel that as long as they are assured of a duplicate of the machine, they don't care who has immediate possession. The only concern is General Motors."

"General Motors? How can they be a problem?" Ted had a confused look on his face.

"Oh, it isn't General Motors that I'm worried about," Gene hastened to assure his listener. "It's the United States Military. You see, General Motors is in bed with our government, and neither entity wants to see free energy released to the world. Therefore, I believe the military; I'm not sure which branch, perhaps the Marines, will come with General Motors to take control of D.A.D. That may cause a scene with the OPEC crowd, but I don't expect any real fireworks. If it plays out as I expect, the U.S. Government will take control and herd everyone else into a caravan, leading to some warehouse or base where it will be destroyed. The other buyers will be out of luck, but our government will try to assuage their feelings by offering to refund their purchase price."

"If that is the situation, what seems to be the problem?" a perplexed Ted asked, finally remembering the beer in his hand.

Gene waited until Ted had taken a large drink of beer before responding. "It's you I'm worried about Ted," Gene waited for those words to resonate.

"The government, and probably OPEC as well, will not want to leave you free to continue working with free energy. There may be others who would like to take you captive to flush out all the information in your brains. Little do they know that you don't have the information they seek, Ted." Gene looked directly into Ted's eyes with a stern look, "The government and OPEC will want you dead."

Ted sat in silence as the words sank into his brain. He had always known there was danger in this role he had volunteered to play, but he never thought about how that danger would manifest. Gene had just made it crystal clear. Some mighty powerful people wanted him dead.

"Oh my God, Gene, what am I going to do?"

"That's really why I'm here tonight, Ted. To help you plan your exit from center stage."

"I guess I always thought I would have to earn that million dollars," Ted said with a chagrined look on his face.

"Pay attention now because the next things I am going to tell you will keep you alive to spend that money." Gene's countenance took on the look of a pleasant hustler, which in a way was his true nature. Ted was concentrating on Gene with his full attention.

"You and Bill will be at Transtec as usual by 9:00 A.M. The guards will keep you safe until all ten buyers are in the building to make the transfer. General Motors will try to bring in a military escort, but our guards will prohibit all military personnel from entering the building. No one may go into the room where we are storing D.A.D. until you have personally verified that all ten billion dollars have been transferred to our Bitcoin account. In fact, I will verify that all the funds have been transferred and leave a message on your computer to that effect."

"Once you see that message, you will delete it immediately, then type in a code that will pop up immediately after you have deleted the message from me. This code will wipe your computer's memory with a unique program. If someone spends a lot of manpower and time, the information could still be retrieved, but you will be long gone, and there is nothing on the computer that leads back to you or our little drama unless one of you entered something personal."

"In the morning, before the buyers are permitted in the building, it is your responsibility to check the computer to make sure that no one entered any information about your real identities. That is the only information that concerns me at this point. Are you aware of any information relating to who the three of you are?"

"No Boss. You made it very clear in the beginning that we were to guard that information with our lives. Bill and I have played a few games on the computer, but no one has sent a personal email as far as I know. I will check that first thing just to be sure."

"That's great, Ted. Now the next part is also crucial. While the guards escort the buyers from the building, Captain Wilson will usher you to a back room where you and Bill will change into guard's uniforms. Remove every article of clothing you are wearing, including underwear and all jewelry, including your watch. Two of the guards your size will dress in your clothes and go back into the office. There will be two makeup kits in your changing room, with a selection of wigs and eyeglasses. Each kit contains a photo of your new appearance. Be sure to get the makeup kit with your name printed on the lid. Change your appearance to match the photo exactly, paying particular attention to your facial features using putty so that any facial recognition software cannot identify you. Are you with me so far?"

Ted was sitting in shock, but seemed to be fully present. "It sure seems like you have gone to a lot of trouble to make us safe."

"Not at all. I have always told you that your safety was of paramount importance to me. Now the really important part. Your wallets, credit cards, driver's licenses, and any identification papers, in fact, all papers in your possession, are to go into a metal-lined bag the guards will provide for you. This bag is a Faraday cage prohibiting any microdot transmitter from reaching the outside world. The guards will dispose of the bag after you leave. You and Bill will leave by the loading dock in the back of the building with two other guards. It will appear as though the four of you will make a routine patrol or perhaps run an errand of some kind. You and Bill will be driven to Westfield Valley Fair, a large shopping mall with a Monroe parking garage."

"The Valley Fair Mall and the Monroe garage are important because if there is any kind of air or satellite coverage of San Jose, and especially of the Transtec vehicles, with the surrounding traffic, your exit from the guard's car inside of the garage cannot be observed."

"Inside of the mall is a Boss store. Ask for Mr. Letterman. He will outfit you with new clothing they will tailor on-site. There, you will purchase a new wardrobe, including shoes, socks, and underwear. Mr. Letterman already has airline carry-on bags for you to pack your new wardrobe. Do you have questions so far?"

"Yeah. If we give up all of our identification and credit cards, how are we supposed to get around and pay for things?"

"It's good you asked because that's next." Gene seemed to enjoy this part of the data dump, and Ted relaxed in response to the more pleasant atmosphere.

"The Boss store is practically in the middle of the shopping mall on the first level. You will return to the Monroe Parking Garage, which is where you entered the mall. Bill will exit at the opposite end of the mall in the Winchester Parking Garage. As you leave the mall and enter the garage, there will be a white Cadillac SUV waiting in the garage, just outside of the mall. This car is an UBER ride already paid for. In the back seat, you will find a package addressed to Fredric Wadsworth; that's you. Inside the package, you will find identification matching your appearance. Included are your driver's license, passport, and credit cards plus five thousand in cash. Also, in the package, you will find a passport in your old name, Joseph Langham. Be sure to keep the two passports in separate locations so they do not get intermixed. In the back of your real passport is a sticky note with a Bitcoin account number with a one-million-dollar balance. You can and should change this account number as soon as possible. You can access this account in almost any country and convert a part or the whole account into some other currency."

Ted was looking a little overwhelmed and seemed in a bit of a daze. "Wake up, Ted, it's almost over." This was said with a smile, showing he was just teasing.

"I'm here Boss. It's just a lot of information. Whew! Man, that's some planning."

"I had a lot of time to work on this script, Ted. Now, your UBER driver will take you to the San Francisco airport, the international terminal. In your package, along with all of your identification cards and papers, you will find a first-class ticket to Sydney, Australia. Your flight leaves tomorrow afternoon at four P.M."

"So, is this goodbye, Gene?" Ted seemed sad suddenly. The reality of the show's closing had finally hit home.

"I'm afraid so, Ted. I appreciate your exemplary performance. You are a gifted actor, and should you wish to return to the theater, just avoid playing any roles that even remotely resemble Theodore Blankenship. Within a few hours of your disappearance, there will be a worldwide BOLO, Be-On-The-Lookout, for the character you brought to life. Once in Australia as Fredric Wadsworth, you can live under that name as long as you desire; however, I don't recommend living under that name for very long. Eventually, the searchers will visit the airports, looking for single men traveling to foreign locations. They may look for the man Fredric Wadsworth."

"You have your passport and plenty of money when you wish to resume your old name and identity. I wish you the best of luck. I will watch everything in Transtec on the television tomorrow, and should I see anything worth mentioning, I'll be in touch."

Gene stood up to leave after hardly touching his beer, which had grown warm. Ted stood up, completely lost for words. His high emotions blocked coherent thoughts from fully forming in his mind. Seeing his CEO's dilemma, Gene went over and wrapped him in a big hug. "Take care, Joseph. You did a good job. Enjoy the money and your life."

Gene turned and left, closing the door softly behind him.

He had one other stop tonight. Hopefully, Bill would not be so emotional. With any luck, he would like his new name and find Athens, Greece to his liking.

CHAPTER SIXTY-SIX

Josh met King and McCutchen at 7:00 A.M. for breakfast at Scrambl'z on Almaden Expressway, near King's home. The meeting was Josh's idea to provide his friends with information about the events planned for today. It was also Josh's farewell to the men who had been supportive of his efforts during the past few days, although neither of his breakfast guests had any idea that they would never see him again.

After they had all eaten breakfast and drank coffee, Josh began describing what he expected to happen during the next few hours.

"You both know what a mess we have on the streets surrounding Transtec; this should all be over before noon. I expect a U.S. military caravan with heavy firepower to arrive soon, and they will clear most of the traffic from Short Creek Drive. There will be limousines and SUVs from OPEC, Russia, China, and the other purchasers of D.A.D. General Motors will be represented by the military, although GM agents will be present to represent their interests."

While Josh paused for a second to catch his breath before continuing, Larry stepped in with a question, "Are we going to have a shooting war, Josh?"

"No, I don't expect any fireworks, although tempers may run hot and someone may get hurt. Many countries, including the Russians and Chinese, already have representatives in the crowd, all wanting a piece of free energy. I am sure there are plans to snatch the device from whoever has control as it leaves the building. I expect the military presence to prevent any outside interest from interfering as they escort D.A.D. from Transtec."

"God Josh," King uttered with a wicked grin, "it sounds like the making of World War III."

"It looks nasty," Josh agreed, "and I wouldn't rule out someone getting pushy, but if my expectations of the military caravan are correct, they should be able to maintain the peace."

"Were you expecting more help from the San Jose Police Department?" Larry asked.

"No, not at all. They have been doing an admirable job keeping that mob under control."

"I suspect those guards just inside Transtec carrying automatic rifles in their hands might have something to do with keeping the peace," Larry added with a wry smile.

"That was my intention," Josh said. "I didn't want any permanent damage to King's beautiful new building."

"That's good to know," King quipped. "I hoped that letting you use the building for a few weeks was not a mistake."

"I was just coming to that King. We will be out of your building permanently by two this afternoon. Everything we used for our Transtec business will be gone. The features we added to the downstairs lobby should convince the city that our contract for fitting out the space inside was real. I hope you like the improvement. Personally, I think it's beautiful."

"Well, in that case, I can't wait to get a look," King responded.

"Oh, and we'll take down the Transtec letters on that swell granite sign out front. I thought we'd just put in your street name and numbers, III SHORT CREEK DRIVE."

"Sounds pretty classy," Larry said. "I thought your Transtec sign shows a lot of class as well."

"Thanks, Larry. I wanted to make sure the King here was not unhappy with our tenancy."

***

In the Cabinet Room, President Carleton met with his entire cabinet, plus Admiral Whittaker, Chairman of the JCS.

"It's almost time for the transfer Admiral, what's the situation."

'Well, as you know, both the Russians and Chinese have agreed to destroy the free energy device and all related drawings, computer data, plus dispose of the Transtec personnel. They will have agents on hand to monitor the disposal of all said items and personnel. I am led to believe that we can expect their cooperation. I'm not comfortable with the OPEC countries. On the one hand, they are ranting about the same kinds of destruction already proposed, but they also suggest an intention to see how the machine works. I believe they would like to have access to free energy once the oil stops flowing. Chevron, Exxon, and Shell are being coy. They could be a problem."

"Is our military on hand to take control of the device from General Motors?"

"Yes, Mr. President," said Secretary Bachelor of the DOD. "General Hutchins has provided a caravan of thirty military vehicles of various descriptions carrying 100 army personnel from Fort Irwin. These men and equipment are presently on site. The expedition is led by Captain Gates, a battle-hardened veteran with three tours of duty. Overhead we have three black hawk helicopters with another 18 marines from the Marine Air Station in Miramar should they be required. Just to monitor things and prevent anyone from escaping our net is the latest observation satellite."

"What about Chevron, Exxon, and Shell, Susan?" the President asked his Attorney General. "What can we do to get them in line?"

"They each legally have a one-tenth interest in D.A.D. Unless we are prepared to fight them for the machine, we must persuade them to sell us their interest. We should see what it will take in money and possibly some oil and gas exploration rights. They all want to drill off the California coast. It is only the environmentalists who have prevented them from drilling in the past."

"I can always count on you for a voice of sanity, Susan. How about leading an effort to see what it will take? I would prefer to buy them out than resort to brute force."

"I'll get right on it, Mr. President," the AG said, trying to hide a smile of satisfaction from her face.

***

Down in Venezuela, Carlos was pacing the room around the table, surrounded by the other OPEC oil ministers. Mohammad Bin Salman had a wicked grin on his face as he taunted the fat upstart to his throne. "What do you propose to do about the Russians and Chinese, Barrera?" Using the last name of his adversary was another taunt.

"Our spies on the street tell me they both want to see the evil machine destroyed just as we do." Barrera spit back at him. He wasn't about to let that evil black-eyed bastard shake him.

"I hear the U.S. military already has a position staked out on the street with dozens of vehicles," Salman continued with his jabs.

"And I have a hundred men in the crowd who can drop every one of those military assholes in a grave if it comes to that," a snarling Barrera retorted.

"What about your plan to blame it all on the dirty Jews?" Salman kept up the pressure.

"The men all have Israeli documentation; their clothes come from Israel and the guns. If any of them get killed or captured, the Jews will be blamed."

The minister from Saudi Aramco asked, "Does this mean we won't get to evaluate the machine for our future use?"

"Yes. We all expected that the machine would probably have to be destroyed. On the bright side, the United States Military will probably take care of that plus those unwanted people from Transtec. And don't forget, we get a full set of drawings. It is up to our representatives at the transfer to make sure our drawings do not get destroyed. They let us look at the first few pages when we had our private demonstrations, showing how the outside ball was assembled. Our operators have prepared a duplicate set of drawings they will switch with the real drawings certain parties want to see destroyed. Our people will smuggle out the actual drawings and bring them here to us where we can decide what to do next."

Salman sneered at Carlos as though he was a beggar on the street. There was still a chance that ugly bastard would fall on his face. He would just wait and see what happened.

***

At the Texaco headquarters in Houston, Lillian was standing in front of the Colonel's desk looking fetching in a blue form-fitting jumpsuit matching her cobalt blue eyes. "We heard from Chevron a little while ago. They seem to think the military is going to take care of our California free energy problem."

Ray smiled at his girl Friday as though she had single-handedly solved their problems. "Excellent Lilly. Is Skipper Walls still on-site monitoring things?"

"Yes, I spoke with him just a few minutes ago. He is hanging around in the background. As we can see from the live television feeds, the area around Transtec looks like a war zone with all the TV broadcast vans and the surrounding mob. He believes the government plans on destroying not only the machine but they will make the Transtec people disappear as well."

"Have Skipper continue to monitor the situation. I don't trust those federal bastards for one second. I know they already have a free energy machine, but maybe not this technology. It wouldn't surprise me to see them confiscate the machine for further study. I just don't want it out into the world."

"As long as it's the government, do we care?"

"Probably not. I know there are too many interests in preserving the energy map as it exists for the government to disseminate the technology. If they can exploit the technology for the military somehow, that's a different story."

"Okay, Ray. I'll monitor the situation. If there are any changes, I'll let you know immediately."

"Thank you, dahrlen." Looking at the backside of Lilly in her form-fitting suit as she left his office, the Colonel fantasized about what it would be like. Sometimes he wished he was single again, but that thought lasted only a second. No way would he jeopardize the life he had for a few moments of pleasure. Glancing at the large screen television on the wall across from his desk, he saw the Transtec guards open the doors to the building. "It's about damn time," he muttered into the silent room.

CHAPTER SIXTY-SEVEN

Josh was in his secret command center, staring at four large television screens. Each screen was dedicated to a different set of pictures. One monitor was focused on outdoor scenes with views from all sides of the building. Twelve hidden cameras displayed images in a four by three grid on this television screen. With a twist of his mouse, Josh could make the image from any single camera fill the entire screen for a better view.

Another screen showed the interior of Transtec from the front doors, up the stairs, and into the holding area for D.A.D. Three cameras were dedicated to different views inside of D.A.D.s room. Josh wanted to observe the transfer of his beloved machine to the buyers.

There were cameras showing the transportation vehicle for Ted and Bill and several cameras along the route to the shopping mall. Josh needed to make sure his actors arrived at the mall safely. He wasn't paying attention to any of these images at present.

The last screen presented images hijacked from airport cameras in both the San Francisco and San Jose airports, where his two actors would hopefully depart from this afternoon.

At the moment, he was riveted by indoor and outdoor scenes at the front doors.

As the doors to Transtec opened, eight guards armed with automatic rifles stood ready with the guns already in their hands pointed at the floor. In the center of the door stood Captain Wilson in full military gear, also holding a rifle. Pushing to get inside the doors was the military escort for General Motors.

"I'm sorry, gentlemen," Wilson barked. "But only the buyers are allowed inside. There will be no military personnel or guns allowed inside of this building."

The Navy SEALs Sergeant leading the military escorts, Sergeant Leo Wolf tried to shove his way inside only to be met with Wilson's rifle stuck in his gut. "One more step Sergeant, and your body will decorate these steps. What about no military or guns, didn't you hear?"

When Wilson stuck his rifle into the Sergeant's stomach, several SEALs and Marines raised their rifles to their shoulders. "I'm sorry, Captain," Wolf said in his most commanding voice, "but my orders are to accompany these gentlemen for the exchange. If we have to shoot our way inside, then we are prepared to do just that."

"Look behind you, Sergeant," barked Wilson. "Do you see those television cameras pointed in your direction? Do you really want the whole fucking world to watch the mighty United States Military slaughter private guards located on private property? And you will be the first to die."

Wolf had been briefed to expect resistance, in which case he was to stand down and let the transfer take place inside without his interference. "Stand down, men," he yelled, dropping the barrel of his rifle so it was pointing down towards the steps. "Step back and let the buyers enter."

Watching the scene unfold, Josh released his breath. He hadn't been aware of not breathing for nearly a minute as he watched Wolf finally back down the stairs. This was what he had expected, but until it happened, you just never knew how the situation might develop.

Wilson strode to the open doors, then shouted, "Okay, listen up, everybody. We will admit two representatives from each of the purchasing companies to enter the building. Every person entering will go through a metal detector and be subjected to an additional pat-down. If you do not agree to these terms, you are free to leave. Those representatives who enter must provide valid documentation."

As the military escort backed away from the doors, several men began shoving their way through the crowd. As they neared the front door, each man was stopped by Captain Wilson. He inspected their documentation before letting them in to proceed through the metal detector. After twenty men had entered, Wilson held up his hand, palm facing outward. "No one else will be admitted to the building today. Please stand back, so when the buyers exit with D.A.D., they will have room to make it to their convoy."

After they had cleared the entrance procedures, the twenty buyers were escorted upstairs, where Bill and Ted were standing by the D.A.D. case alongside four more armed guards.

"I want to see inside the box and watch D.A.D. execute some moves before we will accept delivery." This was spoken by Eli Rimnovitch from Boston, representing General Motors. He spoke in that dry Boston nasal drawl many people find irritating. It sounds like they are somehow superior to the rest of us simpletons, and only those from Boston deserve to be breathing God's clean, fresh air. Even his $75,000 custom gray William Westmancott suit shouted, look at me, one of the chosen.

Ignoring the arrogance, Ted said, "Welcome to Transtec for our free energy machine transfer. Bill, please show these gentlemen what they came to see."

Bill flipped open the transfer case and pulled out the remote. "You can all see the remote," he said, holding it up so everyone could get a good look. "I'll have D.A.D. fly around a little, so you can all get a good look at the machine. It will stop in front of anyone who raises their hand for a better look. This is the same machine you have all witnessed over the past few days."

During the next five minutes, Bill had the machine fly around the room, pausing in front of each group of buyers. When everyone had shaken their heads in agreement, Bill returned D.A.D. to its carrying case and closed the lid after depositing the remote.

"Okay," Ted announced. "There is the machine," he said, pointing, "and behind me on the table are ten sets of rolled drawings in aluminum carrying cases. You are free to open the case and verify that each case contains a roll of drawings. You may not take out the drawings for examination. What would be the point of giving you bogus drawings when you have the original machine?"

While Ted was talking, Tolya Turgenev, a Russian, grabbed ahold of D.A.D.s carrying case carrying it towards the door before any of the other buyers could react. With one member from each buyer's team holding a tube with the drawings, the rest of the buyers hurried out of the room behind the Russian. They were followed by the eight guards who had accompanied them up the steps. The other four guards who had been watching over D.A.D. escorted Ted and Bill towards a back room, out of sight from anyone else in the building.

Josh watched as Ted and Bill entered a back room to pick up a set of guard's clothes and put on their new identities. Knowing that time was precious, it was only a few moments before they were both being escorted out of the back doors into a waiting Ford Explorer SUV. As the Ford left the rear parking lot, Gene watched to see if anyone was following. Satisfied that the only images of the SUV leaving the parking lot would be from the overhead satellite, and those images were just four guards leaving the building, Josh switched his attention back to the front of the building.

Turgenev, followed by his companion Colonel Alexeev of the Russian intelligence agency (SVR) carrying the aluminum tube with their copy of the drawings, was met at the front door by Sergeant Wolf and his Navy SEALs. With his rifle strapped across his back, Wolf held out his hands to the Russian, saying, "I'll take that sir," reaching for the container holding D.A.D.

"Why should I give you the box?" asked Turgenev, pushing past the Sergeant.

Clearly, Sergeant Wolf did not know what to do. He couldn't shoot the Russian in front of the whole damn world. Yet, he couldn't just let the Russians walk off with the free energy machine.

The first ranking officer of the People's Liberation Army (PLA) was just behind the Russians, followed by several members of OPEC. While the Russians tried to force their way past the SEALs and Marines, the other buyers, particularly the Chinese, managed to get in front of the Russians, halting their advance.

"Where do you think you are taking the machine comrade?" bellowed the PLA officer.

Like the Americans, Turgenev didn't quite know what to do in the situation. Surrounded by television cameras, no doubt sending live pictures around the world, he couldn't afford to create a scene making Russia look like the bad guy. He couldn't let the squinty-eyed Chinese control the situation, either. Waiting a few steps from the front doors, swallowed up by the military and television cameras, stood the Secretary of State, Gerry Peacocke, surrounded by Secret Service agents and his aides.

"Gentlemen," boomed the Secretary, in a voice well accustomed to yelling over the crowd noise, "let me interfere for a few moments if you please." There was some shoving and shuffling by the military until all the ten buyers surrounded the Secretary.

Josh was sitting spellbound by the Secretary's appearance. In all the scenarios played out in his mind, seeing the Secretary of State standing amidst the rabble in front of his building was not even close. He could have guessed the Secretary of Defense, but the Secretary of State? Never. Yet, there he was, and damned if he didn't have everybody listening to whatever he was saying. For the first time, Josh wished he had mounted an audio feed outside of the front door. After a few minutes, the large group made its way to the street where the Secretary's long stretch limousine sat in line with the military convoy and another couple dozen full-sized SUVs.

Much to Josh's amazement, the Russian carrying D.A.D. and the Chinese and several other buyers, crowded into the Secretary's limousine. The other buyers scrambled to get into their vehicles while most military personnel were loaded into their transportation. As expected, a contingent of Navy SEALs were left in front of the Transtec building. There were still a few chores to be performed, like securing the computers and any associated equipment such as thumb drives, destroying all paperwork and of course, most important of all, detaining the Transtec personnel for later elimination.

While Captain Wilson and his guards let the Navy SEALs into the building to do their business, Josh watched the Ford Explorer carrying Ted and Bill enter the Westfield Valley Fair shopping mall garage on Winchester Street. Josh watched the garage entrance for several more minutes, trying to determine if his actors had been followed. Satisfied that they were safely inside the confines of the vast Valley mall, Josh stopped watching. There was no way he could pick up either of their UBER cars from all the mall traffic entering and leaving the mall. His actors were now all on their own. Hopefully, they would all live happy lives enjoying their new wealth.

CHAPTER SIXTY-EIGHT

President Carleton was not a happy man. "What in the hell do you mean you cannot find the Transtec people," he bellowed. "Goddamnit, three people cannot simply disappear, and I suppose the ten billion dollars we are on the hook for is not recoverable as well?"

The Attorney General, Susan Whitebridge, who worked with and knew the President when he was still a governor and used to his tantrums, responded.

"The only possible way they could have exited the building was with a black Ford Explorer that left shortly after the exchange. Four individuals dressed as guards left the building. The SUV was tracked to a large downtown shopping mall with covered garages. There was absolutely no way to determine which vehicle or vehicles they left in or where they might have gone."

"Is there any good news?" thundered the President.

"Well yes," said Secretary Bachelor timidly. "The anti-gravity device has been destroyed as you requested, along with all applicable paperwork and drawings."

"Who destroyed the device?" a curious president asked. "I thought there might be some pushback from one of the other buyers. Especially the Russians."

"We'll never know the answer to that question, Mr. President. Everyone was happy to take the device to the Mare Island Naval Shipyard to make the final disposition. Once inside of the Navy warehouse, there was a clamoring to see the inside of the machine. Our military was interested in seeing if what the Transtec people had developed was like what we already possess. A Navy technician was permitted to open up the device. A large screw at the top held the two sides of the ball together.

According to several eyewitnesses, as soon as the screw was turned, it ignited several small blocks of white phosphorous situated around the inside of the machine. Everything inside associated with the device was incinerated in a 5,000-degree flame. There was absolutely nothing left to analyze."

"What about the drawings? Did they get destroyed?"

"There wasn't any need, Mr. President," Bachelor continued. "When the drawings were examined, other than the top three or four sheets which described how the two halves of the ball joined, the rest of the drawings described the design of a sophisticated automatic gate opener."

"You mean to tell me, the whole damn thing was a scam for ten billion dollars?" The President was shaking his head with a weird smile on his face. It was hard to tell if it was a smile of relief or admiration of a clever con.

"It sure looks that way, Mr. President," announced Admiral Whittaker, not afraid to speak now that it looked like the President had settled down.

"What about those smart bastards who made the machine in the first place? Any chance of finding them."

Now that he had found his voice, the Admiral was not afraid to keep the floor. "Our intelligence guys don't believe the people we saw at Transtec had anything to do with building the machine. They believe someone hired professional actors to play their roles with their exit planned way in advance. At this moment, we don't have a clue who was responsible or where any of the parties are presently located."

"For God's sake. They had a brand new building, an elaborate setup, and several guards. Somebody must know something." A subdued President was grasping at straws, and he knew it. Whoever planned this cunning stunt was way ahead of their efforts to find out who he was.

"It's a new building awaiting an occupancy permit from the city," Secretary Whitebridge chimed in. "The building's owner has a contract for retrofitting from Transtec. It's a legitimate contract, and there were extensive inside improvements made, especially in the lobby. Of course, the Transtec people have all disappeared. Oh, and the guards and the rest of the various contract personnel were hired by some mysterious man named Gene Abel, who also does not exist. You have to admire someone with the audacity for pulling off a scam this big."

"That's fine, Susan," the President said with a look of consternation on his face, "but somewhere out there is a brilliant bastard with ten billion dollars who knows how to make anti-gravity machines. That ought to scare the hell out of many people."

CHAPTER SIXTY-NINE

The following day, King had a late breakfast with Detective Larry McCutchen at Bill's Café on The Alameda.

"Did Josh call you?" Larry asked around a mouthful of pancake.

"No, I think he has left the area," King responded after taking a sip of his French roast coffee. "I checked with his housekeeper in San Francisco, and she related Josh asked her to tend to his house for the next few years. After talking with her, I'm convinced that she does not know where he is located."

"Why do you suppose he didn't say goodbye?"

"I believe he did that yesterday at breakfast. I could sense that he was anxious about the upcoming day's events, and for a good reason. A lot of heavy crap went down. I'm just happy that no one got killed."

King seemed relieved while reliving yesterday's events. "Josh couldn't say anything because he didn't know exactly what was going to happen. His whole planned adventure could have gone off the rails, and he didn't want either of us hit with the fallout."

"Yeah, the police officers on the scene reported how they could sense the tension in the atmosphere. They were expecting gunfire at any moment and were afraid of being caught in the crossfire. Did you check out your building yet?" The detective seemed animated while reliving yesterday's events in his mind.

"I did, and you have to see what he did for the lobby, Larry. It really is beautiful. Stunning. The city nor anyone else can claim that Transtec occupied the building just to pull off a clever con."

"When did you figure out it was a con?" the detective asked in all seriousness. "I certainly expected nothing like that to happen."

"I didn't put it together until late yesterday when reports came filtering back about how the free energy model he sold burned up and all the drawings were fake. Our friend wanted, maybe needed, the ten billion dollars to ensure that when he releases free energy into the world, he can do it in a way that no one, especially any government, can stop its progress. He didn't want anyone else messing with the technology until he was ready. We know Josh was not hurting for money, but he was a long way from being a billionaire. He didn't pull the con to make himself wealthy. He needed the money for some other reason."

"I figured that out," the detective responded with a grin. "You do know that I am a detective. Right?"

***

Texaco's Colonel Otto Conrad enjoyed a croissant and black coffee when Lilly came in with the morning's mail. "You're looking chipper this morning, Boss. Are we just a little smug about how things turned out in California?"

"Other than losing a billion dollars, which the government may or may not reimburse, the situation couldn't be better. No damned free energy machine to worry about, at least for a while," he frowned at the realization, "no one got hurt, and we don't have to deal with the California problem until sometime in the future, if ever."

Feeling satisfied with himself and his attentive secretary, the Colonel allowed himself a big grin.

***

Mohammed Bin Salman was once again commanding the closing of OPEC's quarterly meeting in Venezuela. Carlos Barrera had complained of a sour stomach which prevented him from attending the conference, although everyone knew the disgraced minister was too ashamed to show his face. His plans for being OPEC's chairman and ruling the world had gone up in flames. Salman demanded that Barrera and Venezuela reimburse those countries that had lost a billion dollars. He never believed or expected that such a demand would be honored, but it made him look good by simply demanding the payment. While OPEC's influence in the world's oil market had diminished during the past few years, they were still a formidable force demanding attention. Salman was the leader with the strength and determination to see that they got the attention.

***

In St. Croix, Lisa Ogden was on the beach sipping a pina colada. Having shed all of her fake identities, she was enjoying being her own self. Worries about being discovered as the beautiful, talented Janet Hills dissolved with each mile she traveled from San Jose. Enjoying the Caribbean life with plenty of money to ensure her peace of mind, Lisa didn't plan on returning to the New York theater scene for several months, maybe even years.

Joseph Langham and Howard Trent, both disguised in yet another set of identities, were still en route to opposite sides of the world. Langham was sleeping, and Trent was getting sloshed with the complimentary first-class cocktails. Joseph was exhausted after dealing with the pressures of their last day at Transtec, while Trent was relieved that he hadn't been killed, having escaped the wrath of the swindled buyers with a million dollars. It would be several days before either man heard the rest of the story, how the con played out. Trent could not believe he hadn't thought of that scenario, although relieved he hadn't tried to pull a scam himself. He was smart enough to realize that when it came to cons, he had met the master.

EPILOGUE

Somewhere in the northern California foothills, hidden in the coastal range, is an old homestead abandoned many years ago. The nearest neighbor is fifteen miles away, and Red Bluff, the closet town, is twenty-five miles as the crow flies. Collier Springs Road is graded once a year by the Tehama County Road Department and comes within eight miles of the old ranch. For the last eight miles to the ranch, the road was once an old logging trail that hadn't been used since 1950. Accessible only by a four-wheeled vehicle, the track had been cleared of the trees that had grown up in the roadway along with the big rocks and dead tree limbs. Where the old logging road left the country road, it still looked abandoned and was hard to find.

The ranch was situated by a sweet mountain spring, nearly lost among the bay trees surrounding its location. The meadows and hills around the ranch are covered with Sugar Pine, California Coulter Pine, and Foothill Pine, commonly known as Digger Pine, a racial slur for the Indians who used to harvest the pine nuts. Hidden under three large Sugar Pine trees is a log cabin recently refurbished with all the modern conveniences. Nearby are several old-looking weathered buildings, also renovated. Electricity is furnished by Josh's free energy machines, powering all facilities and a water pump providing water to a hidden storage tank high on the mountainside.

On the front deck of the old ranch house is a rocking chair from which it is possible to see Mount Shasta eighty miles in the distance.

The only visitors to this part of the world are occasional bear hunters during the fall. It is possible to go for several years without seeing another living human being. It is to this lonely, remote, hidden property that Josh retreated. His chances of being discovered are nearly zero. Sure, he might get a visitor or two once in a blue moon, but they will not know who he is and cannot see what he is doing in such a remote spot. To them, he is simply a recluse, hiding from civilization.

In the surrounding small towns like Los Molinos, Cottonwood, and Anderson, Josh has contracted with machinists, electronic designers, software engineers, plus other advanced technology burnouts who have fled the big city for a more relaxing lifestyle. Individuals and small companies working for Josh believe they are producing parts for some fancy gate opener.

A few weeks after leaving San Jose, Josh can be found sitting in his rocker on the porch at the end of a busy day, looking at Mt. Shasta. On an end table by his chair is a bucket of ice and a bottle of Johnny Walker Blue, missing a few inches. Holding a drink in his hand and taking a swallow, Josh tilts his glass towards the mountain and utters his usual end-of-the-day toast.

"Here's to you, Dad. We're building your machine."

Serious writing began fifty years ago with a pencil and notebook. Since then, the story has been started and stopped many times with several titles. I remember using an old underwood typewriter for a while before getting my first computer with a word processor. I've lost track of how many word-processing programs I used over the years writing this story until Microsoft Word became available.

All the locations described in the story are as I remember. Some places no longer exist, having succumbed to age and the thirst for more and more immense structures. The northern California ranch is real, along with the miserable road. Most of the restaurants described still exist as well as the shopping mall.

Original Joe's and Joe's special are real. If you ever have a chance to try this dish, don't pass on it. Canaima National Park and Salto Angel, the world's highest waterfall, are real, although I only visited via Google Earth. I drove from L.A. to San Jose several times as a young man, and always found taking Highway 101 preferable to the busy freeway, although that may have changed with the times.

My father was the inventor described in the prologue, and he built the floating silver ball, what he called the anti-gravity device. D.A.D. is a salute to my dad and is an acronym for Dad's Anti-gravity Device. This was before my lifetime, but the machine inserted into a cardboard box was witnessed by many people who described for me how the cardboard box just stayed suspended in the air until the gyroscopes inside lost their momentum.

I do not know how he made this incredible machine; however, he told me when I was very young that his machine could be used as a free energy device, and it was up to me to make that happen. Like the father in the story, my dad died in an accident shortly after that, and as you can guess, his dream never came to be realized.

Over the passing years, I have studied the energy market and realized the impact of free energy on civilization as a whole. I have tried to portray that impact in this story.

Nicola Tesla invented free energy; however, he was shut down and his knowledge buried by the United States Government. That they used his notes to create a free energy machine is an open secret. Like big oil, solar power, wind power and thermal power companies, they are all seriously opposed to free energy. As you discover in the story, most governments are terrified about the prospects of free energy. This is a fact. Free energy frees us all from political constraints. While free energy is a fact, whether it ever becomes a reality for you and me is an open question. My guess is probably not. Too many jobs and companies are affected, with too many others afraid of losing power.

In the world's energy sector, there is a constant churning of players and companies. This is a work of fiction, and any resemblance to actual individuals is purely unintentional.

ABOUT THE AUTHOR

Clark has four previous novels in print including *The Dragon Fly, Hokee Wolf, Hokee II* and *Sage The Reader.* Trained as an actor and singer, Clark entertained until becoming an engineer working as a contractor for the CIA in black ops programs. Clark began metaphysical studies and later trained as a shaman recognized as a specialist in sweat-lodge ceremonies. This rich background provides the ingredients that infuse his work.

NOTE FROM THE AUTHOR

Word-of-mouth is crucial for any author to succeed. If you enjoyed *D.A.D.*, please leave a review online—anywhere you are able. Even if it's just a sentence or two. It would make all the difference and would be very much appreciated.

Thanks!
Clark Viehweg

We hope you enjoyed reading this title from:

www.blackrosewriting.com

Subscribe to our mailing list – *The Rosevine* – and receive **FREE** books, daily
deals, and stay current with news about upcoming
releases and our hottest authors.
Scan the QR code below to sign up.

Already a subscriber? Please accept a sincere thank you for being a fan of
Black Rose Writing authors.

View other Black Rose Writing titles at
www.blackrosewriting.com/books and use promo code
PRINT to receive a **20% discount** when purchasing.